Time of Day

NICOLE PYLAND

Time of Day

Tahoe Series Book #2

Kinsley James has a nice life in South Lake Tahoe. She has a great career in real estate and a great group of friends she's known for a long time. She also has a crush. Things had been easy when the object of that crush lived on the other side of the lake. Kinsley had been able to push her attraction aside. She'd dated other women. She'd even mostly forgotten about that time in college when she'd shared a futon with a girl three years her junior that seemed so much more comfortable in her own skin than Kinsley had ever felt. Then, her crush moved home.

Riley Sanders decided to move back to South Lake Tahoe to settle down with her long-time and also long-distance girlfriend. Her plan was simple: find a real estate agent; find a house. Once she had that house, her girlfriend would move, and they'd be able to finally share a life together.

Riley's plan doesn't quite work out. But, sometimes, the plans people make take paths of their own, taking people exactly where they need to be after all. In Riley's case, her plan took her to Kinsley, a woman she'd known for a while but had never considered herself close to. Things change, though, when she realizes Kinsley may be the woman she hasn't even known she should be looking for.

To contact the author or for any additional information, visit: **https://nicolepyland.com**

BY THE AUTHOR

Stand-alone books:

All the Love Songs

The Fire

The Moments

The Disappeared

Chicago Series:

- Introduction – Fresh Start

- Book #1 – The Best Lines

- Book #2 – Just Tell Her

- Book #3 – Love Walked into The Lantern

- Series Finale – What Happened After

San Francisco Series:

- Book #1 – Checking the Right Box

- Book #2 – Macon's Heart

- Book #3 – This Above All

- Series Finale – What Happened After

Tahoe Series:

- Book #1 – Keep Tahoe Blue

- Book #2 – Time of Day

CONTENTS

CHAPTER 1

SHE HAD THIS LONG and likely soft sable-colored hair. Her eyes nearly matched the color. Her skin was always tanner in the summer, but it also never quite went pale in the mean Tahoe winters. Kinsley James couldn't believe Riley Sanders was back in South Lake full-time. Kinsley tried to avert her stare, but it was difficult. It always was with Riley. Riley left the café with a large coffee in one hand and her cell phone pressed to her ear. Kinsley couldn't hear what she was saying. She just watched her walk along the sidewalk in that long dark-green pencil skirt and matching heels around the corner. Kinsley took a sip of her own coffee as she waited just outside the store.

"James, you ready?" Morgan asked as she locked the door of the sporting goods store behind her.

"What?" Kinsley asked.

Morgan glanced at her inquisitively and followed Kinsley's gaze just as Riley disappeared around the corner.

"Seriously?" Morgan asked and took Kinsley's coffee cup to take a drink for herself. "Riley again?"

"No," Kinsley replied and took her coffee back.

"You know she's back. She's been back for months now. She actually lived with Kellan until Kell moved in with Reese."

1

"What's your point?" Kinsley asked her.

"Nothing, I guess." Morgan took Kinsley's elbow and directed her toward their destination. "Just tell me if you went to the place to get coffee just because you know she goes there around this time nearly every day? We're on our way to dinner, James."

"I had a long day. I wanted coffee. It's decaf, anyway."

"I doubt high-powered attorney Riley Sanders drinks decaf," Morgan teased.

"She's not a high-powered attorney, and I don't know what she drinks," Kinsley said as they walked on.

"Because you never talk to her."

"Why would I?"

"Kinsley, how long have you known Riley?"

"I don't know. A while." She shrugged.

"And how long have you had a massive crush on her?"

"I don't know. A while."

Morgan laughed at her and said, "Come on. Let's go grab dinner. I think you could use a strong drink."

Kinsley did agree with Morgan on that. Her longtime crush on Riley wasn't news to Morgan. She'd kept it to herself all through senior year of college, though. Riley was three years younger and a freshman in Reno when Kinsley met Reese and Morgan. Kinsley hadn't been raised in South Lake like they had. Morgan and Reese had been best friends and later lovers. When they met Kinsley in school, she'd joined their group of friends and had met Riley through that group. Riley was only a freshman, which meant she couldn't go to bars with them and often wasn't at the parties they attended, but she'd hang around coffee houses and libraries with Reese sometimes. Kinsley liked her back then, but she also seemed so young. Eighteen and twenty-one were very different ages after all.

What Kinsley found possibly the most infuriating thing and yet also the most attractive thing about Riley Sanders back then, was the fact that she never gave Kinsley the time of day. She was younger and should have looked up to the seniors she hung out with. She should've wanted to impress them. But she didn't. She hardly talked to Kinsley even after Kinsley came out. Riley came out not long after. Kinsley could have been a confidant for her, but Riley didn't seem to need one. It was so damn sexy and yet so frustrating to Kinsley.

Kinsley had dinner with Morgan, Reese, and Kellan that night. Then, she went home to the two-story, lakeside house she'd bought two years prior. Being a real estate agent in a place like Lake Tahoe had its perks. She knew about listings before everyone else, and she had connections with the other realtors. This realtor, who'd told her about this house, was a friend who'd known she'd been looking for a house to get out of the apartment she'd lived in since college. He'd also known that this particular house was about to go into foreclosure. She'd been able to afford it, thankfully, and loved moving into her dream home.

She'd spent the past two years fixing the place up here and there while using most of her discretionary income to decorate it. The house had four bedrooms along with the master bedroom. It had three baths. It also had both first-story and second-story balconies overlooking the lake, with only the hill leading down to it and the shallowness of the water at its edge preventing her from diving straight into the water. She stared out at the crystal blue of it, as she drank from her mug of tea, and took in the lake at night. She loved doing this. She'd come home from a long day at work and, normally, take in the sunset if she'd timed it just right. Tonight, she'd chosen dinner with her friends. She'd missed the sun, but she'd enjoy the moon all the same. She usually made her tea, wrapped herself into something warm when it called for it, and leaned over the rail of her wood-planked balcony, breathing in the air.

She thought of Riley Sanders, wishing she'd told her back in college that she had a crush on her. She'd pictured Riley's reaction time and time again. Riley had always been so cool and confident. Kinsley had passed her a beer once, thinking Riley would find it cool that the older girl was handing her an illegal beverage. Riley had passed it back saying she wasn't a beer drinker. Kinsley had finished the beer herself.

She moved to lie on her chaise lounge chair that allowed her to comfortably take in the sights and sounds. She turned the lamp on, that was just behind the chair, and picked up her book. She spent the rest of the night reading before her yawns finally took over. She turned the lamp off, covered the furniture to protect it from the elements, and went inside with her empty mug and the book. When she fell asleep that night, it was to the image of Riley Sanders walking out of the café and around the corner until she disappeared.

***

Kinsley arrived at her office around eight the next morning. She was the owner of her business and also the only employee. She managed to run the office, do her own marketing, and help her clients find their dream homes. Her plan was to hire one or two employees within the year to expand. For now, though, she was content in the office she rented on the ground floor of an apartment building just off the main drag downtown. It was convenient. Morgan's sporting goods store was just down the block. Kellan's vet clinic was within walking distance, and Reese stopped by there nearly every day to pick up her girlfriend from work.

When Kinsley heard the bell over the door chime, she turned her head away from the laptop and up to greet the visitor. She was surprised to see none other than Riley Sanders looking down at her. Riley was wearing another business suit, which did not go with the vibe of South Lake at all, but still looked great on her. Today, it was a charcoal gray pantsuit with a matching jacket and a scarlet-colored blouse underneath. Her heels were short but still managed to lengthen her legs. That was what drew Kinsley's attention first as her eyes went from Riley's shoes up her legs to her breasts and then her eyes, which were giving her a confused expression at the moment.

"Hey, Kinsley."

"Riley, hi," Kinsley replied quickly. "Do you need a bathroom or something?" she asked and didn't know why.

"What? No." Riley chuckled a bit and shifted her purse to her other shoulder. "Why would you think that?"

"I don't know. Your office is, like, a mile away. I thought maybe you needed to borrow a bathroom."

She closed her eyes only for a moment, but it was enough to silently scold herself for being a complete and utter weirdo.

"No, I don't need a bathroom." Riley sat in one of the two expensive chairs in front of Kinsley's desk. "I need a house. I ran into Morgan the other day, and she reminded me you're a real estate agent."

"I am," Kinsley replied.

"Sorry, we haven't had a chance to really hang out since I moved back. Things have been a little crazy, trying to get my practice up and running," Riley said. "But I'm still living in that apartment above my dad's old clinic. It was actually great when Kellan was there; I kind of liked having a roommate. But she's been with Reese for a while, and I'm still there." She rattled that all off very quickly.

Kinsley could only focus on the shape of her mouth and those full lips as Riley spoke.

"Anyway, now that I'm staying for good, I'd like to find a house."

"Okay. I can help you," Kinsley said. "Do you have time now or should we set something up for later? I'll need some details before I get started," she added.

"I have a meeting in about twenty minutes, but I'm free for lunch."

"I can do noon. I have a showing after that," Kinsley said as she glanced at the calendar on her computer. For some reason, she was glad she had something to do. It made her feel like less of a loser in front of this elegant creature. "Or, I can do tomorrow."

"I can't do noon. I was thinking more like one, but I can do dinner."

"Dinner?" Kinsley replied with a break in her voice that she was certain would give her nervousness away.

"Seven?" Riley glanced at her cell phone in her hand, and Kinsley assumed she was checking her own calendar. "My place work for you? I can order us something. We can go over everything there."

"Oh, sure," Kinsley answered a little too quickly again.

"Great," Riley said and stood. She gave Kinsley a wide, expressive smile. "I'll see you then."

"Okay," Kinsley said.

She then watched Riley walk in those heels out her front door. Her eyes were so occupied, that her ears didn't even hear the sound of the bell over her door. She was going to Riley's apartment later for dinner. She smiled and tried to make her blush disappear as she got back to work.

CHAPTER 2

RILEY TOOK THE PIZZA from the delivery guy after passing him the signed credit card receipt. He nodded at her, and she closed the door behind him. She turned to see Kinsley sitting at her dining room table, closing her laptop. Riley smiled at Kinsley, who had smiled at her at least three times since she'd arrived about ten minutes prior. Riley set the pizza on the kitchen counter and pulled two plates from the cabinet. She added two slices each to their plates and walked them to the table.

"Wine?" she asked.

"No beer, I take it?" Kinsley took the plate from Riley's hand.

"I have beer, too." Riley sat her own plate down. "It's a dark beer. Is that okay? An import I really like." She headed back into the kitchen.

"I thought you didn't like beer," Kinsley replied.

"Why would you think that?" Riley asked as she set a bottle in front of Kinsley and then opened one for herself, sitting down across from her.

"In college, I offered you a beer once," Kinsley said as she shrugged. "You said you didn't like it."

"I did? I don't remember that." Riley took a drink and placed the bottle back down. "When was that?"

"At some party."

"We hung out a little then, huh?" Riley asked and picked up her first slice of pizza.

"We did, yeah." Kinsley grabbed for her own pizza.

"You were always hanging out with Reese, Remy, and Morgan. Reese and Remy were always so nice to me."

Kinsley took a bite and gave her an expression with her blue eyes that had Riley wondering what the woman was thinking before she replied, "They're nice people."

Riley stared at her for a moment, taking her in. Kinsley had been a transplant to South Lake after they'd all met at college. She'd been from Reno, originally, but after making friends with South Lake locals, she'd moved here after graduation. Riley hadn't heard much from or about Kinsley since her older friends moved on from university and she made new friends that were her age. She'd gone to law school and moved to the north side of the lake in Truckee. She'd wanted to live close enough to her family that she could get to them, but far enough away in order to get some privacy. She loved her parents, but she was their only daughter, squeezed between two brothers. They tended to pay her more attention. It was only recently that she'd decided to relocate back to South Lake permanently.

Her father had retired and sold his vet practice to Kellan. He and her mother were traveling more but were also getting up there in age. Riley wanted to be closer to them in case they needed her. She was also ready to settle down and buy a place. If she was going to do that anywhere, she thought South Lake was the best location for her. It also afforded her the chance to leave behind the law practice in Truckee where she'd specialized in divorce cases. She wanted family law – and sometimes that involved divorce cases, but she wanted more. She wanted her own practice. She would still handle the occasional divorce case, but she wanted to change her focus to helping women who'd been victims of domestic violence. She'd also help in proceedings for adoption, guardianship, and child abuse. She was ready to start this new chapter of her life and needed a home.

"So, I'm thinking... I'd like something with at least three bedrooms." Riley wiped her hands on her napkin and pushed her plate away. "And at least two bathrooms. I love the garden tub in this place. If I can get one of those, that would be amazing. If not, I can always put one in."

"Down to business," Kinsley said, shoving the last piece of crust into her mouth before sliding her plate to the side and opening her laptop. "Okay."

Riley watched as a piece of Kinsley's dark blonde hair fell into her face. She also watched Kinsley attempt to blow it up and away. When that failed, she smiled as Kinsley tucked it behind her ear and stared at her computer.

"Something with a lake view is – I'm sure – impossible on my budget, but I do have a trust with money in it from my grandparents. I just came of age to tap into it. I'm planning to use that for half of the down payment."

"And the other half is in savings?" Kinsley asked.

"No, my girlfriend has the other half."

"Oh," Kinsley said.

"Did I not mention her?" Riley asked. "Shit. Sorry. I'm trying to get my entire life in order, and she's not here to help. I'm a little behind."

"I just didn't know you had a girlfriend. Kellan never said anything."

"I'm not sure I ever told her about Elena," Riley said. "I wasn't the best roommate. I was gone a lot. When I first moved in here with Kell, I had to go back and forth between here and Truckee. I moved slowly. When I finally got settled in, she moved in with Reese. Elena never came down when me and Kellan were still roommates, I guess." She took another long drink of her beer. "But this house is for us."

"I see." Kinsley typed something. "So, three bedrooms? Home office and guest room?" she asked.

"For now. Nursery probably later." Riley tore at the label on her beer bottle. "I'm not in a hurry. That's a good thing."

"For the nursery?" Kinsley looked up at her.

Riley laughed and replied, "To buy a place. I'm not in a hurry for the nursery either, but I meant to buy. I would like to find the right place."

"If you don't mind me asking, where's your girlfriend?"

"Elena lives in Dallas. She's a mayor of a small town just outside of the city."

"Mayor?"

"Elected on her first try. The town is smaller than South Lake without the tourists, but still. She really loves it, but her third term is coming to an end, and we agreed she'd move here when it does."

"Is she going to run for office here?" Kinsley asked.

"I don't think so. She's an attorney, too. She's a bit older than me. She's ready to go a little slower than she did when she just got out of law school and then got elected. I'm thinking we'll just start a joint practice."

"That sounds nice," Kinsley said and smiled, but it didn't meet her eyes.

"I've got another month before she arrives."

"Will she come help house-hunt?"

"Probably not. She trusts me," Riley replied and knew her own smile didn't meet her eyes. "She's pretty busy wrapping things up down there. I probably won't see her again until she moves finally."

"When was the last time you saw her?" Kinsley asked.

"We don't see one another all that often, unfortunately. We're both just too busy to get away. I went there about six weeks ago for the weekend."

"Six weeks without seeing your girlfriend?" Kinsley asked and tucked the same strand of hair behind her ear. "That sucks. The last time I had a long-distance girlfriend was right after college. She lived about three hours away. It lasted only a couple of months."

"Girlfriend?" Riley asked and then she remembered. "That's right. I totally forgot."

"You forgot I was gay?" Kinsley asked and seemed at least slightly offended. "Riley, we've hung out like a hundred times."

"I'm sorry. I knew you were gay. I just forgot that I knew that."

"How do you forget something like that?" Kinsley closed her laptop.

"I don't know. You don't scream lesbian, Kinsley."

"What does that mean?"

Riley thought for a moment before she replied, "You're not exactly the stereotype."

"Did you really just say that?" Kinsley laughed for the first time since she'd arrived, and Riley wondered if that was the first time she'd ever heard Kinsley laugh. She'd likely heard her laugh before, but that would have been years ago. She didn't risk bringing it up, considering she'd forgotten a pretty big fact about Kinsley already. "I came out in college. You knew then. I think I even introduced you to a date once or twice."

"Freshman year is kind of a blur to me, honestly," Riley said. "It's not an excuse, but it's true. I haven't really spent a lot of time with you since then, Kinsley."

"James is fine," she said.

"Huh?"

"You can call me James. Most people do. My first name is kind of a mouthful," she said. "I guess you've always called me Kinsley, though, haven't you? You do remember that, don't you?"

"Yes." Riley laughed. "I like your name," she added. "And, like I said, I knew you were gay. I just forgot that I knew that. I *am* sorry."

"Why was freshman year a blur?" Kinsley asked.

"What?" Riley had been too busy watching Kinsley's fingers toy with her own beer bottle label. They were long and elegant, with short nails that had a light sheen of polish on them. She'd likely just had a manicure. "Sorry."

"You said your freshman year was a blur."

"Oh, right." She met Kinsley's eyes. "It was a big adjustment for me, being away from home. And I was pre-law. I had a terrible roommate in the dorm that–"

"Sylvia, right?"

"How do you–" Riley shook her head at Kinsley's remarkable memory. "Yes, her name was Sylvia, and she was only in college because her parents made her go. She was out late nearly every night, never went to class, and always made a huge mess in our tiny room. She and I spent most of the time either not talking at all or in screaming matches, because she'd slam the door at four in the morning and wake me up."

"That does suck," Kinsley replied.

"I remember hanging out with you guys, sometimes. You were nice to me, too, by the way." She smiled at her. "It's just been a long time."

"And now, you're back and starting your new life with Elena," Kinsley said. "Three bedrooms and at least two bathrooms."

"That's the idea," Riley said.

"How long have you two been together?"

"About three years," Riley replied. "We met through work. I flew to Dallas for a tricky divorce case. She was in the city at some meeting."

"Well, she *is* an important mayor," Kinsley said with a playful smile.

"She is." Riley laughed and finished her beer. "We struck up a conversation and have been together ever since."

"So, you've always been long-distance?"

"We have."

"And you're buying a place together?"

"We are," Riley answered with a hint of suspicion in her tone. "Do I detect judgment, Kinsley James?" She lifted her eyebrow at Kinsley.

"No judgment." Kinsley held up her hands in supplication. "Just that, in my line of work, I see this happen sometimes: people buy a place together too soon, and then they come back to me a year later, needing to figure out how to sell it."

"It makes sense for us to buy."

"Maybe. But you do have this place. Does Kellan make you pay rent?"

"No, but I make her take my rent." Riley laughed. "She tried to shove it back through the mail slot once. I put it back on her desk downstairs. It's a thing we do every month."

"You have this place rent-free, with no lease. Couldn't she just move in here with you? That way, there's no risk."

"She doesn't want to rent."

"Why not?" Kinsley asked.

"Are you trying to work yourself out of a hefty commission there, Kinsley?"

"I'm not." Kinsley leaned back in the chair. "I also don't take commissions from friends."

"Oh, no. I'm paying you for this. This is a job."

"So, we're not friends?" Kinsley asked with a lifted eyebrow.

"We are. That's not what—" Riley was interrupted by the ringing of her phone. She looked down at the screen. "It's Elena."

"I should probably go," Kinsley said.

"No, it's fine. Just give me one second," Riley replied and stood. She took the phone into the kitchen and answered it. "Hey, babe."

"I have amazing news," Elena spoke and sounded a bit slurred.

"Are you drunk?" Riley asked, concerned.

"No. I've had a few glasses of wine, but I'm not drunk. Listen, I have amazing news."

"What is it, Elena?" She turned back to see that Kinsley was packing up her things.

"They want me to run for governor," Elena replied. "Babe, they want *me* to run for governor of Texas."

"What?" Riley asked.

She suddenly realized this was a private conversation, and Kinsley was standing with her laptop bag hanging over her shoulder waving goodbye at her.

"Just one second, Kinsley."

"Who's Kinsley?"

"She's a real estate agent?" Riley told her girlfriend.

Kinsley's eyes met her own, and Riley thought she saw something in them: Kinsley looked disappointed. Like, maybe she'd taken offense to what Riley had just said.

"I'll leave you alone," Kinsley said. "I'll be in touch, okay?"

"Do you have my–"

"I have your phone number, Riley." Kinsley nodded. "Good night."

The woman walked toward the front door of the apartment and closed it behind her. Riley returned her attention to Elena, who sounded tipsy and like she wasn't alone wherever she was.

"Why are you meeting the real estate agent this late?"

"Why are you excited about running for governor of Texas when you're supposed to be moving here with me?" Riley fired back. "I was meeting with Kinsley to start hunting for *our* house, Elena."

"Riley, I didn't think this would happen. You act like I planned this."

"You can't run for governor and live here with me, Elena." She sat back down in the chair at the table.

"Riley, just because I run, doesn't mean I'm going to win. The party thinks the timing is right for a female candidate."

"And a gay candidate?" Riley asked. "In Texas, Elena? Really?"

"Obviously, that wouldn't–"

"You promised me you'd come out." Riley sighed. "You promised me you'd move here and you'd come out."

"Can we talk about all this later? I'm out with a few people. I only called to give you the good news, and this isn't a conversation I want to have right now." Elena hung up the phone without waiting for a reply.

CHAPTER 3

I<small>T HAD BEEN A</small> W<small>EEK</small> since Kinsley went to Riley's apartment and learned that Riley not only didn't remember that she was gay, she also had a girlfriend and was planning on settling down with her. She also, apparently, thought of Kinsley as the real estate agent and nothing more. Kinsley had been wrong to consider Riley Sanders a friend. It was true that they hadn't spent all that much time together in college, and as adults — even less, but still. Kinsley expected more. She'd been wrong.

When Riley made the move back to South Lake, Kinsley had been bouncing around to various cities for work. She'd attended conferences on building a business, how to enhance her online marketing presence, and even a few courses to get certified in different business practices. She also had to take tests to expand her business to commercial real estate, and those often took her out of town. Since Riley had returned, Kinsley had probably spent all of a few hours with her, and that was always in a group setting. Sometimes, she'd be leaving just as Riley arrived or vice versa. She'd built their friendship up in her head. And the crush she'd had forever, all but evaporated the moment she realized Riley had basically forgotten she'd existed and that she'd only sought her out because she'd needed a real estate agent. Hell, she hadn't even remembered Kinsley was a realtor; Morgan had to remind her.

"She didn't remember that you're gay?" Morgan asked as Kinsley helped her stock hiking boots in the store.

"She said she knew, but she… forgot that she knew?"

"How does that happen?" Morgan looked over at her and placed two shoe boxes on top of one another.

"I don't know. Am I crazy, though? Isn't that something you'd remember about someone?"

"I guess, yeah."

"We all hang out together. You're gay; Reese and Kellan are gay, and they're a couple."

"True, but we also hang out with Remy and Ryan. They're straight. Plus, Stacy and Dave are with us most nights." Morgan paused as she considered. "And then, there's—"

"I get it: we hang out with heterosexuals, too." Kinsley shrugged one shoulder as she passed another shoe box to Morgan. "It's just… I don't know."

"It's just that you've liked her for years – decades, at this point, I think. You've liked her, and she doesn't remember you the same way you do her. She doesn't see you the same way you see her, right?"

"Right," Kinsley said. "It's disappointing."

"And she has that girlfriend who's moving here," Morgan added.

"Also, disappointing."

"You can't be disappointed by that when you never exactly tried anything with her. What? Did you expect Riley Sanders to just remain single all these years until you finally walked up to her and asked her out?" Morgan chuckled.

"No, obviously not." Kinsley sat on the bench in the middle of the shoe aisle intended for people trying on shoes. "I don't know. It's just weird."

"I don't even remember her talking about a girlfriend." Morgan sat next to her as she leaned forward to organize the shoes.

"Right? I feel like I would have remembered if she'd said she was with someone."

"Because you're weirdly obsessed with her?" Morgan teased.

"I am not weirdly obsessed with her." Kinsley shoved her lightly.

"How long have they been together?"

"Three years."

"What's her name?"

"Elena Rivera. I looked her up when I got home. She's forty-six years old. She's the mayor of a little town outside of Dallas."

"Forty-six years old?"

"Riley said she was a bit older than her."

"That's not a bit." Morgan leaned back. "That's a May-November kind of thing."

"I know." Kinsley straightened a shoe box for Morgan.

"The oldest woman I've dated was two years older than us."

"Mine was three. But Riley's three years younger than us. So, it's even more of an age difference."

"Well, at least you know she has a thing for older women. If they do ever break up, you might have a chance." Morgan smirked at her and then patted her shoulder. "Sorry, Kinsley. I don't think she's a bad person. It just sounds like she didn't see you the same way you saw her back then."

"I guess so."

"What are you going to do?" Morgan asked.

"Help her find a damn house for her and her girlfriend."

Kinsley left Morgan to go back to her office. She stopped for a late afternoon coffee at the café but, this time, she wasn't there to see Riley. She just wanted the coffee. She grabbed a bagel, too, thinking she'd probably work through dinner, and sat down at her desk. She spread the cream cheese and dove into the bagel just as the bell chimed and the door opened to reveal Riley Sanders.

"Mother fucker…" Kinsley muttered to herself and dropped the bagel to the napkin to use another to wipe cream cheese off her face.

"Hi," Riley said as she walked in farther. "Sorry, did I interrupt? I wasn't sure if you were still open, but the door was unlocked, and the lights were on."

"I'm working through dinner," Kinsley said as she tried to clean her teeth with her tongue and swallow her bagel fully.

"That's your dinner?" Riley asked and pointed at the bagel.

"That and my coffee, yes," Kinsley replied. "Sorry, did you need something? I sent you a few listings yesterday."

"Oh, yes. I got those. Thanks." The woman stood holding her purse in both hands in front of her body. She seemed to be lacking the confidence Kinsley normally associated with her. "I sent them to Elena to take a look at. I'm just waiting to hear back from her before we go take a look."

"Okay. No rush on my end." Kinsley leaned back in the office chair she'd spent way too much money on; but when she saw it in the store, she had to buy it. "I'll send you more listings as they come up, but can you at least tell me which ones aren't worth my time? That way I can move onto others."

"I've done something to upset you, haven't I?" Riley sat down, placing her purse on the floor.

"No," Kinsley lied.

"Yes, I have. I can tell, Kinsley."

"Really? Last week, you couldn't remember that I was gay. But, suddenly, you know me well enough to know when I'm upset?"

"So, you *are* upset about that."

"I'm not upset. I just—"

"What?" Riley asked with concern reading in her eyes. "What, Kinsley?"

"Okay. I am upset. We were friends, Riley. At least, I thought we were friends."

"We *were* friends, Kinsley. That's true. We knew each

other a little in college, but you and I weren't close back then. I've hardly seen you since. I'm sorry I upset you. It wasn't my intention. But can I ask you a question?"

"Sure." Kinsley took a drink of her coffee.

"Why is it so important to you that I remember that?"

"Because I told you, Riley. When I was in school, we were sitting on that futon in Remy and Reese's place. I'd already told them, and Morgan, but no one else knew. I came out to you. It was a big moment for me, and you don't even remember it."

Riley seemed to think for a moment before she replied, "I do remember it, Kinsley. I remember that you told me. I just forgot in that moment. When we were talking the other night, I just forgot. I'm sorry."

"You remember it?"

"The futon was light blue. It had a stain on it that we both tried not to sit on."

"There was a stain?" Kinsley asked. "Wait... That's why you sat so close to me?"

"I guess. There wasn't exactly a lot of space with Remy sitting there, too."

"Right," Kinsley said as the importance of yet another piece of her relationship with Riley evaporated in front of her eyes. "I guess that night just meant more to me than it did you."

"I'm sorry, Kinsley. I don't mean to make light of something that is obviously so important. I mean, I'm gay. I came out right after you, if I remember correctly. I know what it's like to–"

"See? That's what's getting me about all this," Kinsley interjected. "You came out after me. I remember that clearly. In fact, Reese and I both thought you might be gay all along. Morgan, too. They'd grown up with you and knew you better than I did, but I saw it, too."

"Saw it?"

"The way you looked at Morgan sometimes back then. There was also that girl at the theta party. I caught you two dancing. It just seemed like there was something to it."

"Theta party?" Riley tried to recall. "Yeah, I remember her. I hooked up with her that night." She chuckled. "If you could call it that; we mostly just fumbled around in a downstairs closet during the party."

"You had sex in a closet while people partied right outside?" Kinsley asked as she laughed.

"More like my hand went inside her jeans, and she lifted my skirt." Riley laughed at that revelation. "It was intense, to say the least, but that was all it was."

"I guess I wouldn't have thought you'd have that in you."

"Sex?" Riley lifted an eyebrow.

"Sex with a girl you just met at a frat party, where anyone could just open the door and see you."

"The things you don't know about me, Kinsley James." The woman chuckled again, but it was deeper this time, and Kinsley felt it deep in her core.

"I'm starting to realize that," Kinsley replied, trying to move past the feeling inside her. "So, you stopped by."

"Yes, I stopped by to apologize for the other night. I think I gave you the impression that I didn't remember things. I wanted to make sure I'd explained myself properly. I do remember. I was slightly tipsy the night you told me. Remy had just passed me two shots in a row, and that was after – I think – you gave me some mixed drink. We were pre-gaming, if I remember correctly."

"For Remy and Reese's birthday party," Kinsley added.

"Yes. But I remember you telling me that you were gay, Kinsley." She paused. "I'm also sorry for how the night ended. Elena called, and we needed to talk. She had some news I wasn't prepared for; I didn't handle it well. And I'm sorry if I gave you the impression that you had to go."

"You didn't. I just felt like I should. It seemed like a private conversation."

Riley sighed and looked toward the glass door to the

office and the street beyond before she said, "It was, but it was still rude of me."

Kinsley nibbled a bit on her bottom lip before she swiped her tongue across it, tasting rogue cream cheese and wondering why she always appeared to be such a dolt around this gorgeous woman.

"We should just start over," Kinsley suggested.

"We need to go that far?" Riley asked as she leaned forward in her chair. "Kinsley, I am sorry if I offended you."

"You didn't." She waved her off. "It's okay. We're good."

"So, you'll still help me find a house?"

"Of course."

"Can I do something?" Riley asked as her expression turned thoughtful. "Let me take you out to dinner tonight to make up for what an asshole I was the other night. We won't talk about house-hunting. We'll just be two friends at dinner."

"You don't have to do that," Kinsley said, lowering her eyes immediately to her bagel that had likely cooled and hardened and now looked like the most disgusting thing in the world to her.

"Come on. You can't just eat a bagel for dinner. We can go to *Bradley's* and grab some burgers."

"How do you eat pizza and burgers and still look like that?" Kinsley asked with light laughter before she realized she'd said it out loud.

"Well, thank you; I think." Riley smiled and nodded. "You ate pizza the other night, too. And a bagel is all carbs. Look at you." She pointed at Kinsley. "You seem to be doing alright."

"I work out a lot," Kinsley said. "To balance it all out. Morgan kind of makes me."

"You and Morgan are pretty close, huh?" Riley asked. "Wait." She stood abruptly. "This is good dinner talk for two friends. Let's go. I'll drive."

"I really should—"

"The work will be there when you get back, right?" Riley asked. "I have a mountain of it on my desk, too. But I'm determined not to try and climb it tonight."

Kinsley nodded, and after packing up, she locked the office and walked around the block to where Riley had parked her car. Before she climbed into the passenger's seat, she saw Kellan and Reese walking toward them hand in hand.

"Hey, guys," Reese said and waved with her free hand.

"Hey," Riley replied. "What are you two up to tonight?"

Kinsley lowered her head and stared at the ground. She knew what was coming next.

"I'm just picking this one up from work, and we're heading home for dinner," Reese said and rested her head on Kellan's shoulder.

"Join us." Riley tossed her designer bag into the back seat of her car. "We're going to *Bradley's.*"

"Burgers?" Kellan asked Reese, who nodded against her shoulder. "We're in."

"Morgan was meeting us at our place, though. I'll text her the change in plans," Reese said as she pulled her phone out of her pocket.

"Want to invite Remy, too?" Riley asked.

Kinsley looked up and met Kellan's eyes as Kellan smiled at her. Kellan then glanced toward Riley and back to Kinsley, and gave her a knowing expression followed by one that expressed a silent apology that they'd be interrupting her dinner plans.

CHAPTER 4

"WAS THIS MEANT TO BE a date?" Kellan whispered into Kinsley's ear.

"What?" Kinsley turned to her. "No. We're not–" She stopped herself. "She's with someone."

Kellan nodded and leaned over to Reese to whisper in her ear, likely, telling her that they hadn't interrupted a date between Riley and Kinsley. Morgan had decided to join them, but Remy and Ryan had made other plans. Morgan sat across from Kinsley and next to Riley. She'd offered Kinsley that spot when they'd first arrived, but Kinsley had opted to sit next to Reese and Kellan instead. Riley smelled so good. Kinsley had been able to catch the scent when they'd left the office. She wasn't sure she'd be able to sit next to her and not give herself away.

"How's the new practice?" Reese asked as she snagged a fry from her girlfriend's plate.

"Coming along. I'm still wrapping up a few of my longer cases from before I moved back, though. They were complicated divorces. Now, I'm taking on new cases. It's a lot, but it's coming along. I like working for myself," Riley offered in response.

"And you're thinking about buying a house, right?" Morgan asked.

"That's the plan. Kinsley is helping, thanks to your recommendation," Riley said to Morgan as she smiled at her and then winked at Kinsley.

"She's the only realtor I know," Morgan replied. "But I hear she's pretty good."

"So, how is it: living together and without me, Kell?" Riley asked.

"You were hardly ever there when we did live together," Kellan replied and laughed. "But I love living with Reese. I miss my friends in San Francisco, but we're going to visit them next month. I love it here, though."

"Morgan, what's going on with you lately?" Riley asked her. "Anyone in your life these days?"

"If you mean friends, I'm all good in that department. If you mean family – still all good. If you're asking if I'm dating anyone, the answer is no."

"What about that woman you went out with last week?" Reese asked her best friend.

"Didn't work out," Morgan replied.

"Why not?" Riley asked.

"Just not my type."

"What *is* your type?" Riley pressed.

Kinsley stared at Riley, who was staring at Morgan. What was happening?

"I don't know. I just know she's not it," Morgan answered. "Pick on James for a minute. She's single, too." Morgan nodded in Kinsley's direction.

"Hey," Kinsley retorted and tossed a fry at her. "Leave me out of this."

"What about you, Kinsley?" Riley turned to her to ask. "What's your type?"

Morgan nearly choked on her soda. Reese glanced down at the table, and Kellan played with the remnants of her hamburger. Kinsley tried to look away from Riley's stare, but she couldn't. Something told her to keep looking at her. Something told her to defy her thundering heart and her foggy mind, because Riley's dark brown eyes were remarkably beautiful to stare into.

"I don't know that I have one."

Morgan nearly choked again. Kinsley glared at her,

planning her murder inside her head for later that night.

"Really? Nothing? Not even blonde over brunette or something like that?"

"She prefers brunettes. The darker the hair color, the better," Morgan answered for her.

"Morgan!" Kinsley exclaimed.

"Dark hair, huh?" Riley sipped her soda through her straw and looked so damn sexy, Kinsley was just about ready to pull it away from her, because she couldn't take it anymore. That damn button nose just did things to her when it combined with those lips making that shape. "What else? Tell me all her secrets, Morgan."

"Morgan does not know my secrets," Kinsley retorted and dropped a fry back onto her plate, suddenly not wanting to eat it.

"I know most of them," Morgan argued.

"Really?" Riley smirked at Morgan and then turned her head to Kinsley.

No, this wasn't happening. Kinsley stood and removed her wallet from her pocket. She tossed enough cash to cover her meal onto the table.

"I need to go. I have work. I'll see you guys all later."

***

"I fucked up again," Riley said mostly to herself.

"What are you talking about?" Morgan asked her.

"I keep messing up with her." Riley motioned with her open hand toward the door just as Kinsley headed out. "I need to talk to her."

"What's going on there?" Kellan asked.

"I don't know. I just feel like she doesn't like me," Riley said. Morgan nearly choked for the third time. Riley turned and slapped her on the back. "Are you okay?"

"Fine," Morgan replied. "I'll go talk to her."

"No, I think this is something I need to do. Besides, I drove her here."

Riley rose and was grateful she'd hit the ATM earlier and had cash. She tossed enough to cover her meal and Kinsley's on the table, before picking up Kinsley's money. She said her goodbyes to the people she'd invited to dinner and moved to the door.

"Kinsley, wait up." She moved quickly down the sidewalk toward Kinsley and stopped as the woman turned around. "I'm sorry."

"Sorry for what? Trying to set me up with Morgan Burns?" Kinsley asked.

"I wasn't trying to—"

"Yes, you were. Riley, Morgan is one of my closest friends. That's all she's ever been, and I don't want her to be anything more, okay?"

"Okay. I'm sorry."

"Why is this so important to you?" Kinsley asked her and ran a hand through her dark blonde hair that fell around her face in layers.

"It's not. I just thought..." She stopped herself. "I'm sorry. You just mentioned Morgan before. She makes you work out; she recommended you to me. You two hang out a lot. I don't know... I guess I just went a little crazy there for a minute. I'm trying to be a friend to you, and I'm doing a terrible job at it." She held out Kinsley's money. "Here. I said I'd buy you dinner."

"What? I don't—"

"Please, just take it. I've screwed up your night. The car is around the corner. Let me at least take you back to your office. Then, I'll leave you alone and stop embarrassing myself."

"I'm going to walk," Kinsley replied and tucked the cash into her front pocket. "I think I'd like to be alone if you don't mind."

"Sure. I'm sorry."

"Can you let me know about the listings I sent you already? I'd like to hear back before I find more for you and Elena."

"I'll look at them again tonight," Riley replied.

"Thanks," Kinsley said, and the word sounded even shorter than just its one syllable. "I'll see you later."

Riley stood on the sidewalk, watching Kinsley walk away from her. Kinsley's hands were in her back pockets. Riley watched Kinsley's ass move in those jeans and turned her head to the side, as if to take the view in even more. She shook her head and snapped out of it. Why was she always managing to upset Kinsley James? Kinsley had been nothing but kind to her. They'd known one another for over a decade. Riley rolled her eyes at herself and walked to her car. The drive to the apartment was short. When she arrived, she quickly reviewed the listings Kinsley had already sent her, and emailed back that two were options. The others, she knew she didn't like. There was no point in waiting for Elena to finally take a look at the links she'd sent her.

She let out an exasperated sigh and headed into the bathroom, where she took a long hot bath. When she finally emerged, she went back to the kitchen table, where she'd laid out files, and opened her computer. It was nearly midnight when she finally closed her computer and decided to go to sleep. For the fifth consecutive night, Elena hadn't called to wish her good night. That part of their relationship had long since passed, but Elena hadn't gone this many nights without at least calling to say good night to her.

They'd been together for three years, but they hardly ever actually saw one another. In the beginning, Riley was in Dallas for three months. They'd had that time to get to know one another and to fall in love. She hadn't expected to fall for an older woman like Elena, but Elena had won her over with her elegance and charm. The part where she was still in the closet wasn't ideal back then, but Riley understood. Elena was a politician in Texas of all places. And, as a lesbian, it was hard enough to get elected in one of the blue states. Riley had understood, because Elena had promised this would be her last term. She'd leave Texas and move to Tahoe. They'd finally be together for more than two weeks at a time when they could get it.

Things hadn't been the same this past year. They hadn't had the chance to take a vacation. They'd only seen one another every couple of months, and Elena still wasn't out of the closet. Riley had been holding onto the promise of their move. She was still holding onto the promise of this move. If Elena decided to stay in Texas, Riley didn't know what she was going to do. She wasn't sure she'd be able to go on for another four years like this; eight years, if Elena got re-elected. With the campaigns, that would be more than ten years living in two different states, with a woman who was straight to the rest of the world. Hell, if she got elected, the party would likely try to convince her to remarry. Elena's husband had died in a car accident just before she ran for a city council position. They'd probably want her to find another man to make an honest woman out of her. Riley fell asleep to the thought of Elena, arm in arm with a Mitt Romney lookalike, as she took the stage and waved at the adoring crowd after winning the election for governor.

CHAPTER 5

KINSLEY NOTICED the paper bag from the café on the desk in her office when she came out of the bathroom. Next to the bag was a large coffee of some kind. She'd heard the bell chime, which was what had made her rush out of the bathroom as quickly as possible. She hadn't heard it chime again, though, likely due to the toilet flushing. There was no one in the office now. She moved behind her desk and opened the white bag. Inside were half a dozen bagels and just as many small containers of cream cheese along with one plastic knife. Kinsley glanced at the coffee and noticed a napkin underneath it. She moved the cup to read the words scribbled there.

"For the dinner I interrupted the other night. I am sorry." Kinsley read it out loud and liked the way Riley wrote her name with a large letter R and a curly Y at the end.

Riley wasn't there, though. Kinsley sat down in her chair and didn't know what to do. Should she rush after her to say thank you? Should she text her a thank you? Maybe she should send her an email, since their relationship was more professional than personal at this point. Kinsley had sent her a few more possibilities that met the limited criteria Riley had provided. When Kinsley checked her email, she noticed Riley had replied to her last message. She smiled and sent her own reply.

***

"You ready?" Kinsley asked Riley when she got out of her car.

"I only have an hour." Riley approached and tucked her car keys into her purse. "Sorry, the day kind of got away from me. I thought I'd have more time."

"That's okay." Kinsley motioned for Riley to head up the driveway and toward the front door. "I don't think it'll take that long."

Riley looked up at the modest size house before meeting Kinsley's eyes and saying, "It's nice so far."

Kinsley smiled at her, unlocked the door, and motioned for Riley to follow her inside. Kinsley explained the layout and features of the house as they walked from room to room. Riley would smile and nod every so often. She asked a few questions, which Kinsley answered, but the woman gave nothing away. When they finished looking around the house, Kinsley took her out the back door.

"Wow," Riley said as she looked at the lake view. It was through a lot of trees, and she could barely see the water, but it was still technically a lake view. "This is amazing. This is within my budget?" She turned to ask Kinsley.

"It's been on the market for a few days. It'll go fast. There hasn't been an offer yet, but there will be; probably by the end of the day today or tomorrow. Any house here where you can see even a sliver of the water goes quickly, and generally at or above asking price," Kinsley explained.

"I don't know if I'll be able to get Elena on board that fast." Riley swatted at a bee as it buzzed between them.

"Most houses go pretty fast around here though, Riley. How fast is she realistically going to be able to make a decision? I mean, should we try FaceTime or something, since she can't be here in person?"

"No, she couldn't even if she wanted to." Riley rolled her eyes.

Kinsley wondered what that reaction to her question was all about. She didn't want to ask, though. She didn't want to push Riley where Elena was concerned. She knew she didn't want to hear about their amazing love story and the fact that they were looking for their dream home together.

"She's been busy lately," Riley offered next.

"Wrapping things up, I'm sure. Moving isn't easy. I can't imagine what it's like if you're the mayor of a town."

"Right," Riley replied but appeared to be thinking of something else in that moment. "Well, I should be getting back to the office. I have a client meeting."

"So, this is a no?" Kinsley asked. "Or will you talk to Elena about it and get back to me?"

"I'll try to talk to her about it tonight. Can I call you or—"

"You can call me, but we should try to sit down soon to talk more about what you're really looking for. We could have Elena on speaker or something if she can spare the time. If I don't get more specifics, I'm kind of just shooting in the dark."

"Right. I'm sorry. I don't want you to think I'm wasting your time." Riley held her head in her hands. "I just keep messing up with you, Kinsley. I keep trying to show you that I can be a friend, after my monumental error that night at my place, and I keep messing up. I promise you, I'm not a horribly selfish person. I'm also not normally a mess like this either. There's just a lot going on."

Kinsley wanted to hug her in that moment. She wanted to pull Riley into her and hold onto her, but she knew that would be strange. Riley wasn't in tears. She wasn't sobbing uncontrollably. She was just stressed out. She'd just moved back home. Her girlfriend lived in another state and would soon be relocating to join her. She had a thriving new law practice. She had to buy a new house without Elena's help. This wasn't a hugging moment. It was a helpful friend kind of moment. Kinsley could do that for her.

"What are you doing tonight?" she asked.

"Working, probably."

"Why don't you come over to my house? I'll cook you something. My guess is you're not much of a cook if you're living on burgers and pizza."

"I'm not much of a cook. That's correct." Riley laughed.

"I'll make dinner. You bring wine or that imported beer you like. We can look at listings, maybe narrow a few down, and just – I don't know – hang out."

"Hang out? When was the last time we've done that?"

"Just the two of us? Never." Kinsley realized it as she said it. "I guess we tried to, the other night, but that didn't go well."

"Then, let's try it again. No house talk. We'll just hang out." Riley smiled at her.

"We should probably talk about the house. If we don't, I won't be able to find you a place to live once Elena gets here." Kinsley tried to laugh. "But we can do that part first and then hang out if you want."

"That sounds nice," Riley replied. "What time should I be there?"

***

Riley rang the doorbell. A few moments later, Kinsley opened the front door of her house and smiled so warmly to Riley, that it caused Riley to smile back immediately. She held out the bottle of wine and the six-pack of beer she'd brought with her.

"I brought both."

"I guess we're getting drunk tonight," Kinsley replied and motioned for Riley to enter. "Come in. I'll give you a quick tour."

"This place is great, Kinsley." Riley looked around the open foyer with gorgeous redwood beams visible all over the place. "Really great."

"Thanks," Kinsley said. "Can I take your coat?" she asked, pointing at the light blue pea coat Riley had worn over her black cardigan.

She'd paired it with skinny jeans and black heels. She'd had a hard time picking out what to wear tonight. She was just hanging out with her friend, Kinsley. This wasn't a date. If anything, it was a working dinner with her realtor that happened to be someone she knew from college, and a little more recently. Did that make Kinsley an acquaintance? That didn't seem right. Riley placed the drinks she'd brought on the table by the door where Kinsley, apparently, kept her keys and a nice-looking candle centerpiece. Kinsley moved behind Riley and helped her with the jacket. When was the last time a woman helped her with her coat? Riley watched as Kinsley hung it up for her in the closet before grabbing the beer and wine and carrying it for her into the kitchen.

"Damn, Kinsley. This place is amazing," she said when she noted the wood notes continued throughout the kitchen and mingled with the stainless-steel appliances effortlessly.

"Thank you. I'll take you around in a minute, but let me get you a drink first. I knew you were probably bringing wine, but I put one out to breathe just in case. Would you like some of that or should I open the one you brought?"

Well, this was different. Riley nodded toward the decanter of red wine resting on the kitchen counter and watched as a very well put-together Kinsley James poured them two precise glasses. Kinsley was wearing jeans, which Riley had noticed she pretty much always wore, even when she was working. She was also wearing a light gray scoop neck shirt with the logo of some 80s rock band on it in navy blue. The look made Riley feel slightly overdressed, but it also seemed perfect for the occasion and looked really good on Kinsley. She wore it with a confidence Riley hadn't seen her possess before. Every time she'd seen the woman recently, she'd always seemed caught off guard by her. This was a different Kinsley. Both versions of the woman were charming, but Riley had to admit that she liked this version more than the one that had uttered *'mother fucker'* at her the last time she'd walked into the woman's office to meet with her. That reaction had been why she'd dropped her gift of coffee and bagels and ran the last time.

They carried their wine around Kinsley's home. Kinsley had pointed out the things she'd done herself to improve it since purchasing it. She added the things she'd like to do in the future, and the things that were the highest priority, like re-staining the decks outside. It was on the patio balcony that Riley took in the beauty she sometimes forgot about: the lake. When she grew up here, she knew tourists came to town specifically for the views, the outdoor activities, and the summertime fun. But she thought of the place as home. It wasn't a vacation spot for her. As a busy adult, she also forgot the beauty of this place. The sun was just about to fully set. The sky was alight with pinks, purples, and oranges. Riley stood against the railing with her wine glass and just took it all in. Kinsley moved next to her but left enough space to stay in this moment. She didn't say a word. After a few minutes, Kinsley moved to sit on her patio chaise. Riley turned around and noted it was the only piece of furniture on the balcony, save the table and lamp next to it.

"Mind sharing?" she asked and headed toward the chair.

"Oh, sure. Sorry. I have another one of these. I just had to stain it. It's downstairs, in the yard," Kinsley stated, and Riley wondered why she felt the need to do so.

"Your place is perfect, Kinsley. Really. I can't believe you can do all this. You really replaced the tile in your own bathroom?"

"It's not too difficult. I read a book. It's mostly just time-consuming."

"I can barely boil water, and you're replacing the tile." Riley laughed.

"When I go to do it in the downstairs bathroom, you can watch. Maybe you'll learn how." Kinsley smiled at her as Riley sat on the end of the lounge. "It's kind of fun in the beginning: you get to beat the old tile into submission with a hammer."

"Count me in," Riley replied and took a drink of her wine. "This is great."

"I thought it would pair nicely with what I'm making."

"Where'd you learn about wine pairing?" Riley asked and crossed her legs, turning more toward Kinsley.

"In culinary school," Kinsley said with a smile that told Riley she should have known that. "Do you not–"

"No, I remember." Riley pointed at Kinsley as if to tell her that, this one, she knew. Kinsley didn't have to remind her. "You majored in…" She thought for a moment. "You majored in finance, didn't you?"

"I did."

"And you hated it," Riley added.

"Completely." Kinsley took a drink. "I went to appease my parents. As soon as I graduated, I enrolled in culinary school. I thought I'd run my own restaurant one day. But – I don't know – that just seemed impractical. I knew how most of them were unsuccessful. Plus, I had that finance degree, that crusher of dreams."

Riley laughed and almost spat her wine out at that.

"I ended up getting my real estate license. And now, I run my own business; it's just not a restaurant," Kinsley finished.

"And you're okay with that?"

"I am. I love what I do. I didn't expect to, but I do." She shrugged. "It's how I was able to find this place, and I love this place."

"I love it, too," Riley said as she stared out at the sun disappearing into the horizon.

"Is this something you'd like? This place?"

"Oh, I don't think I'd be able to afford anything like this. You know my budget," she replied.

Kinsley stared at her thoughtfully for a moment and said, "Right. Well, I got a great deal on this place."

"I'd hope so, or I would consider taking you up on that friendship deal of no commission," Riley said.

"I already told you: I'm not taking a commission," Kinsley replied. "Come on. Dinner's just warming up. We can talk more about it as we eat."

Riley nodded, and they carried their wine downstairs back into the kitchen. When Kinsley pulled some chicken dish out of the oven, it both looked and smelled delicious. Riley had missed lunch. She'd also skipped breakfast. She'd subsisted on a protein bar and a bag of chips. Kinsley walked them to the table, carrying the dish. That was when Riley noticed Kinsley had set the table. Their plates, silverware, cloth napkins, and salads awaited them along with brimming water glasses. Kinsley placed the dish in the middle of the table and nodded for Riley to sit, which she did. Kinsley disappeared into the kitchen and returned with the decanter and their wine glasses. She set them down and then sat down herself, across from Riley.

"I don't know what to say."

"I thought you could use a home-cooked meal," Kinsley said.

"I haven't had one of those since my mom cooked for me before they went on their trip." Riley picked up her fork. "Kinsley, you didn't have to do all this."

"I wanted to. I like to cook, and I don't often get a chance to do it for others."

"How do your friends not take advantage of this love of yours?" Riley smiled at her as she dished out a healthy portion for herself.

"They do. But that's mainly for parties. I don't get to cook for them like this all that often."

"Well, I'm lucky I get the pleasure," Riley said.

They ate in relative silence for a few minutes before the requisite small talk began. Kinsley talked about her business and a few difficult to please clients. Riley did the same, leaving out some details to protect confidentiality. It was pleasant. Riley found herself trying to remember that this was not a date on more than one occasion. By the time they'd finished the chicken, they'd also nearly finished the wine. Kinsley stood and insisted Riley stay at the table. God, Riley hadn't been pampered like this in years. Maybe she'd never been pampered like this. It was nice, but she couldn't get used to it. This was two friends hanging out. She'd have to find a way to repay Kinsley for this kindness and amazing food.

Kinsley came back out first with another decanter of wine, filled their glasses, and disappeared back into the kitchen. When she came out again, it was with two plates that contained some type of pastry dish. There were beautiful berries on top of it, and a dollop of whipped cream next to them.

"I didn't know if you were a dessert person or not." Kinsley sat back down across from her. "If you're not, you don't–"

"I am. This looks so damn good. What *don't* you do, Kinsley?" Riley dug in with her fork.

Kinsley laughed and replied, "I liked pastry the best in culinary school."

"It shows." Riley took a second bite. "I'm not even ashamed of how much I like this and how I'm going to eat all of it."

"I made four. I can give you the other two. You can take them home with you."

"You keep them. Maybe I'll come over again, and we can eat them together."

"They won't keep beyond tomorrow, I'm afraid." Kinsley laughed and took a bite.

"Then, I'll be back tomorrow." Riley meant it as a joke, but she also meant it, period.

"I'll make fish and pair it with a nice white," Kinsley replied.

They left it at that, and the conversation drifted a little to the topic of their friends. Kellan and Reese were doing well. Remy and Ryan were doing well. Morgan was doing well at the store and trying to expand her family's business but was still looking for love. When it came time to do the dishes, Kinsley again tried to make Riley sit down, but Riley wouldn't hear of it. They did them together, and it was nice. It was nice doing this with someone. When they finished, Kinsley carried the half-empty decanter into the living room, where she also started a fire, and they sat staring for a few minutes as it burned.

"So, should we talk about the house you two want now?" Kinsley asked after some silence.

Riley looked over at her, taking her eyes away from the fire, and replied. "Right. I guess I should stop wasting your time."

"I don't think you–"

"No, it's my fault." Riley felt the wine she'd consumed hit her in that moment. "I've been putting it off. I shouldn't be. I asked you to do this, and I keep not answering your questions."

"Is something wrong?" Kinsley asked. "If you want to hire another–"

"I don't want to hire anyone else. I just might not need a realtor after all."

Riley took a long drink of her wine, finishing it. Moments later, her glass was full again, and Kinsley had topped off her own as well. Though, Riley hadn't been paying attention as they'd drank. It might have been her consuming most of the wine tonight, because Kinsley did not appear even the slightest bit tipsy.

"I think maybe you should discontinue your search. I can let you know to pick it back up again if I need it."

"Did something happen?" Kinsley asked.

"Elena might be the first lesbian governor of the state of Texas." Riley took another drink and knew she'd regret this in the morning.

"What?" Kinsley laughed a little. "Are you serious?"

"The party wants her to run for governor. The current governor's term is up in about a year and a half. It's perfect timing to start a campaign."

"But what about your plans?"

"That's what I've asked her about. She hasn't answered me yet."

"What do you mean?" Kinsley took a drink.

"I mean, I sent her the links you sent me right after I got them. I got a short email back that she'd take a look when she could. She hasn't told me how she feels about them yet."

"What did she say when you talked to her?"

"That's the thing: we haven't talked since that night."

"The night I was there?" Kinsley asked.

"She told me about possibly running for governor, and I didn't take it well."

"I can see why," Kinsley replied. "She's really thinking of staying?"

"She's changing our entire plan if she does," Riley said. "I gave her three years. That was the deal. She wanted this term, and then she'd give it up and move to Tahoe with me."

"And if she runs?"

"Well, that's a year and a half of campaigning without me, and then four years in office without me."

"So, basically another six years until she's here. Would you consider moving there?"

"What's the point? We wouldn't be living together. She's not out."

"Oh. I guess that would be a problem," Kinsley said.

Riley took another drink and added, "It's been a problem all along. I've just put up with it."

"Why do you?"

"Why do I what?" Riley asked, feeling a little fuzzy.

"Put up with it?" Kinsley paused and set her glass on her beautiful coffee table. "I mean, I don't know if I could do what you do. How does it even work?" She paused again. "And I'm not judging or suggesting it doesn't work; I'm honestly just curious."

"It worked really well in the beginning. But that was probably because I was there for three months. We spent every free moment we had together. She was in the closet and always had been. She'd married young to try to push the gay away. When her husband died, she finally decided to date women. I was – and still am – the first long-term relationship she's ever had with a woman."

"Really? She's forty-six."

"How'd you know that?" Riley asked.

"I may have Googled her." Kinsley shrugged. "There's only one mayor in Texas named Elena."

Riley laughed so hard, she nearly spilled her wine and said, "You Googled her?"

"I did. I'm not crazy, I promise. I was just curious."

Riley took another drink of her wine, felt the immediate hit of it to her already tipsy brain, and set the glass down next to Kinsley's on the table.

"Yes, she's forty-six. She was forty-three when we met. And yes, I was her first serious girlfriend. She'd dated women but hadn't found anything real until me."

"She waited a long time for you," Kinsley said with an expression Riley couldn't read.

"And now I'm waiting a long time for her," Riley replied. "I don't know if I can do it, honestly."

"Can I just say something and you won't hate me?"

Riley laughed and said, "Of course."

"You deserve better," Kinsley said and shifted closer to her on the couch.

Or maybe it just seemed like that to Riley.

"She hasn't even called you in what? A week? If I had a girlfriend like you, and we had to be apart like that, I'd call you every night. I'd call you every morning, too, probably. I'd also probably text you a lot. Like, if I found a cute animal video online or something, I'd have to send it to you. If something funny happened at work, or even something bad happened, I'd have to tell you about it. I don't know... That's what a relationship is to me, I guess. I'd want to make dinner for you and sit by the fire. Maybe even just go out on the patio and sit in the evenings while the sun goes down."

Riley thought she heard Kinsley gulp from where she was sitting.

"I'm sorry," Kinsley said then.

Riley could only sit and stare as Kinsley's expressive eyes lowered to her wine glass. She lifted it up to her lips, finished the wine, and lowered the empty glass back to the table.

CHAPTER 6

KINSLEY HADN'T MEANT to say all that. She hadn't meant to say anything at all. She'd just planned on listening as Riley spoke about her relationship. But hearing how Elena had been treating Riley had Kinsley's blood boiling. She'd tried to hide it, but then she'd blurted all that out. Now, Riley was staring at her.

"That sounds nice," Riley said so softly, Kinsley almost didn't hear it.

"I guess I just meant that you deserve someone that makes you a priority. I don't know Elena, and I don't know much about your relationship, but from what you've told me, I'm not seeing that from her. I mean, it's a home she's buying with you. It's not just a building made of wood and stone, right?" Kinsley asked, feeling fired up again.

"Right."

"It's a place you'll share with the person in your life. You'll build onto it. Your blood, sweat, and tears will be in that home. You might even raise children there. It's not just a house."

"No, it's not."

"I know I wouldn't want my partner to find a house for us on her own. It would be something we'd share together, just like the house itself."

"But you have this perfect place," Riley said and looked around.

42

"Yeah?" Kinsley asked and followed Riley's eyes.

"It's gorgeous, Kinsley. I wish I could find and afford a place like this."

"You'll find something you love," Kinsley said.

"You know what the hardest part is?" Riley asked.

"What?"

"Finding someone I love to share it with," Riley replied.

Kinsley didn't know what to make of that statement. Did that mean Riley no longer loved her girlfriend? Did that mean she did love her girlfriend, but that said girlfriend likely wouldn't be living in that house with her?

"More?" she asked nodding toward the wine.

"No, I shouldn't. I can't even drive myself home. Looks like I'll be calling for a ride," Riley said.

"I'd offer to drive you, but I've had a couple of glasses myself." Kinsley didn't feel drunk, but she also didn't trust herself on these windy mountain roads after drinking a couple of glasses. "You can stay," she suggested softly.

Riley met her eyes and replied, "I shouldn't."

"I have the space. I have this nice, big house to myself. Sometimes, it gets lonely." Kinsley lowered her eyes, trying not to think about what it might feel like to fall asleep next to Riley. "You can take the guest room."

"I'm sorry. I shouldn't have driven over here and then basically got drunk." Riley laid her head back on the sofa and closed her eyes. "I always seem to be messing up around you, don't I?"

"What? No, you don't." Kinsley slid a little closer to her on the couch. "Why do you say that?"

"You were so cool back in college," Riley said, apparently changing the subject.

"What? No, I wasn't." Kinsley couldn't help but laugh at that. "I was a mess back then. I was such a baby gay and didn't know how to flirt with women. Plus, I was in school for something I didn't even want to do."

"Kinsley, you were gorgeous back then." The woman

paused, and her eyes got big. Kinsley swallowed hard. "You are now, too. I realize how that sounded. Did you really not notice that girls were all over you?"

"Girls were not all over me. When would you have even noticed that?" Kinsley laughed. "I thought you didn't remember I was gay."

Riley grunted in frustration and stared at her intently before replying, "I said I forgot that I knew that. It's different than just not knowing. Do you ever hear a song on the radio after, like, a million years, and you sing the lyrics out loud in the car? You realize you've forgotten you knew them all this time."

"I guess, yeah."

"Kinsley, I haven't talked to you in over a decade. I mean, *really* talked to you. This is probably the first time we've had a conversation that's lasted this long. It's definitely the longest we've ever been alone." She paused. "I remember you, Kinsley James. I remember that theta party and that girl that was all over you when you sat on that battered orange sofa. Didn't she do a body shot off you later?"

"Oh, yeah." Kinsley chuckled. "God, what was her name?"

"Girl number three that night." Riley lifted an eyebrow. "There were at least two others I remember nodding in your direction or asking me about you when we all walked into the party together. That was just that night."

"You remember that now?"

"I think our talk the other week kind of shook some things loose for me. I felt like a bad person, Kinsley. I don't want you to think you're someone I don't remember."

Kinsley gulped again. She smiled sweetly at Riley after hearing those words. It had hit her hard that night. The days that followed weren't much easier. Riley had been someone she'd cared for. Crush or no crush, they'd been friends. Hearing that Riley hadn't remembered something so important to Kinsley had been enough to make her cry.

"You're not a bad person," Kinsley replied.

"I feel like a bad person around you. I brought you bagels and coffee to try to make up for it," she said with a smile.

"I ate two of those bagels and drank all of that coffee. I gave the rest to Morgan and the people at her store. I'm sure they enjoyed them."

"I'm sorry about Morgan, too," Riley said. "I was out of line."

"What was that?" Kinsley took the chance to speak on this subject since Riley had brought it up. This woman was clearly more open with a few glasses of wine in her. "Why Morgan?"

"You two used to get along so well in school. You're still talking to one another now. And it seemed like you were close. You said she makes you work out with her. You also have dinner with her a few times a week, I think."

"How do you know that?" Kinsley asked.

"I see you sometimes. You come into the café, or I'll see you leaving with Morgan when she's closing up for the night."

"You've never said anything," Kinsley replied.

"You were always so cool," Riley said again. "I still sometimes feel like the lowly freshman around you guys. Even though we've been out of college forever."

"I'm not cool, Riley." Kinsley laughed. "I always thought *you* were so cool. You never seemed to care about us. You never tried to hang out with us or ask to be invited places. You just sometimes showed up and sometimes didn't. You seemed so comfortable with who you were and in your own skin. Even when you came out, it was just like, *'Okay, I'm gay, everyone.'* And that was it."

"You guys made it so easy. Reese and Morgan were both gay. I knew them a little growing up. Not a lot, but enough that when I got to campus, I reached out. It was like a safe place where I could just be myself. Maybe that's why I appeared that way. I wasn't, by the way."

"Wasn't what?"

"Comfortable in my own skin. I can talk the talk, though. And, apparently, I'm a great actress." She smiled at Kinsley. "I am also incredibly tired all of a sudden. I'm going to call that ride now."

"Riley, sleep in the guest room. I'll get you towels and stuff. You can sleep it off." Kinsley stood. "And I'm not taking no for an answer."

"Fine. But you're the one that'll have to deal with my bed head and hangover in the morning," Riley replied as she stood, too.

"Really not a problem," Kinsley said mostly to herself as the butterflies in her stomach flew around in there, bashing into walls, apparently, trying to escape at the thought of seeing Riley Sanders and her bed head in the morning.

Kinsley laid out a few towels in the guest bathroom after lending Riley something to sleep in. She also found a new toothbrush deep in the recesses of her own bathroom drawer. She usually had one or two travel toothbrushes from when she'd go on a work trip and forget she already had one, ending up buying one she didn't need. She made sure there were toothpaste and a hairbrush in there, too, before checking to see that the bathtub was stocked with guest soaps and shampoo. When she left the bathroom to make her way down the short hall and say a quick good night to Riley, she overheard Riley on the phone and stopped in her tracks.

"Elena, we haven't talked in a week. I'm starting to wonder if I even have a girlfriend." There was a pause. "I'm starting to wonder if I even want one." There was a second pause that came with an exasperated sigh. "Do you want one? I'm going to sleep. Call me tomorrow."

Kinsley waited another few moments before she knocked on the door and said, "I just wanted to say good night. Do you have everything you need?"

"No, but that's not your fault." Riley tossed her cell

phone on the bed and sat on the end of it, wearing an old t-shirt of Kinsley's and a pair of her workout pants. "I'm sorry. Yes, I have everything I need. Thank you. I had a great time tonight, Kinsley."

"You're just never going to call me *James*, like everyone else, are you?"

"Why? Your name is beautiful," Riley answered so sweetly, Kinsley had to lower her eyes and look away from her. "Where does it come from?"

"My name? I don't know."

"You don't know where your name came from?" Riley asked.

"Where did your name come from?" she asked back and sat next to Riley on the bed.

"I had another brother once. He was a year older than me, but he died when he was a month old." The woman lowered her head and clasped her hands together. "Riley was his middle name."

"I'm sorry."

"I didn't get a chance to meet him. I think that giving me his middle name was my parents' way of keeping his memory alive."

"What's your middle name?" Kinsley asked.

She couldn't help herself. Riley's long hair was down around her face. Kinsley couldn't see her. She had to reach out and slide Riley's hair back behind her ear. When she did, Riley immediately looked up and over at her. Kinsley's eyes went wide when she realized she'd made a mistake. She opened her mouth to say something, but Riley smiled at her.

"What's your middle name?" Riley asked.

"Elizabeth. Nothing fancy," Kinsley replied.

"Kinsley Elizabeth James," Riley said it to try it out.

"You're not getting off that easily." She shoved at Riley's shoulder lightly. "What's your middle name, Riles?"

"Riles?" The woman laughed and fell back onto the bed, still somewhat tipsy, apparently. "My middle name is Hope. Riley Hope Sanders. I guess it's Riles Hope now."

She chuckled again.

"Okay, it's time for bed there, Riles." Kinsley stood.

For a moment she just stared down at Riley, who was still laughing to herself. Then, she realized she probably looked creepy. She moved to the top of the bed and pulled down the blanket and sheet for Riley before moving the decorative pillows out of the way.

"Hey, Kinsley?"

"Yeah?" she asked and turned her head.

Riley was still lying down, face up on the bed, but her eyes were on Kinsley now.

"Thank you for taking care of me tonight."

CHAPTER 7

RILEY WOKE UP the following morning in a strange bed. It took her several minutes to remember where she was. Then, the splitting headache took over her thoughts. She opened her eyes halfway to find that the curtains on the window had been closed. She turned slightly and noticed there was a full glass of water along with a couple of pills on the table next to the bed. She smiled, took the pills, and climbed regretfully out of bed. She showered, enjoyed the soft towels Kinsley had left behind, and dressed in the clothes she'd arrived in. She left the clothes Kinsley had lent her folded neatly on the bed. That was when her nostrils smelled the most delicious smell in the world.

She made her way toward the kitchen, where there was, undoubtedly, coffee brewing. But after her nose adjusted to the smell of that, her eyes took in something else, too. Kinsley was standing at her stove, cooking something. Her hair was pulled up. She was wearing dark jeans and a nice long-sleeved shirt that, Riley guessed, was a button-down. She watched Kinsley cook for a moment. There was something elegant about the way she held the spatula. Riley watched her for another moment before she cleared her throat and smiled when Kinsley turned around. She smirked when Kinsley's cheek turned a soft shade of pink.

"How long have you been standing there?" she asked.

"Only a minute or two. What are you making?" Riley asked as she moved over toward the stove.

"French toast."

"God, Kinsley." She hovered over the pan and took in the sights and smells of French toast. "Some woman is going to be lucky when she gets you; some lucky woman you'll undoubtedly fatten up with all this cooking."

"Well, whoever she is, she's not here right now. So, this is for you," Kinsley replied with a smile so genuine, Riley had to take a step back, because it almost hurt to look at it.

Elena's smile recently had been that fake one Riley had seen on her campaign commercials or at the occasional party they'd attended together, but not *together*. Riley had gotten very used to being the *'friend'* Elena had in town, staying for the weekend. It had become almost second nature to her, to be holding Elena's hand one minute in private, only to let it go the instant someone else entered a room. She'd also gotten used to seeing that false smile directed at herself the last few times she'd been able to see her girlfriend on FaceTime and, unfortunately, even in person. As she took in Kinsley James, though, there was just nothing about her that was fake.

***

"Once all the paperwork is signed by him, we'll wrap this up for you," Riley told her client.

"Thank you. I never should have gone to Vegas. I went there a single woman and came back a married one, with a man I hardly know."

"It's happened more than you'd think," Riley said as the woman stood. She stood with her and shook her hand. "I'll call you when I receive it."

The woman nodded at Riley and left her office. Riley sat back down in her desk chair and stared at the flashing screen on her phone. She actually rolled her eyes and then picked it up.

"Hi," she said.

"Hey, babe."

"Elena, you can't just *'hey, babe'* me right now," she retorted.

"I called to talk to my girlfriend. I can't lead with hello?"

"You haven't called your girlfriend in over a week."

"Riley, don't start. I'm exhausted. I've had a crazy week. I just called to say hello."

"You just called to say hello? Are you kidding, Elena?"

"Well, I didn't call to get yelled at." The woman paused. "Jesus, Riley. I'm sorry. I'm sorry, I've been so busy trying to figure out if I'm going to run for governor. Things are moving quickly here."

"You're just deciding?" Riley asked softly. "Like, you're just deciding on your own?"

"Well, not on my own. I'm working with—"

"For a woman who is so intelligent, you are so dumb sometimes, Elena." Riley paused. "What the hell happened to us?"

"What are you talking about?"

"We were crazy about each other when we first met. Do you remember that?"

"Of course, I do."

"Well, what happened?"

"Are you saying you're not crazy about me anymore?" Elena asked.

"I'm saying I don't understand how it got this far." She breathed out and leaned back in her chair. "Do you even love me?"

"Riley…"

"Do you?"

"Yes, I love you."

"Then, why are you acting like this?" Riley asked.

"Like I'm trying to make a huge life decision?"

"Like you already made one, and now you're thinking about backing out of it. Oh, and you're not even talking to your girlfriend of three years about it. You're talking to advisors, party leaders, and politicians. I'm your girlfriend. This impacts my entire life, Elena. Don't you get that? If you run, that's at least six more years of you living there and me living here."

"You could move here instead. I own my place here. It would be so much easier."

"And if you actually won the election?"

"I'd move into the governor's mansion."

"And I'd stay in your old house? Alone, right?"

"You know I can't come out right now and win an election, Riley."

"You've made the decision already, haven't you?" Riley asked, knowing the answer.

"I haven't made any decision yet, babe. I'm sorry I've upset you with this. I wasn't expecting it. You know that, right? I love you, Riley."

Riley's eyes welled with tears. She'd loved this woman so much once, she couldn't imagine her life without her.

"I don't think I can keep doing this anymore, Elena."

"What do you mean?" Elena asked softly. "Riley, don't do this."

"Don't do what? You want to be the governor of Texas. I want to live a simple life in South Lake Tahoe. I want to buy a home with my girlfriend. I want that girlfriend to become my wife one day. I'd like us to raise children together."

"We talked about kids. I'm past that point–"

"I know. I know." Riley wiped at her eyes. "You said you're too old. You don't want kids even if I'm the one that has them. I know."

"But you said that was okay before. You're changing your mind now?"

"You changed your mind about moving here."

"That's not the same thing, Riley."

"It isn't?"

"Changing your mind about wanting to move in with someone is one thing. Changing your mind about wanting to have children is something else entirely."

"Well, both of them end up with us going our separate ways, Elena. In that way, they are the same."

"Hold on. Going our separate ways?"

"It's better this way, don't you think?"

"No, I don't think. Riley, I love you."

Riley's next appointment entered the outer room of her office. Her assistant greeted the man, and Riley wiped at her face.

"I have to go. A client just walked in."

"Wait. Riley, let's talk about this. I'll make time tonight, okay?"

"I don't want you to *make* time for me, Elena. I want you to *have* time for me because you can't *not* do that. I've got to go." She hung up the phone moments before her assistant led her next appointment into her office.

***

"I think if I drink tonight, that would give you a very bad impression of me," Riley said as Kinsley passed her the beer she'd just opened for her.

"You brought them last night. We didn't get a chance to drink them."

"You drink it. I'll stick to water," Riley replied with a laugh. "You really didn't have to make dinner again."

"I told you, I don't mind. I love cooking. And I hate cooking for one. This works out."

"Can we eat outside, or would that be too much trouble?"

"We can definitely eat outside. It's a nice night," Kinsley replied and passed her a plate.

They made their way outside to the lower patio. Kinsley had a round glass table there, with four metal chairs.

They chose to sit next to one another in order to enjoy the view. They ate in silence for a few moments, with Riley staring out as the sun began to set.

"This is perfect."

"It's not bad." Kinsley smiled over at her and offered a wink.

"Is that a path down to the water?" Riley asked and pointed with her fork toward stones Kinsley had set in the ground. "I didn't notice it last night."

"To the sand, yeah. I had them put in last year. I don't go straight down there all that often, though."

"Why not?"

"Usually, I just sit here, or up there." She pointed at the balcony over them. "When I'm alone, that is. If I'm with my friends, we're usually playing football on the beach down the road. Sometimes, I go hiking with Morgan, but we take one of the trails."

"Do you have a boat down there?" Riley paused. "I've always wanted my own boat to take out on this lake. We couldn't afford one when I was growing up here."

"No, I don't have a boat," Kinsley answered and laughed. "I think you might think I'm rich. I'm not." She continued laughing. "I got this place because it was going into foreclosure, and I had the inside scoop. I picked it up before anyone else heard about it. No way I'd be able to afford this place otherwise."

"It's beautiful, Kinsley. Have I said that yet?"

"Once or twice." Kinsley took a drink of her beer. "How was your day?"

Riley stopped eating at that and thought about the last time Elena had asked how her day was when they'd eaten dinner together. She couldn't remember it. What did that say about their relationship?

"Can I ask you a question?" she asked Kinsley.

"So, you're not going to answer mine, I take it?"

"I will. I just want to ask you something first, if that's okay." She took a bite of Kinsley's delicious dinner.

"Okay."

"What's the longest relationship you've ever had?"

"Oh, wow." Kinsley set the beer bottle down onto the table, and the sound was thundering against the near silence of the setting.

"You don't have to answer."

"It's not that. I just wasn't expecting that."

"What *were* you expecting?" Riley asked.

"I don't know. How did you get your lawn that green?"

Riley laughed and replied, "You can tell me that later."

"My longest relationship…" Kinsley looked out at the trees as she considered.

Riley wondered what she was considering exactly. It seemed like a pretty simple question to her. Her longest relationship was Elena. They'd been together for three years.

"I guess it was about a year and a half. I've had a couple of those, technically," Kinsley supplied.

"A couple?"

"One was about a month longer than the other, if you need specifics." Kinsley looked back at her with a smile. "Abigail was her name."

"Where'd you two meet?"

"Culinary school."

"Another student?"

"Instructor." Kinsley lifted both eyebrows. "She was one of the reasons I fell in love with pastry."

"I bet she was." Riley laughed. "Why'd you two break up?"

"She took a job in Spain. It was amicable."

"That's good."

"Can I ask you a question now?" Kinsley lowered her fork again.

"Fair is fair."

Riley waited for Kinsley to ask her why she'd ask that question.

"How was your day?"

CHAPTER 8

"So, YOU GUYS are hanging out now?" Morgan asked.

"I guess."

"And that's okay with you?"

"Why wouldn't it be?" Kinsley asked.

They were hiking one of the more difficult trails. Kinsley's thighs were already starting to feel it, and they'd only been at it for a mile.

"Because you're all in love with her, and she has a girlfriend."

"I'm not all in love with her," Kinsley replied with a laugh. "I like her, yes, but I'm not all in love with her."

"But?" Morgan said as she stopped to take a long drink from her water bottle, apparently feeling the burn, too.

"But nothing."

"It won't bother you, being just friends with her?"

"I've always been just friends with her." Kinsley took a drink of her own water.

"But this is different. You're spending time alone now. You never used to do that."

"I'll admit it's different."

"Different good or different bad?" Morgan took a seat on a large rock.

"I don't know yet. I like spending time with her. But we've been hanging out a lot lately, and it is weird sometimes."

"How so?"

"We'll be eating dinner or just talking, and I'll get this urge to touch her or kiss her. I can't explain it."

"You've always been that way with her. I never understood it either." Morgan chuckled.

"I never understood how you felt that way about Reese. I mean, I love Reese. She's one of my closest friends. But I don't see her the way you used to see her. You two were over the moon for one another. Now, she has Kellan. They're that way with each other. I like Kellan, but I don't get it. I don't think you're meant to understand fully how that works with another couple."

"But, James, you and Riley aren't a couple." Morgan gave her a sympathetic look. "She's in her own couple with someone else."

"I know." Kinsley stared out at the expanse of the wilderness. "I don't understand that."

"You just said you're not meant to." Morgan stood.

"It's different."

"How so?" Morgan chuckled as she motioned for Kinsley to join her and continue the hike.

"Her girlfriend treats her like crap," she replied.

"She's been with her for three years, James."

"So? I stayed with Abigail even though I wasn't feeling it at the end. The last six months with her weren't good. She was working all the time, trying to figure out if she even wanted to stay in the country, and she hardly noticed me."

"Why'd you stay then?"

"Because we'd had a great first year. It seemed like we just needed to get through the rough patch. We loved each other once. We'd get back to that. Then, we didn't."

"You think Riley's doing that? Trying to get through a rough patch?"

Kinsley walked behind her, regretting this difficult hike idea, and replied, "I don't know. It might be. I feel like she deserves better, Morgan. She's so nice. She's smart, and funny. She brings me coffee now."

"What?" Morgan laughed and turned around to look at her, walking backward up the tricky hill.

"Turn around, Morgan." Kinsley pointed. Morgan

obeyed and turned to continue walking. "And it started on Monday."

"Today's Sunday."

"Yes, thank you. I know what day of the week it is." Kinsley avoided a rock in the path that she nearly tripped on. "She dropped by around lunchtime, but I was with a client. She came back, like, twenty minutes later with coffee for me. On Tuesday, she came around ten, and when she found I wasn't with anyone, she stayed for a while, and we talked. It's like a thing we do now: she comes in, we have coffee, we talk, and then she goes back to work."

"And she brings you this coffee that she pays for?"

"Yes."

"And you've had dinner a couple of times?"

"Three times, yes."

"Do you talk about your hopes and dreams, plans for the future, kids and grandkids?"

"We've talked about that stuff some," Kinsley replied.

Morgan stopped abruptly and turned around.

"James, be careful. Okay?"

"What? Why?" Kinsley looked around, thinking that Morgan had seen something on the trail ahead.

"Because she has a girlfriend."

"I'm aware of that," she tried to laugh it off.

"Kinsley, you're doing things couples do. You think her girlfriend isn't good to her. I don't want her taking advantage of the fact that you *are* good to her. I don't want you to get your heart broken." Morgan's expression was serious. "She belongs to someone else, Kinsley."

***

"Hey," Riley greeted when she entered Kinsley's office on Monday morning holding two cups of coffee. "Are you busy?"

Kinsley checked her schedule and noticed it was ten on the dot. She also noticed the block she'd already put on her calendar for every day this week in order to prevent herself from booking something at this time. She'd wanted to make sure she was there when Riley arrived. She smiled up at Riley as she deleted that block.

"Hi, I have a few minutes, but I have to head out soon for a showing," she lied. "Thank you. You don't have to keep bringing me coffee."

"I know. I wanted to." The woman sat in the guest chair Kinsley now considered to be Riley's chair. "How was your weekend?"

"Good." Kinsley moved the coffee to the other side of the desk. "Yours?"

"I had a chance to look at those listings you sent over. I really liked the one with the porch swing."

"It's a nice house. Good bones." Kinsley leaned back in her chair. "It's been on the market for a while, because it's not in one of the best locations."

"I don't mind. Do you think we could go take a look at it?"

Kinsley leaned forward again and looked at her calendar.

"I can do tomorrow at three," Kinsley replied.

"I have to be in court."

"I can do Wednesday at five. Is that late enough?"

"I can do that. Maybe we can grab dinner after." Riley leaned forward in her chair. "Have you been to *Dante's* in Truckee?"

"Truckee? Up north?"

"Yeah, it's one of my favorite restaurants up there. My treat."

Kinsley wanted to say yes so badly.

"I can't. I have another showing at six, actually."

"Oh," Riley replied, seemingly disappointed. "Right. Well, five is good for me, then."

"Okay. I'll put it on my calendar. I should probably…" She pointed at the front door.

"Go. Yeah, sorry." Riley stood.

It was an awkward goodbye, to say the least. Mainly, because Kinsley didn't actually have anywhere to go. She followed Riley out and locked the door behind her before climbing into her car. Once Riley disappeared, she climbed out and went back into her office. She kept the lights off, though, and made her way back to the bathroom. She stayed in there for another ten minutes or so, just to make sure Riley was really gone. Then, she emerged, feeling like a complete idiot; but at least she was an idiot that wouldn't risk getting her heart broken by a woman who was with someone else.

***

"Is it weird, being back here now that you don't live here?" Riley asked Kellan as they sat at her table, sharing Chinese food.

"A little, but not a lot. I'm at home where I am. This place was always temporary," Kellan explained.

"And your place with me is permanent," Reese said as she smiled at her girlfriend.

"That's the idea," Kellan replied.

"Can I ask you guys something?" Riley asked.

"What's up?" Reese asked back and slid a shrimp into her mouth.

"What was it like when you found each other?" she asked. "You two, I mean." She motioned with her chopsticks between the two of them.

"Confusing," Kellan said with a laugh. "She has a twin sister."

"Stop it," Reese replied and laughed at Kellan. "It *was* confusing. But that was because she was a tourist."

"And I had a broken heart," Kellan added. "I thought it was broken, at least."

"And it just worked?" Riley asked.

"Well, it is still working. But, yeah, it just worked." Reese nodded. "It *took* work. We had to figure things out.

Kellan moved here. She started a vet practice. I had to open up about something I hadn't told anyone else about. She had to get over some stuff as well. We worked it out, and now we're here. We love each other. We're not just planning our lives together; we're living them together." Reese took Kellan's hand with her free one on top of the table.

"How did you know?" Riley asked.

"Know what?" Kellan asked. "That Reese was the one?"

"Yes, how did you know?"

"Is something going on with you and Elena? Is that where these questions are coming from?" Kellan asked.

"No, we're fine," she lied. "I was just curious."

"So, it's a curiosity because the girlfriend is about to move here, and you'll be living together for the first time?" Reese asked.

"I guess."

"Well, pick your socks up off the floor; that I can tell you," Kellan said. "Oh, never run out of mint chocolate chip ice cream."

"Or whatever Elena's favorite ice cream is," Reese suggested. "Maybe she's a Rocky Road kind of girl." She glanced in Kellan's direction.

Riley didn't say anything for a moment. She stared down at the cardboard container and poked around at her noodles with her chopsticks.

"You don't know what her favorite ice cream is, do you?" Kellan asked.

"I don't, actually," Riley answered. "She eats ice cream. We've had it together a few times. But I don't know what her favorite kind is. I think she's ordered chocolate a couple of times, but I don't know if that's her favorite kind or if that's just what she wanted in the moment." She let out a deep exhale. "I don't know my girlfriend's favorite ice cream, and we've been together for three years."

"What was the longest you've ever been in the same place together, though?" Reese asked her.

"Three months, when I went to Dallas. But that was right when we met. We've only had a couple of weeks together each visit since then," Riley replied.

"Kind of hard to get to know that stuff if you're only on the phone, huh?"

"Maybe she told me once, and I just forgot. I've been forgetful lately," she said.

"Forgetful?"

"I forgot Kinsley was gay," she said and met Reese's eyes.

"What?" Reese laughed. "How'd you forget that?"

"I don't know." She laughed at herself. "I know I knew that. I remembered her telling me for the first time as soon as she said it. I just hadn't thought about all that college stuff in years."

"But she's one of our closest friends," Reese said.

"Not really," Riley replied. "She's one of *your* closest friends. She wasn't one of mine back then. And since I've moved back, I hardly spent any time with her. If I did, it was with all of you. Up until recently, I hadn't spent time alone with her at all."

"Our friend group is like 75% lesbians," Reese said.

"And while I knew that, I honestly hadn't thought about Kinsley in the longest time. I know that makes me sound like a bad friend, but you guys were ahead of me in school. Once you left, I was there on my own. I made new friends. Then, I went to law school and made more friends. I moved to Truckee after that and had my own life there. Moving back here has reconnected me to you guys, but Kinsley was always one of your friends that I hung out with, until the past few weeks."

"And now you'd say she's one of your friends?" Reese asked.

"She's become one of my closest friends, oddly enough."

"How'd that happen?" Kellan asked. "She's helping you find a house still, right?"

"Yes. We saw one yesterday," she answered. "It was kind of weird, though."

"How so?" Reese asked.

"We've been hanging out a lot lately. We've had dinners, coffee, and just talked. It's been nice. I was actually kicking myself for not realizing how great Kinsley was before and trying to spend more time with her. Yesterday, though, she was all business. She pointed and described and told me everything about this house that I like, but don't love. Then, she left. And I haven't talked to her since. She sent me an email today, asking if I'd talked to Elena about the house we saw. It's just strange. We've been texting and talking on the phone regularly; and, now, I get an email."

"That's about the job, though," Kellan said. "It's her keeping that part of things professional, probably."

"Does it bother you?" Reese asked her as she set down her carton.

"I don't know. I guess it does."

"Why?" Reese asked. "She's doing a job for you, right?"

"Yes. But it's been more than that, too. These past few weeks... It's just been more."

"More?" Kellan asked. "Are you and Kinsley–"

"What? No," Riley objected. "We're not."

"Okay." Kellan held up both hands after placing her carton next to her girlfriend's. "It just seems like you two are getting close."

"We are, but we're just friends."

Riley finished her dinner and said goodbye to her friends. When she went into her bedroom later that night, she had a text from Elena. It was her goodnight message. She was at an event and couldn't call. At least she'd texted, though, Riley thought. Then, she thought about how nice Kinsley's smile was, and how she'd already found out that her favorite ice cream was strawberry, preferably with sliced bananas on the side.

CHAPTER 9

"HI," KINSLEY GREETED Riley through the phone after stepping away from her client. "What's up? Did you talk to Elena about the house?"

"Oh, hi." Riley sounded strange, but Kinsley didn't know why. "Not yet. She's been pretty busy."

"I've got another client that might be interested in it. I'm actually with him now. We're at another house right now, but we saw that one this morning. He might try to–"

"Let him have it. It wasn't a slam dunk for me, anyway," Riley replied. "Listen, I was calling to see if you wanted to come over for dinner tonight."

"Dinner?"

"Yes, at my place. I'm going to attempt to cook you something to thank you for always cooking for me."

"Are you trying to burn down your apartment," Kinsley said while laughing.

"No, I'll be extra careful. What do you say?"

"I probably shouldn't."

"Why?" Riley asked.

Kinsley glanced behind her and found her client waiting and watching expectantly.

"Can I get back to you?"

"I'm at the store now. I was hoping to find out what you'd want me to make."

Kinsley smiled at her client and held up her index finger to the impatient guy before she turned around and replied, "Whatever you want to make is fine. I'll be there at seven. Is that okay?"

"Oh, yeah. That's fine. Great. Okay," Riley said all of that in rapid succession.

"I'll see you then," Kinsley replied hurriedly and hung up the phone. "Sorry about that."

***

Two hours later, Kinsley found herself standing at the door of Riley's apartment, wondering how she'd ended up here. She'd done her best to try to avoid the woman in these kinds of situations. She had ducked out of her office a few minutes before ten in the morning every day the rest of this week. She felt terrible about doing it, but she needed some separation. She and Riley had become good friends recently. Riley had a girlfriend. Kinsley wanted Riley to be her girlfriend. It was all very confusing. Kinsley had done her best to keep things professional between them in order to figure out how she could just be a friend to Riley and want nothing more. Riley was making that difficult.

"Hey there," Riley said when she opened the door. She smiled wide and looked Kinsley up and down. "Did you come straight from the office?"

"Yes. Is that okay?"

"Of course, it's okay. Come in. I haven't burned the place down yet. I did have a mild smoke detector issue about ten minutes ago, but I opened the windows and waved a towel. It's fine now. Don't mind the smoke smell."

"You're kidding, right?" Kinsley lifted an eyebrow.

"I'm half-kidding."

Kinsley laughed and entered the apartment. She made her way to the living room, where she noticed a bottle of wine uncorked with two empty glasses next to it on the coffee table. There were also two candles lit on either side of that display. She looked to her right and saw the kitchen table set for two. There were candles on that table as well. Kinsley looked at Riley, who had made her way into the kitchen.

"Need any help in there?" Kinsley asked, following her in.

"Yes." Riley laughed. "But no. I'm trying to do this myself."

"Why? I can help." Kinsley walked up next to Riley, who now stood in front of the stove.

"Are you worried I might kill you with my cooking and trying to save your own life?"

"Yes." Kinsley nodded, earning another laugh from Riley.

"It's pasta. I don't think I can kill you with pasta."

"You might be the first person in history to murder someone with pasta," Kinsley replied.

"Go pour the wine," Riley ordered while laughing.

Kinsley obeyed and made her way toward the living room. She smiled as she poured red wine into glasses. It all felt so perfect to her. This felt like a date between two women that were getting to know one another. She had to put that out of her mind. She had to find a way to think of Riley only as her friend.

"So, how's Elena?" Kinsley asked. *That should do it.* "What didn't she like about the house? It'll help me narrow down the search."

"She's fine." Riley entered the living room. "She didn't say, specifically. She just didn't like it."

"Oh," Kinsley replied. "It's kind of a slow process without feedback, Riley. Does she understand that?"

"She does. I tried to get her–" A sound came from the kitchen. "Shit."

Riley ran toward it. Kinsley followed her. The pan had boiled over, thrusting foamy water onto the burner and stove, surrounding it at the same time as the saucepan also boiled over, causing a vibrant red to join the water and speckle the white stovetop.

"I've got it." Kinsley moved quickly, having dealt with this kind of thing before.

"God, I'm sorry," Riley replied and grabbed a towel. "I can't do anything right these days, can I?"

"Riley, it's just boiling over. It's fine. It happens all the time."

Riley began wiping at the sauce stains after turning the burner down. Kinsley lifted the pan lid and allowed the water to lower before she turned her burner down and reached for the fork next to the pan. She stirred the pasta briefly and turned her attention to the sauce. Then, she placed her free hand on Riley's hip to lightly move the woman out of her way. Kinsley stirred the sauce for a moment and looked up to smile at Riley in an attempt to reassure her. What she found was a beautiful woman with tears in her eyes.

"I'm sorry," Riley said after a moment.

"For what? Riley, what's wrong?" Kinsley moved toward her, but Riley backed away and moved into the living room. "Hey, come on. Talk to me."

"I wanted to cook a nice dinner for you, and I messed it up. God, I can't even get pasta right. What's so hard about it? Put pasta in water. Boil water."

"Actually, its boil the water first, and then put the pasta in." Kinsley met Riley's glare. "But that's not important. Let's sit down. The food isn't ruined."

Riley wiped at her eyes and sat on the sofa. Kinsley joined her a moment later.

"The sauce came in a jar." Riley wiped a few stray tears and turned her face to Kinsley's.

"I know, Riles. The jar is still on the counter." Kinsley smiled at the woman, reached for her cheek, and wiped a rogue tear away.

Riley laughed, but it wasn't a real laugh. It was a laugh that held back a light sob. She smiled at least, though it was weak. Then, she looked over at Kinsley, who had no idea what to do now. Riley was still so beautiful even when she cried.

"Elena and I aren't doing well," she said finally. "We hardly talk these days. I get a text every night, if I'm lucky, and a phone call every few days, where all we do is fight." She paused to try to gather herself. "I moved back here for a few reasons. I wanted to spend more time with my family, as my parents get older. They aren't even here right now and won't be back for a while. My two brothers have both moved away. In fairness, they both did that before I moved here. But they used to come home a lot because our parents were here. And now, they're not. So, my brothers aren't just going to come here to visit me. They're busy, too." She glanced at the wine glass on the table, picked it up, and took a sip. "I moved here to start my own practice, but I could have done that in Truckee, too. It's going well. I like my work. I always have."

"But?"

"But I wanted to move here and settle down. I planned on having Elena here for that. And now, she's not even coming for a visit. She's too busy."

"I thought she was going–"

"We made this plan that she would come here and help narrow down the house options, spend time together, since we rarely see one another, and then pick where we'd live out the rest of our lives together. I just don't think that's going to happen."

"Because she's running for governor?" Kinsley asked and leaned back against the sofa.

"When we first started dating, we thought it would be short-term." Riley took another drink of her wine and placed the glass back down. "We figured we had three good months together. I'd return home, and that would be the end of it."

"That obviously didn't happen," Kinsley said and reached forward for her own wine. She suddenly had the need to consume alcohol. "How'd it keep going then?"

"We talked a few weeks after I got back. It was one phone call, but we talked for hours, and it changed everything." Riley smiled, but it still didn't meet her eyes. "We decided to try long-distance. For a while, it was great. It was what I needed. I was just starting out at work. Things were hectic. It might be weird to say this, but I kind of liked that I could have a girlfriend but also have my place to myself at the same time. There's no pressure to go out on a date or make plans. We each had our own lives, but we also had each other. It worked for us."

"What changed?" Kinsley asked with another drink.

"I don't know." She shrugged. "I guess, it got to a point where it wasn't enough for me. I asked her to move here because I couldn't move there. There would be no point. She's not out and doesn't seem to want to be there. We made an agreement that she could start over here. I thought that was what she wanted. But now, when we fight all the time, she keeps bringing up that it's what I wanted."

"So, you changed, and she didn't," Kinsley stated.

"What do you mean?"

"Your visions changed. That's normal, isn't it? You want one thing when you start dating. Then, as time goes on, you want something else."

"And she doesn't, it seems." The woman placed her head back on the sofa. "Maybe I should just move there and be a governor's mistress."

"What? No way." Kinsley set her wine glass down. "Riles, you're not someone's mistress. You're not someone's dirty little secret. You're someone's girlfriend, and you deserve to be treated like that. God, Riley, you deserve so much," she said, and her voice broke at the end.

Riley stared into her eyes for a moment, and Kinsley wasn't sure if maybe there was recognition there. Then, Riley smiled at her.

"I'm always such a disaster around you." She slapped Kinsley's knee lightly.

"Really? I think I'm always such a disaster around you."

"No, you're not," Riley replied. "Why would you think that?"

"Giant chunk of bagel in my mouth and cream cheese all over my chin."

Riley laughed loudly at that and replied, "Did you

mutter *'mother fucker'* under your breath that day?"

"I did, yes." Kinsley chuckled. "I couldn't believe you'd chosen that moment to walk into my office, looking how you always look; and me, looking like someone who hadn't eaten in a month and doesn't know how to chew properly."

"How I *always* do?" Riley asked.

Kinsley gulped and replied, "You're always so put-together, Riles. You have this way about you that just – I don't know – gets me." She paused and looked down at her own hands in her lap. "It always has. You just always seem confident to me and put-together. I'm always sitting on a stain on some futon or wearing a wrinkled shirt."

Riley just kept staring at her. Kinsley could feel it. She couldn't meet Riley's eyes, but she could feel her.

"I think you're put-together, Kinsley. I think you're very well put-together," Riley replied.

Kinsley looked up at that and met Riley's searching eyes. She bit her lower lip, because her instincts told her that this was the perfect moment to kiss Riley Sanders for the first time. Her body wanted it. Her mind wanted it. Her heart wanted it. And, God, her soul wanted it.

"Riley, we should have dinner." Kinsley moved to stand, but Riley's hand met her forearm.

"We should talk," the woman replied. "I have some decisions I have to make."

"Like, what to have for dinner now, because that pasta is most definitely ruined?" Kinsley asked, trying to lighten the mood.

"Not exactly," Riley answered with a look that lacked assurance. "Bigger decisions; like, about my relationship."

Kinsley wanted to kiss her again. Riley's lips looked like they were made for kissing. She'd thought that long ago, when they'd first met. She still thought that now. But Riley wasn't her girlfriend. Riley had a girlfriend named Elena. They'd been together for three years. They were going through a rough patch in their relationship, but Kinsley wouldn't take advantage of that.

"I'm sure you guys will work it out," Kinsley replied.

"I got strawberry ice cream and bananas for dessert, Kinsley," Riley shared. "For you."

Kinsley looked down at those lips again before her eyes met Riley's.

"I can't be a substitute girlfriend to you, Riles." She couldn't believe she just said that, but it had slipped out before Kinsley could stop herself. She'd said it softly, but she'd still said it. "It's starting to feel like that for me, and it can't be that."

"You're not a–"

"I know. I know. But it's starting to feel that way, and it can't feel that way, because I..." She didn't say anything for a long moment. "Do you know why it hurt so much when you didn't remember I was gay?"

"I didn't forget. I just–"

"Because I liked you, Riley. Back then, I had such a crush on you. You were eighteen, and I was twenty-one. It was stupid – and it doesn't matter now – but I did. I liked you."

"I didn't know that." Riley turned to her.

"I didn't tell you," Kinsley said. "We've been hanging out a lot recently, Riley. I'm worried it's not just a crush for me. I don't want to get hurt, and I think that's what's going to happen if we keep doing this stuff. It just feels so much like a date, sometimes."

"Is that why you haven't been around for coffee and didn't want to do dinner?" Riley asked.

"Yes," Kinsley answered honestly. "And I should probably go, because this is getting really awkward." She laughed in an attempt to lighten the mood. "You're in a relationship." She stood. "I shouldn't be the one wiping your tears away. She should be."

Kinsley turned and began walking toward the door.

"But she's not," Riley said.

CHAPTER 10

RILEY STOOD AND STARED at the back of Kinsley's body. The woman had yet to turn around.

"I'm going to go, Riles. I'll see you around," Kinsley said.

"Kinsley, wait."

The door unlocked the moment Riley made her way to Kinsley and attempted to take her hand. She hadn't been expecting anyone. Three people had the key to the apartment. Her father had one, but he was out of the country. Kellan had one, but she had no reason to just stop by, and she hadn't ever done so uninvited. The only other person, who could unlock the door like that, was her girlfriend.

"Hey, babe." Elena opened the door and met Riley's eyes before glancing at Kinsley and their slightly linked but not entwined hands. "And someone I don't know."

"Elena, what are you doing here?" Riley asked and dropped Kinsley's hand.

"I'm here to see my girlfriend. I thought I'd surprise you. I didn't know you'd have company." Elena made her way quickly into the living room, leaving her roller bag by the door as if she'd done it a thousand times before, and approached Kinsley. "I'm Elena; Riley's girlfriend. And you are?"

"Real estate agent," Kinsley said. "Kinsley James." She held out her hand for Elena to take. "I'm helping Riley find a house for you two."

"Kinsley is a friend, Elena." Riley stood next to Kinsley and placed her hand on Kinsley's shoulder. "She wasn't here to work tonight. We were hanging out and about to eat dinner."

"Maybe I could join you. I'm starving. I caught the next flight after my meeting and didn't get a chance to grab dinner," Elena said.

Riley noticed Elena still hadn't taken her eyes off Kinsley. The woman also hadn't attempted to reach for Riley in any way. They hadn't seen one another in weeks. Maybe Riley could measure it better in months at this point. Still, Elena had hardly met her eye.

"Well, dinner's kind of ruined," Kinsley said. "My fault. I showed up early and distracted her with house stuff." She turned her face to Riley's and gave her a smile. "It would have been great otherwise, I'm sure."

"You cooked?" Elena asked Riley, meeting her eyes finally.

"I tried," Riley replied. "Pasta."

"I should get out of your hair," Kinsley said. "It was nice to meet you, Elena."

"You don't have to go, Kinsley," Riley stated. "I can order instead."

"Riley, I just got here," Elena said and lifted her eyebrows.

"It's not like I knew you were coming. I had plans with Kinsley. It's rude, Elena."

"I'll send you those links tomorrow," Kinsley said. "For the listings we were discussing. I hope you two have a good night."

"Nice meeting you," Elena said.

Kinsley moved to the door, pulled it behind her, and left without turning around.

"Elena, what are you doing here?" Riley asked the moment the door was closed.

"I told you. I came to surprise you. What the hell was that, by the way?" She hooked her thumb to the front door.

"What was what?"

"Kinsley James? That's the realtor trying to find *us* a house?"

"Yes. She's the realtor, working hard to try to find us a house that you don't even care about." Riley turned around. "I have to clean the kitchen."

"Why did you cook for her? I can count on one hand the number of times you've even *attempted* to cook for me," she said, following Riley into the kitchen.

"That's because we've had just over a handful of days together during a three-year relationship," Riley retorted, tossing the rag she'd just picked up into the sink.

"That's what you wanted. We were long-distance, and it worked for a reason, Riley. You wanted it, too."

"Well, I don't anymore." Riley stared at her. "Don't you want to be with me?"

"I'm here, Riley."

"That's not what I asked." Riley lowered her head and raised it again a moment later. "Elena, this isn't working anymore."

"Because you're sleeping with the realtor?"

"What? I'm not sleeping with Kinsley."

"You had her hand in your hand, Riley. I saw it," Elena said. "What was that about then?"

"She's a friend. I've told you about her."

"Yes, you have. During the few phone calls we've actually had where you're not yelling at me, you've mentioned her at least ten times. And I don't remember hearing anything about how hard she's working as our realtor, Riley." Elena leaned against the counter and folded her arms over her chest. "But nothing's going on between you two?"

Riley didn't know how to answer that question. She didn't want to lie, but she couldn't exactly say nothing was going on either. Kinsley had become important to her. She also wasn't 100% certain she was only important to her as a friend.

"Elena, do you want to move here and live with me in a house that we own?" Riley changed the subject. "That's the question that matters. If you don't, then what are we even doing here?"

"I came here to talk to you about moving to Texas with me," Elena said after a moment and uncrossed her arms. "I still think it could work with us, Riley."

"In Texas," Riley said.

"Yes, in Texas. If I run, it'll be a brutal campaign."

"I thought you were running."

"I plan to," Elena shot back. "I want this, Riley. I didn't realize it until they asked me just how much I want it. I won't apologize for wanting something."

"We had a plan, Elena."

"And we can still have it," Elena moved forward and took her hands in her own. "Move to Texas with me."

"I just started my practice here."

"And you can start one there, too. People get divorced in Texas," she said and laughed, trying to make the mood light.

"What happens if you're elected? We can't exactly buy a place together and—"

"You'll stay at my place if I win, and I'll move into the governor's mansion. If I lose, we'll still have my place. It's in my name. No one will—"

"Know?"

"We can—"

"Hide?" Riley finished for her again. "You want us to keep hiding, don't you?"

Elena dropped Riley's hand and said, "You never had a problem with it before."

"Because I thought we'd stop at some point." Riley took a step back. "Elena, I can't do this anymore."

"Okay. Let's talk," Elena replied. "We have things to talk about, obviously. We keep fighting on the phone. Now that I'm here, we can talk in person and clear the air. We'll make a plan for if I win and if I don't."

"I don't want that," Riley said after a moment and met Elena's brown eyes. "Elena, I don't want that."

"What do you want?"

Riley thought for a moment and said, "Not this."

***

"Hey there," Riley said. "Is it okay that I'm here?"

"Oh. Hi." Kinsley looked up from her computer.

"I brought coffee." She placed the cup on Kinsley's desk. "As an apology. No strings. No conversation required. They were out of sesame bagels. I got one blueberry, one everything, and one plain." She then set the white paper bag on the desk next to the coffee. "And now, I'll be on my way."

"Riley, wait. What's going on?" Kinsley leaned back in her chair.

"I feel bad about dinner the other night. I ruined the food, and then Elena showed up. This is just me saying *'thank you for putting up with me, and I'm sorry for what happened.'* But it's not me thinking you're a substitute girlfriend, I promise."

"I'm sorry. I shouldn't have said that." Kinsley leaned forward again.

"No, it's fine." Riley waved her off. "I should get going, though. I have a meeting in ten minutes."

"Do you really have a meeting?" Kinsley chanced.

"I do, yes," she said. "It's in an hour, though." She lowered her head. "Sorry, I don't know how to do this with you now."

"It's okay," Kinsley replied. "I'm not sure I know how to do this either. I thought it would be easier if you knew how I felt. But, it turns out, that was wrong."

"Can we talk?"

The front door to the office opened. A man and a woman walked in hand in hand. Kinsley both wanted to and didn't walk to talk to Riley at the same time. Elena had been beautiful in her online photos, but she'd been gorgeous in person. She looked older, yes, but not old. Her hair was dark and had been swept back in an elegant bun. Her eyes were dark as well. Kinsley remembered thinking that they looked good together. They both had similar hair and eye color. Elena's skin was darker, though. She'd thought as she'd driven home that night, after the failed dinner, that their skin probably looked good pressed together: the paler skin of Riley meeting Elena's darker shade. Then, she shook her head violently to eliminate that thought from her brain.

"Hi," the woman said as she approached. "We're a little early."

"No problem," Kinsley said. "You're the Hermans, right?"

"That's us," the man said.

"I'll let you get back to work," Riley replied. "She's great. You guys will love working with her."

Kinsley watched as Riley didn't look her way again. She made her way toward the front door, and just as she was about to exit, Kinsley worked up the courage she needed and stood up in her chair.

"Riley?"

"Yeah?" Riley turned, surprised.

"I'll call you, okay?"

Riley smiled and gave her a light nod before she left the office.

CHAPTER 11

WHEN KINSLEY ARRIVED at the store, Morgan was with a customer. She waited off to the side until Morgan was free. Morgan gave her the nod that told Kinsley she understood she'd need some privacy for this chat. They made their way to the back office, where Morgan sat behind her desk and Kinsley stood behind the only guest chair in the room.

"You requested my presence," Morgan began mockingly.

"I have a Riley problem," she said.

"Of course, you do." Morgan leaned back in her chair. "Go on."

"Her girlfriend is in town," Kinsley said and crossed her arms over her chest. "And I don't know how I feel about that."

"Yes, you do. You don't want her to have a girlfriend unless it's you," Morgan replied. "That's the problem."

"It's not like that."

"What is it like, then?"

"I want her to be happy," Kinsley offered.

"With you."

"Morgan, come on." She sat in the chair. "You and Reese used to be together. Then, she found Kellan. I know that was hard for you. But you wanted her to be happy, right? Kellan is that person for her. It hurt you, yes. But you also know Reese is happy, and that's what matters."

"I know that," Morgan replied. "It sucked at first, that's true. I assume that's what you're dealing with? You want her, but she wants someone else?"

"No," Kinsley replied. "That's actually the problem. If that was it, I think I could deal with it, assuming she was happy."

"You don't know that she's happy?"

"I don't." Kinsley sighed. "It's not my place to judge someone's happiness; I know that. But it just doesn't seem like she wants this. Elena is non-committal, at best, these days. And Riley's ready for that next step."

"But they're still together, James," Morgan reasoned.

"I know."

"It's hard to see them together in person, I take it."

"It's not just that. I only saw them for a moment before I left the other night. It's more that… I might have told her I can't be her substitute girlfriend and possibly confessed that I have feelings for her, right before her actual girlfriend walked into her apartment unannounced and saw us kind of holding hands but not *really* holding hands."

"Hold on!" Morgan exclaimed and shot out of her chair with that rapid-fire confession. "You what? You told her? You held her hand?"

"She held mine," Kinsley replied.

"She held your hand as a friend or as something more? Did you do the thing where it's just two friends clasping hands, or did she slide her fingers between yours?"

"It wasn't like that," Kinsley said. "It was like a second. She reached for my hand, and our fingers touched. Then, Elena was there, and it was over."

"But it was her? She did that?"

"Yes," Kinsley replied.

"I'm going to kill her," Morgan said.

"What? Why?"

"Because you just told her how you felt, and she took your hand when she has a girlfriend," Morgan answered.

"It wasn't like that. She didn't say anything. It's not like she confessed her undying love for me. It was just a friend thing. But it's weird between us now."

"So, what's bothering you the most? Is it that she has a girlfriend? Is it that the girlfriend isn't good for her?"

"It's both." Kinsley stood. "God, it's both. Morgan, I like Riley so much. I always have. It's not like this epic love story where I've loved her forever and stood in the shadows waiting for her to realize it or anything. It's more that I liked her in school, and I left when I graduated. I didn't see her for years, dated other women, fell in love, and then saw her again and remembered how it felt to like her."

"And now she's back, and you still like her," Morgan understood.

"Yes. But I can't like her. She has someone, and they're working through things."

"James, maybe you and I should go out. That lesbian bar, about a half hour from here, is calling our name."

"We haven't been there in forever," Kinsley said with a chuckle.

"The last time I was there was with Reese, I think."

"I haven't been there since you and I went. I ended up making out with that woman."

"That wasn't a woman. She was twenty-one, Kinsley James," Morgan replied with a glare. "That was a girl."

"How was I supposed to know she was still in college?" Kinsley laughed again. "I don't know if a bar is the right way to go."

"We can invite Reese and Kellan. They're all boring and settled down. They have no need for hot ladies at the bar. They can be our wing women," Morgan suggested.

"Saturday night?"

"Let's do it."

***

When Riley arrived, it was just as she expected. The place had the requisite DJ with a sideways haircut, tank top, and low-slung jeans. She also had a nose ring and two lip rings along with an eyebrow ring. She had headphones on her ears, but she likely also had at least three earrings in each ear, too. The music was loud. It was very loud, and Riley actually grimaced when she walked further into the space. She was too old for a bar like this.

She'd been invited by Reese and Kellan, when she'd run into them at the café that morning. They'd only chatted for a few minutes, but they mentioned they were going out. She'd needed to get out of the apartment after the week she'd had. She'd also specifically been interested in seeing Kinsley tonight. When they'd mentioned it had been Morgan's idea, and that Kinsley would be in attendance, Riley had told them she'd be there. She had to drive on her own, thanks to the day she'd had, but it would be worth it if she could just see Kinsley and talk to her alone for a few minutes. Kinsley hadn't called her as she said she would. Riley didn't want to press her, but she missed spending time with her.

"Oh, we invited Riley tonight. I hope that's okay?" Kellan said.

"Riley's coming?" Kinsley replied. "I didn't know she was coming."

"Is it a problem? I thought you guys were friends now," Reese said.

"We are, but we're not at the same time. I don't know," Kinsley said.

"James, just tell them," Morgan said.

The booths at the bar were hardwood and tall. Thanks to a slight break in the song where the DJ introduced a contest of some sort, Riley could hear the conversation her friends were having without them knowing she was there.

"I told Riley how I feel," Kinsley said. "Well, sort of. It was weird."

"Weird?" Reese asked.

"She was talking about her girlfriend, Elena. I was having a hard time listening to her tell me how Elena treats her, because she deserves so much better than that. And I may have blurted out that I like her," Kinsley said. "I told her I can't be her substitute girlfriend, basically, because I wish I was her real girlfriend."

"That's so cute, James," Reese said.

"It's not cute. It's terrible. It's all awkward now. I like her. She loves someone else. She knows I like her, and now I don't know what to say when I'm around her. Is she going to think – if I compliment her hair or something – that I'm flirting? What if I do that thing where I slide the hair behind her ear just because it's in her face? Am I still allowed to do that? Was I ever allowed to do that? Should only your girlfriend do that if you have one?"

Riley smiled and shook her head at Kinsley's minor rant. She was beginning to get used to them, and she liked that.

"That's so lesbian, isn't it?" Morgan said. "The hair-tuck thing."

Reese and Kellan laughed, but Riley didn't hear Kinsley laughing with them. She was beginning to feel bad about eavesdropping, but she couldn't resist hearing Kinsley tell this story.

"I told her I'd call her. But I have no idea what to say," Kinsley said.

"You could say *hello*," Riley said as she made herself known and moved to stand in front of the booth. "Hi, guys."

"Hey, Riley," Reese said first.

"Riley, hi. How long have you been there?" Morgan asked from her seat next to Kinsley.

"Not long." Riley decided to save Kinsley the embarrassment. If the woman's expression was any indication, she hadn't done that completely. But there was no need to tell Kinsley she'd heard everything either. "Do you guys need another round? I'm buying."

"I think I'd like to go find someone to dance with. Kinsley, you want to come along?" Morgan asked. "There's the blonde over there that's been staring at you for the past five minutes."

Riley turned to follow Morgan's finger only to notice that a blonde woman was indeed looking over at their group; and, possibly, at Kinsley. She turned back to watch Kinsley finish her martini before standing and moving quickly past her.

"Let's dance," Kinsley said as she walked toward the woman.

Morgan stood, too. She held onto Riley's forearm for a moment and whispered into her ear, "If you like her, don't hurt her."

Then, Morgan was dancing with a redhead she grabbed from the bar. Kinsley was dancing with the blonde. Riley was now a third-wheel at the table with Kellan and Reese.

"How much did you actually hear?" Reese asked.

"All of it. Am I screwing this up?" Riley asked and took a drink of Reese's cosmopolitan.

"You're not screwing it up. But you shouldn't lead her on if there's nothing on your end of things, Riley," Kellan said. "She doesn't know, though, does she?"

"She said she'd call. She hasn't yet. I was hoping I could talk to her tonight. But she seems busy." She turned to see the blonde wrap her arms around Kinsley's neck and lean in. She must have said something into Kinsley's ear. "Very busy."

"Riley, she's just dancing. James doesn't do one-night stands. She won't take anyone home tonight," Reese explained. "Why don't you ask her to dance next? You could try talking to her then."

"I've got a better idea." She took another drink of Reese's cosmopolitan, for some liquid courage, before she stood somewhat confidently, exhaled a deep breath, and walked toward the dance floor. When she arrived at Kinsley and the blonde, she asked, "May I cut in?"

"With which one of us?" the blonde asked.

"I'd like to dance with her if you don't mind," Riley replied, pointing at Kinsley.

"Oh," the woman said and glanced in Kinsley's direction.

"I'll grab you later for another dance," Kinsley told the blonde. "My friend just got here," she added, likely to make the woman not feel as bad.

When the blonde kissed Kinsley's cheek slowly and whispered something to her Riley couldn't hear, Riley gulped and considered just going back to the table. The blonde walked off the dance floor just as a slow.

The next song started. It was one of those songs that still allowed people to dance at a bar but also to pull someone close and rock their body against them. It was just the kind of song they should *not* be dancing to right now. Riley wanted to talk to Kinsley. She wasn't sure they could do that with this song playing, but she'd started this. She'd have to finish it now. Riley pulled Kinsley's hips toward her before placing her arms around Kinsley's neck.

"Is this okay?"

"It's fine," Kinsley replied but didn't sound so sure.

They weren't pressed against one another. In fact, Riley thought, they must have looked like two kids at a seventh-grade Catholic school dance, where they were told to leave room for the Holy Spirit. She hadn't danced in a long time, though. Riley wasn't a big dancer, but she liked to go out occasionally and dance with a woman. She hadn't been able to do that with Elena. Even when she'd tried to just dance with her in the kitchen, where they had privacy, Elena had thought it ridiculous.

"I needed to talk to you. You didn't call. Reese and Kellan told me you'd be here. I shouldn't have just shown up, though," Riley said.

"It's fine," Kinsley repeated.

"Are you just going to keep saying that?"

"No," Kinsley said. "I'm answering your questions, Riley."

"You're being short with me, because you're upset. Will you tell me what you're upset about?" She swayed as Kinsley's hands gripped her sides but weren't really holding her. "Kinsley, I wanted to talk to you for a reason. That day I dropped off coffee and bagels, I wanted to talk, too. I just lost my nerve."

"Why?"

"I told you. I always feel like such a mess around you," Riley said as she chuckled.

"I wish you'd stop saying that. I don't think you're a mess."

"You might take that back in a minute," Riley said.

"What? Why?" Kinsley lifted a sexy eyebrow.

"Kinsley, will you go out with me?" she asked.

CHAPTER 12

SHE HADN'T heard that correctly. Kinsley pulled her body away from Riley's and just stood in the middle of a semi-crowded dance floor.

"That's not funny, Riley. That's actually pretty mean," she said.

"Hey, everything okay?" Morgan leaned over and away from the redhead she'd been dancing with.

"Everything's fine, Morgan," Riley said.

"I'm going to get a drink," Kinsley said.

"Kinsley…"

"Riley, come on." Morgan let go of the redhead. "What are you trying to do?"

"Morgan, can you just mind your own business?" Riley snapped.

Morgan moved to where Kinsley had been standing before she'd walked off the dance floor. Kinsley made her way toward the bar where she thought about ordering another drink. Then, she decided she needed air more than alcohol. She'd driven Morgan here, but Morgan could get a ride with Kellan and Reese. She texted Morgan as she made her way to the door and outside. She knew she'd been rude not to say goodnight to Reese or Kellan, but she needed oxygen, and she couldn't get any inside that bar. What the hell had just happened? Had she heard Riley correctly, or had she just imagined it? She'd imagined it, for sure. She was overreacting to something she thought she heard. Riley probably thought she was crazy now.

"Kinsley James, stop!" Riley yelled.

Kinsley turned around to see Riley standing just outside the bar's bright red door.

"Riley, I'm going home, okay?"

"No, it's not okay." Riley rushed toward her.

She looked good tonight. She'd worn a light blue cocktail dress with white two-inch heels. Her hair was half up and half down, and it looked great. Her makeup was light and matched the lightness of her dress. Her lips only had gloss on them with no shade and looked just as kissable as they always did.

"What the hell was that, Riley? I've been a good friend to you. I've listened to you talk about your girlfriend. I've tried to help you find a house that you two will share. I've done everything I can to try to help. And it's like, you can't even respect my feelings. You remember what happened the other night, don't you?"

"Kinsley, I absolutely remember." Riley moved toward her. "And this is crazy, and probably a bad idea, but I am asking you out on a date. I meant what I said in there."

"You are—"

"Single," the woman interrupted her. "Newly single, technically."

"Wait. What?" Kinsley asked. "Elena is—"

"Gone. She left yesterday."

"But—"

"We broke up that night, Kinsley. She stayed in Kellan's old room for a couple of nights. I think she thought she could convince me to take back the breakup by staying an extra night, but I didn't. We're over. Elena is back in Texas, living the life she wants. And I'm living the life I want here."

"But—"

"But what, Kinsley?" Riley moved another step closer

to her as they stood in the near-empty parking lot. "But what?"

"You're single?"

"Yes, I'm single." Riley smiled at her. "And I'd like to go out with you if you'd like to go out with me."

Kinsley was standing in front of the woman she'd liked for pretty much her entire adult life, and she didn't know what to say. Riley was single. She was asking Kinsley on a date. Kinsley should say yes. She'd love to go on a date with Riley. The woman was smiling at her, patiently waiting for an answer, and Kinsley had yet to give her one, because she didn't know what to say. She had thoughts about her parents and their troubled past that always had her on edge when it came to the endings and beginnings of relationships. Of course, that ex-girlfriend of hers had caused some problems for Kinsley, too. Kinsley had started that relationship after the assurances that the woman's previous relationship was definitely finished, only to find out too late that it wasn't. She wasn't just gun-shy because she'd always wanted Riley. She was gun-shy because she wasn't sure Riley wouldn't break her heart and end up back with Elena.

"Riley, we shouldn't."

"Shouldn't go out?" Riley asked, seemingly hurt by the words.

"You were with Elena for three years. You were planning a life with her, buying a house, settling down. And now that's not happening. It's a lot. It's something you need time to deal with. Maybe you'll even reconsider once you've had more time to think about it."

"You know what I've been thinking about?" Riley asked as she reached her hand out and took Kinsley's the same way she had that night. "How nice your hand felt that night. It didn't last long – I know, but there was this little spark I felt when I touched you. I think that means something, Kinsley."

"Riley, you have no idea how much I want to say yes to you right now."

"Then, say yes," Riley implored. "Say yes. We can go back inside and dance like two single people who want to dance with one another, instead of the way you just tried to dance with me."

"Because I thought you had a girlfriend, and I had to protect my heart, Riles," Kinsley said and dropped Riley's hand. "That's all I've ever done with you."

"Protect your heart," Riley said it as if trying out the words. "But I'm here now, and I like you. I like you, Kinsley," she added.

"But I can't trust that right now, Riley," Kinsley began. "I wish I could, but I can't. You just broke up with Elena, but I know a lot of people who end their long-term relationships only to begin them again days or weeks later. I can't start something with you thinking that's a possibility."

"I'm not going to get back together with her. You were the one that showed me what I was missing, Kinsley. You show me what a real girlfriend is supposed to be."

"I need to go," Kinsley said.

"What am I doing wrong? Please, tell me. I'll fix it. I thought you'd be glad to hear that Elena and I were over."

"I am glad to hear that, but not because I think we should date. I'm glad to hear it because you do deserve better, Riley," Kinsley offered.

"And *you* are better, Kinsley," Riley replied. "You are, and I like this. I want to try this with you."

Kinsley lowered her head before raising it back up and meeting Riley's confused eyes.

"I don't want you to try with me, Riley. If you feel the same way after some time has passed, we can talk about this again. But I can't be with you now."

"I'm telling you I don't need time. Why don't you believe me?" Riley asked, her voice slightly raised. "I think I know how I feel better than you do, Kinsley."

"And I know how *I* feel better than you do, Riley. As much as I want this between us, I don't want to be a rebound for you. I don't want to be someone you try with because I cooked you a few meals and listened when you talked."

"Fine," Riley said and shook her head sideways several times. "I guess I'll go then. You should stay. I'm sure Morgan is worried about you. She just gave me an earful about how I need to be careful with you. I told her I'd never hurt you. Because, in the past month, I've thought about you way more than I thought about the woman I was actually in a relationship with. But if you feel this way, and you can't see this happening right now, there's no reason for me to be here tonight."

"Riley, please don't be—"

"Upset?" Riley interrupted. She took a few steps past Kinsley and said, "I am upset. But you have every right to feel how you feel, Kinsley. I get it. I just didn't see tonight ending like this." She turned back to face Kinsley then. "I thought I'd take you home. I thought I'd make you strawberry ice cream and sliced bananas, since I didn't get a chance to do that last time. I thought we'd talk a little or a lot, and I thought we'd share our first kiss. I actually thought the whole night through as I drove here tonight, and I smiled the whole time."

"I'm sorry. I don't know what else to say," Kinsley replied, feeling like the worst and dumbest human being alive.

"Nothing," Riley replied. "I'll see you around, I guess."

Riley unlocked her car with her key fob. Kinsley heard the two consecutive beeps interrupt the near silence before Riley climbed into her car and drove off without another glance in Kinsley's direction.

"Hey, are you okay?" Morgan had somehow ended up behind her.

"No, I'm not," Kinsley replied without turning around.

"What happened?"

"She asked me out."

"That's good, right? Why is she driving off then?"

"Because I said no," Kinsley answered.

"What? Why? She told me she's single now, and she likes you, James. You like her, too. What's the problem?"

"She's been single for a few days, Morgan."

"Oh, you think she needs time?"

"Who wouldn't in her situation?"

"Did she say that?"

"No, she said she didn't need time," Kinsley replied.

"But you don't trust it?"

"No." Kinsley turned around. "How many couples do we know that broke up and got back together?"

"A few, but that doesn't mean that would happen with Riley and Elena."

"I can't risk that, Morgan. I like her too much."

"You keep saying you like her, but you're not acting like someone who likes someone," Morgan suggested.

"Because I don't want to go out with someone that's on the rebound?"

"Because you don't just *like* her, do you, James?" Morgan asked. "It's more than that, isn't it?"

"It can't be. Not right now, at least," Kinsley said.

"You can't help that, James. You can't help falling in love."

CHAPTER 13

"I ASKED HER, REESE. She said no. I don't know what you expect me to do now," Riley said and took a long pull from her beer. "I feel like such an asshole."

"I don't understand," Reese replied. "She's liked you forever."

"But it is a little weird with the timing," Kellan added.

"It's definitely weird with the timing," Morgan added as she made her way into Kellan and Reese's living room. "And it's weird that we're in here talking about James, but James isn't here." She sat on the floor and faced Riley. "You really screwed it up, didn't you?"

"Morgan!" Reese exclaimed. "Come on."

"What? She broke up with her girlfriend and, like, two days later, she's asking James out on a date."

"I want to go out with her," Riley argued. "I like Kinsley. She's amazing."

"She is. And she's nobody's rebound." Morgan glared at her.

"Damn, Morgan. Are you sure *you* don't want to go out with her?" Riley tossed back.

"I love that girl. She's like my sister. I'll always try to protect her, just like I did with Reese when Kellan first got here," Morgan said.

"That's a little different, though," Kellan suggested. "You used to date Reese. Kinsley isn't your ex."

"Kinsley James was the first friend I met when Reese, Remy, and I got to school. She's been a shoulder to cry on for me ever since. She's also been there when I needed work advice, help handling every breakup I've ever been through, and she's a person I know I can always rely on. So, I'm protective, but I'm protective for a reason."

Riley sat on the floor on the other side of the sofa that Reese and Kellan shared. She stared at Morgan and knew she'd have to say something to get her to understand Kinsley wouldn't be a rebound for her. She took another drink and set the empty beer bottle on the coffee table before she took a deep breath in and then out.

"Morgan, I like that you're so protective of her. I mean, I think Kinsley is completely capable of taking care of herself, but I like that she has someone like you in her life. It's important to have someone looking out for you."

"What's the catch?" Morgan glared again.

"There is no catch," Riley replied and laughed a little. "I like her, but... I don't know. Maybe she's right. Maybe you're right."

"About you needing time to think about Elena?" Kellan asked.

"No, that's over," Riley said instantly.

"What happened exactly?" Morgan asked and leaned back against the sofa. "I only heard the basics."

"She came by unexpectedly. Kinsley and I were in the middle of a pretty important conversation where she told me she liked me. I was about to tell her that I liked her and was thinking about breaking up with Elena."

"Because of James?" Reese asked.

"I broke up with Elena because I wanted to. I didn't want to deal with everything she brings with her. We had this plan for us, but she doesn't want that anymore. I'm not willing to do what she wants."

"Which is?" Kellan asked.

"Be a mistress, basically," she replied. "I'd move there and stay out of her way. She'd run for office. And win or lose, nothing would really change. She'll probably be in the closet forever."

"I don't understand that. Why date women at all if you're going to remain in the closet? You can always find a woman to hook up with. She led you to believe that some time down the road, you two would be out. And now, that's changed," Reese said.

"Even that, I probably could have lived with. It would have sucked, but I probably could have made it work."

"Then, what was it?" Morgan asked another question, seemingly interested.

"I guess it was a bunch of things." Riley leaned back against the empty chair behind her. "Elena and I have been fighting for the better part of a year. I didn't realize until that night that her moving here was a last ditch effort to save us. I'd put so much work in relocating here, starting my practice, and trying to make it a home for us, that I failed to listen to her talk about how much she loves Texas, and how excited she is to possibly be its governor. Even though I don't agree with her decision to stay in the closet, it's still her decision." She paused. "I want to live here. I've always planned on settling down in South Lake. I want a home I share with a wife and our kids. I don't want to be with someone who wants to hide from all that or keep the best part of themselves away from everyone else. Hell, she's probably going to find some guy to marry before the election."

"Really?"

"It'll help her win."

"That's messed up," Kellan said.

"I know. But it's true," Riley said. "If that's the life she wants for herself, she can have it."

"And you can have James?" Morgan asked with a lifted eyebrow.

"Morgan, Kinsley is part of the reason I figured all this out and had the guts to break up with my girlfriend of three years. Kinsley James is amazing, and I'm crazy about her, okay? Is that enough for you? Does that prove anything to you, or do I need to pass some sort of a test?" She stared at Morgan confidently. "I like her, Morgan." She softened. "I don't know how I never saw it before, but I like her. I like how she is with me, and I want to be that way with her. I can't cook at all. Maybe I'll be the one that does the dishes or something." She laughed. "She's adorable." She smiled. "And she's sexy as hell sometimes. Saturday night, for example: she was wearing that shirt and those tight jeans."

"Wow," Reese said and laughed as she pointed at her. "You *do* like her."

"I wouldn't have asked her out if I didn't like her," Riley replied and glanced at Morgan. "I understand why she thinks we should wait. I get it; I do. I'm good with waiting for her."

"She's been waiting for you for a while, it seems." Kellan leaned forward on the sofa.

"She has," Morgan agreed. "So, no more Elena? That's over for good?"

"Yes, Morgan."

"And you like her enough to wait for her?" Morgan asked.

"Yes, Morgan."

"What if she finds someone else in the meantime?"

"She's found someone else?" Riley leaned forward and looked to Morgan for confirmation. "It's been like a week."

Reese and Kellan both laughed. Morgan looked surprised at her near-outburst and then smiled at her.

"I'll let you know about that test thing later. I might come up with a few questions, but I think we're good for now." Morgan winked at her.

Riley laughed and replied, "So, I'm okay for now?"

"For now," Morgan agreed.

"When are you going to talk to James?" Reese asked.

"I tried calling her twice. I also sent a few texts, but she's not responding. I think I need to leave her alone for a while, unfortunately."

"Maybe that's a good thing," Kellan suggested. "You take some time to move on from Elena, and she takes some time to get ready for you," she said with a smile.

***

"You're on her side now?" Kinsley asked.

"I'm on your side always, James. I know you know that," Morgan replied. "This is stupid. There are no sides. I'm friends with Riley, too. I love you both."

"But you're sitting there telling me I should have said yes to her," Kinsley said.

"That's not what I said," Morgan argued. "Look, I think you were right in saying no. I just talked to her this weekend, and I believed her when she said she and Elena were done."

Morgan stood up from the chair opposite Kinsley's desk. She placed both hands on the back of the chair and stared down at Kinsley.

"It takes time to get over something like that," Kinsley suggested.

"And you don't want to be a rebound. I think that's smart. I'm only suggesting that when you're both ready, you finally give this a chance. You've wanted to date that girl since senior year, James. I remember how you looked at her the day you met her for the first time."

"Her freshman orientation," Kinsley said wistfully and remembered at the same time.

"See? I'm right. This is more than some crush. It always has been for you," Morgan pointed out. "Just give it some time, but you should talk to her. Just be friends for now or something. I think it's important you two keep talking," she said. "Maybe if you do, things will move quicker. She already knows how great you are, but it can't hurt to rub it in her face. It might make it easier for her to get over the ex when she's constantly watching you be awesome."

"Did she ask you to come here?" Kinsley squinted at her. "Are these bagels from her?" She held up the white paper bag she'd come to associate with Riley Sanders. "And this coffee? Is this bribery coffee, Morgan Burns?"

"She asked me to bring it by, yes. She said you're terrible at eating while you're working," Morgan replied. "But that has nothing to do with me speaking slightly on her behalf."

"Slightly?"

"Yes, slightly." Morgan shrugged. "What? James, she likes you. It's obvious."

"So, you think I'm crazy now?"

"No, I told you. I think you were right to turn her down. I just think it's cute that she came by the store and asked me to drop this stuff off, because you're not returning her calls and she wants to respect your space."

"That is cute," Kinsley replied with a shy smile.

"Okay. I'm done. I have to get back to work. Do what you want about Riley. I'll see you later?"

"Yeah," Kinsley replied.

Morgan gave her a wave and headed out the front door of the office. It was then that Kinsley noticed Riley standing across the street looking into the window. Her eyes followed Morgan, who turned back toward her store. Then, she must have noticed Kinsley stand and head toward the front door, because she turned quickly and disappeared around the corner. Kinsley laughed at the display but couldn't follow her. She had clients coming in to sign paperwork. It was a blessing in disguise, because she did want to follow her. She wanted to follow Riley around that corner, slam her up against the wall, and kiss her. It hurt her not to do that, but she knew that it would hurt her more if she did follow her. She couldn't be led on by Riley. She couldn't be someone Riley needed while she was trying to get over her girlfriend. She couldn't just be her friend, either, but she guessed she'd have to try. Riley, it seemed, wasn't great at giving her space. At least she was adorable while she tried.

CHAPTER 14

IT HAD BEEN TWO WEEKS since she'd tried dropping bagels and coffee off at Kinsley's office, lost her nerve, and asked Morgan for her help instead. Kinsley still hadn't spoken to her. Elena, though, had. She'd called more since the breakup than she did during the last six months of their relationship. Riley had to pick up the phone at some point. There were still things they'd needed to iron out. While they'd never had joint accounts or shared any property, they had planned a life together. They'd ordered custom made furniture for their future home in an impulsive move when they were riding high immediately after making the decision. The furniture was expensive, and now – unnecessary. Elena had used that as her first excuse to call. They'd decided to just take the loss and tell the designers to keep it and sell it to someone else.

The second call had been because Elena had had a flight purchased for both of them to take a weekend away in New York. She'd also prepaid for the five-star hotel. It had been a surprise for Riley. The woman had planned it completely without her knowledge for the month after Elena had been slated to move. It was meant to be an exciting whisk away, complete with a Broadway show and couples massage. She hadn't expected Riley to pay for it. Riley knew she was using the details of her plan to attempt to win her back. She'd even offered to let Riley keep the trip and take a friend. Riley had turned it down and suggested Elena still go and take a friend. The last time they'd talked, Elena had actually gotten Riley to laugh as she recounted an event from a fundraiser held that night in her honor. It was nice sharing a laugh like that. They hadn't done it in so long.

"Riley, I want to see you," Elena said.

"Elena, we're not together anymore. You know that," Riley replied as she grabbed a beer from her fridge and heard the microwave ding. "My dinner's ready. I should go."

"You cooked?"

"No, I–"

"Did that realtor cook?" she asked. "I remember you telling me how she liked to cook for you."

"I'm making a TV dinner, Elena."

"So, no realtor?"

"Elena, you don't get to ask that anymore. You're not my girlfriend," she pulled the meal out of the microwave and removed the thin plastic quickly, as to avoid burning herself. It didn't work. "Damn it."

"What happened?"

"Nothing. I have to go, Elena."

The doorbell rang. She turned at the unexpected sound and left the meal to deal with later. She sucked the tip of her index finger into her mouth to try to stop the pain, and then moved to open her door.

"I'll call you tomorrow," Elena said. "Before I have that meeting with the senator and his wife."

"Kinsley?" Riley said with her finger still in her mouth when she opened the door to her apartment and found Kinsley James standing in the hallway.

"Kinsley? The realtor?" Elena asked.

"Elena, I've got to go." She hung up the phone.

"Elena?" Kinsley asked.

"It's not what it looks like," Riley said and lowered her hand from her mouth.

"Why is your hand in your mouth?" Kinsley asked while pointing at her.

"I burned myself," Riley answered and shrugged.

"Cooking?"

"Yes," Riley replied and smiled.

"Do you need help?" Kinsley asked, clearly trying not to laugh.

"No, it's just a TV dinner." Riley lowered her head. "I gave up trying to cook something real after that night."

"I guess I should leave you to it," Kinsley said.

Riley's head snapped up, and her eyes met Kinsley's.

"Why did you stop by?"

"I was hoping to talk to you, but now's not the right time."

"Because I burned my finger?" She held it up.

"Because you were on the phone with Elena. But that doesn't look good, Riles. You should take care of that." Kinsley took Riley's hand. Riley wished it was for another reason, but she loved the touch of Kinsley's soft hands. "Run this under room temperature water. Do you have a first aid kit?"

"I might," Riley said. "I think Kellan left the one she bought in the bathroom."

"I'll go get it. I'll take care of this for you, and then I'll go, okay?"

"Kinsley, you don't have to go. I was just–"

"One second," Kinsley replied as she made her way toward the bathroom.

"Damn it, Elena." Riley sat on the sofa. "You had to call tonight of all–"

She heard a scream, jumped up from the sofa, and rushed into the bathroom, where she saw Kinsley standing completely still, holding the small first aid kit in one hand and staring at the floor.

"There's a spider," she said.

Riley lowered her gaze to see the world's tiniest spider on the tile next to the bathtub. She glanced up at Kinsley's terrified expression and burst out laughing.

"That's why you screamed?" Her laugh continued. "I

think that's a baby spider, Kinsley. It's hardly even visible. How did you see it?"

"It moved. I saw it when it moved. I don't like spiders, Riley." Kinsley still hadn't moved a muscle.

"Go out there, and I'll take care of it," Riley ordered.

"If I move, it will move," Kinsley replied.

Riley gripped Kinsley's hips from behind. She held onto them a little longer than necessary because of how good it felt. Kinsley's t-shirt was soft and thin, which meant she could feel the skin beneath it. She took advantage of the moment and wrapped her arms around Kinsley's waist. When Kinsley's muscles tensed even further, she held onto her, rested her head on Kinsley's shoulder, and breathed her in. *God, this felt good.*

"I guess I'll be the spider remover for us, huh?" she asked.

Kinsley stood still a moment longer before she nodded, turned, and fled the bathroom. Riley picked up the spider in a Kleenex and tossed it into the toilet. She flushed it, feeling bad for killing the tiny thing. But she guessed Kinsley didn't want to watch her carry it outside and release it into the wild. She didn't have to worry about that, though, because by the time she got out of the bathroom, Kinsley was gone. The first aid kit was sitting on the table open and ready for Riley to use.

***

Kinsley needed to get away. She did this sometimes. She'd go hiking on her own or would take a long drive. Today, she'd decided to do both. She drove around to the north side of the lake, ending up at a trailhead. She hiked for over a mile, trying to use the sounds of nature to calm her heart and mind. She'd gone to Riley's to talk to her. She probably should have called first. She hadn't expected her to be on the phone with her ex. She also hadn't expected Riley's arms around her to feel so good. In that moment, she knew how hard it would be to get over her if it went wrong. Riley's reference to being the spider killer in their relationship had also terrified her enough to run. She'd been running for the past two days. She'd avoided Riley's attempts to contact her. She'd worked from home when she wasn't doing a showing. She was being immature. But when Riley had held her like that, it felt too real. Unfortunately, it was while thinking about that feeling and wishing she could have it again that Kinsley missed the giant tree root in the middle of the path and tripped.

Her ankle ached immediately. She tried to stand on it and found herself in excruciating pain. She cursed herself several times. Then, she cursed herself some more for thinking that hiking alone – on an unfamiliar trail about forty minutes away from her friends, who could come and pick her up – was a good idea. She had no first aid supplies in her small day pack. She had no choice. She hobbled back down the trail, thankful at least, when she got to her car, that it was her left ankle, which meant she could drive. She knew it wasn't broken, but it was at least a sprain. She also had a pretty nasty cut on her knee that would need to be cleaned up. Her relaxing day had turned into a train wreck. She found the nearest urgent care on her phone and drove the three miles there, parked the car, and walked inside.

"Can I help you?" the receptionist asked.

"I tripped on a trail. I think I sprained my ankle," Kinsley explained.

"Just fill this out, and we'll be right with you," the receptionist replied and passed her a clipboard with the requisite paperwork.

After she completed it and sat for an additional ten minutes in the waiting room, a woman emerged from the back with a clipboard of her own. She was wearing blue scrubs with the standard white coat. She had long blonde hair, parted in the middle with two long braids lying against her shoulders. Her eyes were brown, and her smile was welcoming.

"Kinsley James?"

"That's me." Kinsley raised her hand unnecessarily.

"Can you walk on it?" the woman asked.

"I'm okay, yeah."

Kinsley made her way into the exam room, where she slid onto the table and waited for the woman who hadn't yet introduced herself.

"I'm Dr. Ash." The woman held out her hand for Kinsley to take. Kinsley shook it. "I understand you tripped while hiking."

"I did. I wasn't paying attention," Kinsley admitted.

Dr. Ash smiled at her and replied, "It happens to the best of us. I took a fall a few years ago. I ended up with a dislocated shoulder and a bruised ego."

Kinsley laughed and said, "My ego definitely took a hit today, too."

"Well, let's get you checked out."

Dr. Ash examined her ankle gingerly before sending her for an x-ray. While they waited for the films, she cleaned the cut on her leg and bandaged it up. She took care of Kinsley silently and carefully before she left to review the x-rays. When she returned, she had a bandage in hand and sat on the rolling stool.

"Give it to me straight, doc," Kinsley said.

"You have a mild sprain. I'm going to wrap it up, and you should stay off it for a few days if you can. Ice every four to six hours, take some ibuprofen, and you should be fine," the woman replied.

"Great. I'm a real estate agent. It's kind of hard to stay off my feet when I'm doing showings," she said as Dr. Ash began wrapping her ankle.

"I can give you crutches here."

"Crutches? Really?"

"It's better than you overextending yourself while you're healing."

"Fine. I guess I'll take one set of crutches along with the pain and humiliation. I can't wait to tell Morgan about how I managed to go out of my way to injure myself. Literally, I went out of my way."

The doctor laughed and replied, "What do you mean?"

"I live in South Lake. I drove up here to go hiking, and here I am."

"And Morgan is your… girlfriend?" she asked.

"Oh, no. Morgan is my best friend. I don't have a girlfriend," she said quickly.

"And you're from South Lake?"

"Not originally, but I've lived there since college," Kinsley answered the soft smile this doctor continued to give her as she bandaged her up. "You?"

"Here. I'm a native," she replied with a small laugh. "I left for medical school but came back. I volunteer here two days a week, but I have my own practice."

"How old are you? You have your own practice?"

"I'm thirty-six. And yes, I do," she said. "I'm very lucky."

"And successful," Kinsley added.

Dr. Ash looked up at her and said, "I'm doing okay. And you're all done." She lowered Kinsley's ankle. "I'll get you those crutches and some ibuprofen to help with the inflammation."

"Thank you," Kinsley replied.

"Who drove you here?"

"No one. I drove out of my way, remember?" Kinsley laughed at her own mistake.

"Right," the woman replied. "Well, you're lucky it's your left ankle, but I still don't like you driving."

"I don't really have much of a choice. I can call my friends and try to see if someone can pick me up, but it's not my right leg. I should be okay."

"If I asked you to call someone to pick you up, would you think I'm crazy?" Dr. Ash asked. "It would just make me feel better."

"I can make a few calls and embarrass myself for you. How's that?"

The woman laughed and replied, "Sounds great."

"But if none of them can get me, I'll drive myself. Is that a deal?"

"Deal. Let me get your crutches while you do that."

Kinsley called Reese first, because she knew Morgan would only yell at her for being stupid before she laughed at her for missing a giant tree root they could probably see from the space station. Reese didn't answer. She called Kellan next. Kellan did answer, but she had two more patients. She said Reese was with Remy and Ryan at the beach and, likely, couldn't hear her phone. She called Remy, thinking maybe she'd get lucky. Then, she called Ryan, for good measure. She called Stacy, but she and Dave were out of state. Finally, she gave in and called Morgan.

"You did what?" Morgan asked.

"I know. I'm stupid. Can you just come and get me? The doctor doesn't want me driving."

"But it's your left ankle."

"I know that, Morgan. If you can't, it's fine. I told her I'd call everyone I knew first, and if none of you can get me, I'll drive myself."

"Well, that would make me a terrible friend, wouldn't it?" Morgan asked. "I can't believe you went all the way up there and hiked an unfamiliar trail on your own. That's so dumb, James. You know how dumb that is."

"And if I wanted a lecture, I'd call my mother."

"Give me about forty-five minutes, and I'll be there, okay?"

Kinsley hung up after she told Morgan the address of the clinic and lowered her phone.

"Any takers?" the doctor asked when she came back into the room with crutches, leaning them against the wall.

"My friend Morgan."

"Did she lecture you, like you thought?"

"Yes, she did." Kinsley laughed.

"At least you got it out of the way already," the woman said and handed her the pills and a small cup of water.

"Please, I'll have to listen to it all the way home," Kinsley replied and took the medication.

"Well, I'm done with my shift. I can keep you company until she gets here if you want," Dr. Ash said.

"I'd like that, but you don't have to. I can just wait in the waiting room."

"You can't, actually. We're closing. Technically, we're closed already. You were the last patient of the day. Jackie already went home."

"Jackie is?"

"The receptionist, sorry."

"Oh, I'll wait in my car, then."

"There's a bar down the street. If you want, we can go there and wait. If you're not driving, you can have a drink with me."

Kinsley smiled softly at the doctor and said, "I probably shouldn't walk down the street."

"I have a car." The woman blushed a little. "If I'm being honest, I might have insisted you have someone drive you because I was kind of hoping to talk to you more."

"What? Really?"

"Yes. And it's completely unprofessional." She laughed. "But if you are…"

"Gay?"

"Yes," Dr. Ash said.

"I am. You?"

The woman nodded and said, "Drink?"

"Sure."

CHAPTER 15

RILEY WATCHED them for a minute before she approached. She gritted her teeth when she saw them both laugh, and then again, as the woman she didn't recognize helped Kinsley shift her injured ankle on the chair she was propping it up on before the woman sat back down in her own chair. Riley knew this was jealousy. She understood this feeling all too well. She'd been jealous before, but she was pretty certain she'd never been this jealous.

"Kinsley," she greeted.

"Riley?" Kinsley was obviously surprised to see her. "What are you doing here?"

"Morgan's in the car. We're here to pick you up."

"You're both here?" Kinsley asked and turned to the other woman.

"One of us has to drive your car back." She turned to the woman. "Hi. You are?"

"Courtney Ash," she said and held out her hand.

"She's the doctor that helped me," Kinsley added.

"Nice to meet you," Riley replied and shook her hand reluctantly. "Are you ready?" She turned her attention to Kinsley.

"Yeah, I guess." Kinsley lowered her ankle to the floor. Riley watched as Courtney moved to the crutches leaning against the wall behind the table, helped Kinsley stand, and passed them to her. "Thanks."

"You'll call me?" Courtney asked Kinsley.

Kinsley looked at Riley before looking back at Courtney, giving her a smile and nodding.

"Thanks for the drink," she said.

"Anytime," Courtney replied.

Riley watched the exchange as Kinsley settled into her crutches. Riley let her walk over to where she was standing before she put her hand on the small of Kinsley's back and ushered her out of the bar.

"I texted Morgan this address. I didn't expect you to be here," Kinsley said when they got outside.

"Obviously," Riley replied.

"What does that mean?" Kinsley turned her head toward her.

"Drinks?"

"She was nice enough to wait for Morgan with me. The closest place to wait was the bar. She was nice."

"I could see that," Riley said.

"Are you jealous?" Kinsley asked.

"Are you going out with her?" Riley asked back.

Kinsley stopped walking abruptly. Riley's hand went to the small of her back again to help steady her.

"She asked me to look over the paperwork for her. She's thinking about moving offices for her medical practice and isn't sure about the new building. I offered to help her, since she was so nice to me."

"Oh," Riley replied, feeling a little foolish.

"Hey, just how injured are you?" Morgan asked as she approached them. "And why were you in a bar? Where's your car?"

"It's back at the clinic," Kinsley explained.

"Well, let's go then. I'm hoping to get back early enough so I can catch Steph before she closes up," Morgan explained.

"Steph from the café?" Kinsley asked.

"She's hot," Morgan replied. "And she may have suggested I stop by tonight. She said she'd give me a free cappuccino if I did." She wiggled her eyebrows.

"I do not want to know what you think a cappuccino is," Riley said.

Kinsley laughed. Riley loved the sound of it and helped her into the back of Morgan's car. They drove while Morgan lectured Kinsley about the dangers of hiking alone and how much worse it could have been. Riley didn't say anything until they arrived at the clinic. Kinsley climbed out of the car. Riley helped her into the passenger's seat of her own vehicle. Before she could turn around, Morgan was waving at both of them and driving off. Riley had failed to consider that she and Kinsley would be driving alone for over forty-five minutes. In a way, she was very happy. Kinsley would be trapped; they'd be forced to talk. She was also still slightly jealous. Kinsley had been laughing at Courtney Ash in that bar. She'd smiled and laughed, and seemed to be having fun, despite the fact that she'd injured herself and was clearly in pain.

"Can I just say that I agree with Morgan?" Riley asked as they pulled out of the parking lot.

"About?"

"You, hiking on your own like that. That's dangerous, Kinsley. Why'd you do that? Why'd you come all the way out here to do that? We live in South Lake. There are trails next to your damn house you could have used. You could have hobbled your way home, for crying out loud."

"I needed to get away." Kinsley leaned her head against the side window. "I misjudged my hiking ability, apparently."

"Yeah, apparently," she replied angrily. "God, Kinsley. What if something had happened to you?"

"Riles, I'm fine. It's a mild sprain. I'll stay off it for a few days and be fine."

Riley sighed and asked, "Are you hungry? We could stop on the way back."

"No, I'm okay. Courtney and I shared a couple of appetizers."

"And that was all you shared?" Riley asked without glancing in Kinsley's direction.

"She's gay, Riley. If that's what you're getting at, she's gay, and she did ask me out to drinks. We shared one and some laughs. She's very nice."

"You said that already," Riley pointed out.

"And yes, she asked me out."

"You said she asked you to look into some paperwork," Riley said, looking over at Kinsley, whose eyes were now meeting hers.

"She asked me out and also asked me to look at the paperwork."

"And you said?"

"I said I'd think about it."

Riley's eyes went to the road as she replied, "Got it."

"You can't be mad at me for this, Riley," Kinsley said.

"I'm not mad."

"Then, what are you?"

"Tired of talking about this," Riley replied. "Let's just listen to music." She turned the volume up. Kinsley reached forward and turned it back down. "What, Kinsley?"

"You were on the phone with Elena, Riley."

"I had my arms around *your* waist, Kinsley," Riley reminded.

Kinsley didn't say anything for a moment. Riley let out an exasperated sigh.

"Let's just listen to music, like you said," Kinsley suggested.

The rest of the ride was silent. It wasn't that comfortable silence Riley liked so much in a relationship, though. It was that tense, awkward silence between two people who obviously had things to talk about but neither of them was ready to do so. When Riley pulled up in front of Kinsley's house, Morgan's car was there, waiting. She pulled into the driveway and put Kinsley's car in park before turning it off and passing Kinsley the keys.

"Well, Morgan is waiting. I guess I should go."

"Riley, I don't like this," Kinsley said.

Riley turned to her and took in Kinsley's face before her eyes moved to Kinsley's leg.

"Kinsley, you're bleeding," she said as she placed her hand just above the bandage that blood was soaking through.

"It's just a cut. I'll take care of it when I get inside."

"Wait. What don't you like?"

"Huh?"

Kinsley was cute when she was confused.

"You said you don't like this," Riley reminded.

"Oh, I don't like whatever we've turned into."

"What's that?" Riley asked.

"I don't know, but I don't like it."

Riley stared into Kinsley's blue eyes for a moment before she said, "Neither do I."

"Hey, I need to get out of here if I'm going to make it to Steph in time," Morgan said as she stood next to Kinsley's car and Riley's open window. "I've got to drop you back at the office to get your car."

"You were at work?" Kinsley asked her.

"I was meeting with a client when Morgan came in and told me what happened."

"I needed someone to drive your car back," Morgan explained.

"You were in the middle of a meeting with a client and you left?" Kinsley asked Riley.

"I'll finish the meeting tomorrow." She looked down at Kinsley's leg. "You need to get inside. Come on. I'll help you take care of that."

"So, I'm not meeting Steph tonight, am I?" Morgan asked when Riley opened the door.

"You can go." Riley closed the driver's side door. "I need to take care of her." Morgan lifted her eyebrow. "Not like that," Riley whispered.

"Whatever you say," Morgan replied and smirked. She also offered an eye-roll. "Should I stay? Does she need me?

I don't really care about Steph. I can catch her tomorrow night."

"She'll be fine. I'll stay," Riley replied and placed her hand on Morgan's arm. "Thank you for coming to get me."

"I could have grabbed any one of my friends from the beach. I chose you, because I know you two need to talk. Make sure you take care of her, okay? And I don't mean that in a dirty way."

"I'll make sure she's okay," Riley said with a light laugh.

Morgan turned and made her way back to her car. She drove off as Riley helped Kinsley out of the car and into the house. She got Kinsley situated in bed with a pillow to elevate her ankle. Then, she went into the kitchen and got her something to drink and a bag of chips she found in the pantry, in case Kinsley got hungry. She dropped it off with Kinsley before she went into the bathroom and found a much larger first aid kit than her own.

"Is this because you're so injury prone?" Riley asked when she emerged from the master bath, holding up the first aid kit.

"It's because I'm a single woman and I did a lot of these home improvements myself. I had a few cuts and bruises along the way," Kinsley explained. "You can just leave it here. I'll bandage it back up. If you want to take my car home, you can. I'll come by tomorrow and get it. It's not like I'm going anywhere else tonight anyway."

"Kinsley, can you just let me help you? We don't have to talk about anything we really should be talking about. I can just fix your leg."

Kinsley nodded. Riley removed the existing bandage, revealing the cut beneath. She cleaned it again, wiping the blood from Kinsley's leg. She applied a topical ointment and rebandaged it. When she finished, she grabbed the kit and the trash. Once she'd put that all away, she made her way back into Kinsley's bedroom, suddenly remembering she had no other reason to stay at the house. She didn't want to leave, though. Kinsley wasn't in bed. The pillow was still in place, as was the water and bag of chips, but the woman was gone. Riley looked at the opened door and made her way to it. She found Kinsley lying in one of her chaise lounge chairs.

"Come out here?" Kinsley asked.

Riley moved outside, leaving the door open behind her. There was another chair there this time, but she chose to stand against the railing instead, turning to face Kinsley and not the nighttime view.

"You should be lying in bed. It's getting late."

"I was out there because of you," Kinsley said.

"Hiking?"

"Sometimes, I go for a drive to clear my head. Sometimes, I hike. Today, I decided to do both, and it clearly backfired."

"You needed to clear your head of me?" she asked.

"I can't ever seem to clear my head of you."

CHAPTER 16

"I'D SAY IT'S THE PAIN MEDS making me more direct, but I don't think ibuprofen does that," Kinsley said and chuckled.

"Kinsley, just talk to me. That's all I want."

Riley stood there, leaning her back against the railing of Kinsley's patio and looking great while doing it. She wore black slacks with matching short heels that had a small silver flourish on them. Her blouse was silk and a bright blue that wasn't quite navy but also wouldn't be described as light blue, either. The top button had been undone. There was a nice view through that V between her breasts, but not enough to be considered revealing. Her hair was down. Riley ran her fingers through it as the wind had gusted around them moments ago, causing the hair to fly in her face.

"You look beautiful," Kinsley replied as Riley smiled and looked away from her eyes. "And I am scared," she added.

Riley's eyes returned to Kinsley's, and she said, "Because of me?"

"Because I don't want to get hurt by you," Kinsley explained.

"Why are you assuming you will?"

"When was the last time you talked to Elena?" Kinsley asked.

"Yesterday," Riley answered. Kinsley lowered her head. "We were together for three years, Kinsley. There are still things we need to work out."

"Like what?" Kinsley looked back up at her.

"She's having a hard time," Riley replied.

"Not being with you?"

"Yes. But that doesn't mean I want to be with her," Riley said and moved toward her. "Kinsley, you helped me realize I didn't want a life with her. Why can't you see that?" She sat on the side of the chair, causing Kinsley to shift a little.

"I guess I can see that. It's just hard to believe it's over between you two when you're still talking on the phone every day," Kinsley said. "My worst nightmare is you and I getting together only to have your ex-girlfriend come back into the picture, Riley. Maybe I should be a better person than that, but I've never been able to be friends with my exes. I don't understand how Morgan can do that with Reese."

"Your worst nightmare is us getting together and then Elena coming back? That's the worst thing you can imagine?" Riley asked.

"Why does that matter?" Kinsley shifted to sit up.

"I'm trying to put things into perspective, Kinsley."

"Well, my actual worst nightmare involves bears and sharks, but this is pretty close," Kinsley said and laughed.

"Bears *and* sharks?" Riley laughed.

"Yes," Kinsley replied, getting serious again. "Riles, can you be 100% honest with me?"

"I've only ever been that with you, Kinsley," Riley said.

"Do you still love her?" Kinsley asked with a gulp.

"Yes, but not in the way you're thinking or worried about," Riley answered and placed her hand on Kinsley's thigh. "I'm not in love with her anymore, Kinsley. I'm not sure I've been in love with her for a while, actually." She paused, looking down into Kinsley's eyes. "Kinsley, I realize we haven't gotten off on the best foot, and part of that is definitely my fault, but I like you. I meant it when I asked you out. I loved dancing with you, being that close to you, holding you, and being held by you. It felt good. It felt right to me."

"Me too," Kinsley replied softly.

"Can I sit behind you?" Riley asked. "I don't want to hurt your ankle, but–"

"Yes," Kinsley interrupted.

She shifted forward as Riley stood, kicked off her shoes, and moved to sit behind her, pressing her back to the chaise. Kinsley waited the length of several breaths before she allowed herself to lean back against Riley's front between her legs. Riley's arms wrapped around her middle. Kinsley laid her head softly against Riley's shoulder and breathed in the scent of her.

"Can we just stay like this for a while?" Riley asked.

"I'd like that," Kinsley replied.

They stayed that way for several minutes. Neither of them spoke. They seemed to be enjoying the silence between them, along with the sounds of the birds, crickets, and the distant sound of people playing in the water below. Neither of them moved, either. Kinsley wondered if Riley wasn't moving for the same reason she wasn't moving. Kinsley wasn't moving because she was afraid if she did, this might end. Riley would pull back, and Kinsley didn't want Riley to pull back. She wanted Riley to squeeze her tighter and hold onto her forever. That scared her. It was one thing to like someone since college. It was a whole other thing to more than like that person, and to possibly have them like her in return. Riley liked her. She knew that. She could trust that Riley meant what she said. She still had something aching in her gut, though, that told her if she trusted her all the way, if she gave into this, she'd end up getting hurt.

"Can I ask you something?" Riley finally broke the silence.

"Sure," Kinsley answered as she continued to listen to Riley's quickening heart beneath her.

"What are you so afraid of?" Riley whispered it in her ear before her right hand slid under Kinsley's shirt just slightly to touch the skin of her hip.

She suddenly felt very self-conscious. She hadn't worked up much of a sweat on her hike. She'd been taking things slowly, because that helped her think. She also hadn't gotten that far. But she still didn't feel comfortable sitting there with this gorgeous woman, who was still dressed for work, when she was dressed in shorts and a shirt she usually wore when she hiked that was stretchy and tight in certain places. She didn't move Riley's hand, though. She couldn't. She needed Riley to be touching her right now. Riley's hand started to move, but not up. It moved over and stayed still on her stomach, under her shirt.

"You didn't even remember me, Riley," she said finally.

"I've always remembered you, Kinsley. Are we really going back to this?"

"No, that's not it. That's not what I meant, I mean."

"What did you mean then?" The woman placed her lips against the skin of Kinsley's neck; not kissing her, but pressing there.

"I remembered you, Riley. Even when you weren't living here, I remembered you. I'd think of you. Maybe not every single day, but I'd remember you, and I'd smile thinking about something from back then."

"So, you're saying no to me because I didn't feel the same way about you when I was a freshman in college?"

"No, it's not that," Kinsley said. "I'm not saying this right. It's more than one thing."

Riley's lips went back to that same spot on her neck before she gently kissed her there and said, "Keep talking."

"It's that, yes. I'm having a hard time understanding how you're, all of a sudden, interested in me. It's just also something else, too." She paused as Riley's hand slid up ever so slightly. "I watched Morgan after she and Reese broke up. I saw what happened to her and how long it took her to get past it. In some ways, I'm not even sure she is past it. She and Reese were so close before they started dating. Then, they were together for a long time, and everyone thought they'd get married one day. Reese had her accident, lost her parents, and broke up with Morgan. I assumed they'd get back together. I think everyone did, right up until Reese and Kellan moved in together. I know Reese and Kell love each other. But I still didn't trust it for sure until Reese smiled so wide when she told me she and Kellan were moving in together and taking all those important steps. I took Morgan out drinking that night. She still wasn't over Reese even then. Now, they're friends, and it's not awkward anymore, but it was a process. Like I said, I still don't know how they did it."

"And you're worried that if we try this, and it won't work out, you'll be in Morgan's shoes?"

"I worry I'll have to watch you with someone else. And I don't think I can do that," Kinsley answered. "Even now – we're not together, and thinking of you talking on the phone to Elena drives me crazy."

"Thinking of me talking on the phone to Elena drives me crazy, too," Riley said and laughed lightly into Kinsley's ear. "Kinsley, let me take you out to dinner. I don't know what's going to happen with us. I don't know if we'll be together forever, or if we'll go on one terrible date and that's the end. I do know that I'm going nuts right now, keeping my hand still, because I want to touch you. I want to kiss you right now. But I don't think you're ready for that. I don't think you trust me enough or trust this." She paused. "This feels so good to me. It's never felt this good. Just your body, pressed to mine like this, feels like it's supposed to be this way." She kissed Kinsley's neck and patted her stomach. "Come on. Let's get you into bed."

"That's it?" Kinsley asked as Riley lightly pushed her up from behind and stood, straightening her clothes next to the chair. "You're just going to say something like that and get up?"

Riley held out both hands for Kinsley to take and said, "It's all I can do until you trust me, because I really want this, Kinsley. I don't want to rush it if you're not ready."

Kinsley took both hands and stood. They were so close now. Riley's lips were inches away. Her dark eyes were staring at her. Then, she smiled, leaned forward, and kissed Kinsley's cheek.

"That wasn't exactly what I was hoping for," Kinsley said and laughed at herself.

"What *were* you hoping for?" Riley asked.

"A real kiss," Kinsley replied.

"You get that after a real date." Riley slid her arm under Kinsley's shoulder to help her into the bedroom. "And you can have a date with me whenever you're ready."

Kinsley lowered herself onto her bed and looked up at Riley, who was still adjusting her pillows.

"Whenever I'm ready?" Kinsley asked, smiling up at her.

"Yes, because I *am* ready. I know you don't believe that; and until you do, this won't go anywhere, Kinsley." Riley paused after adjusting the pillows and met her eyes. "And neither will I. I'm going to sleep in the guest room tonight if that's okay," she added.

"It's an ankle sprain. I'm okay, Riley," she said.

"I'd still like to be here to help." Riley sat on the side of the bed. "I'll just be down the hall, okay?"

"Riles, just sleep in here," Kinsley said as she patted the bed beside her.

"You have no idea how much I want to do that." Riley moved away from the bed. "But when I do, I don't want it to be because you have a sprained ankle, Kinsley."

CHAPTER 17

RILEY SAT behind her desk, closed her laptop, and packed it away. She climbed into her car a few minutes later, drove to the restaurant she'd ordered food from in advance, climbed back into the car, and drove. When she arrived at Kinsley's, she was surprised to find another car in the driveway. It wasn't Morgan's or anyone else's she knew. She'd texted Kinsley telling her she'd bring her dinner. Kinsley had replied with a happy face emoji. She'd been working from home for the past two days and had been going stir-crazy, according to their text message exchanges. She made her way up the driveway. She wasn't proud of it, but she glanced into the driver's side window of the car, and her heart sank. She noticed an ID badge for a Dr. Courtney Ash sitting on the passenger's seat.

Riley held onto the bag of food she'd bought for her and Kinsley to share as she knocked on the door. She'd planned to have dinner with Kinsley. But seeing Courtney's car in the driveway, after what she and Kinsley had discussed the other night, had her in actual pain. She thought they were working on something. She hoped Kinsley was getting to a point where she could trust her. She'd been wrong.

"Oh, hey." Courtney Ash stared back at her. "She's in the kitchen. Riley, right?"

"Yes. I didn't know you'd be here," Riley commented as she briskly entered Kinsley's foyer.

"That's because I was supposed to be gone already. I was just rewrapping her ankle," the woman replied.

"You came all this way to wrap Kinsley's ankle?" Riley asked as they made their way toward the kitchen.

"No, she didn't." Kinsley sat in one of the chairs at the kitchen table. Her laptop was out, and there were papers strewn about, with pictures of buildings from what Riley could see. "She's here for a client meeting."

"Right," Courtney said, but Riley caught her face drop when Kinsley said that. "She's helping me find a new office. We would have met at my current space, but I didn't want her to drive."

"We were just finishing up," Kinsley revealed. "She wanted to wrap my ankle again."

"And now, I've done that." Courtney moved to the chair next to Kinsley's; they'd been pushed very close together.

Riley swallowed hard. Courtney grabbed her purse hanging off the back and slung it over her shoulder.

"I'll leave you two to your meal."

"Thanks for coming all the way here, Court," Kinsley said. "I'd walk you out, but—"

"Don't move. You've been doing so well staying off it; letting me get you your coffee, paper from the printer, and everything. You're healing fast because of that."

"I know. Riley's been taking care of me." Kinsley smiled in Riley's direction. Riley gave her a smile back that didn't reach her eyes. "I'll talk to you later," she said to Courtney.

"Call me?"

"I will," Kinsley smiled as Courtney left the kitchen.

Moments later, the front door opened and closed behind her. Riley set the bags on the counter and turned to Kinsley.

"I'm just going to take my stuff and go. I'll make you

a plate first so you don't have to get up," Riley said.

"I thought you were staying for dinner," Kinsley replied.

"Kinsley, that woman wants to date you. It's written all over her face. Did you see it when you told me she was just a client?" Riley turned around, leaned back against the counter, and folded her arms over her chest.

"She was here for a meeting, Riley," Kinsley said.

"She was here for more than just a meeting." Riley turned back around to the bags of food. "You called her *Court*. Do you always shorten your clients' names like that?"

"Yes, I called you Riles when you were my client," Kinsley argued.

"That was different. We were friends first," Riley said.

"Are you jealous?" Kinsley asked, her voice sounding closer now.

"Should I be?" Riley risked.

"Riles…"

"She asked you out, Kinsley." Riley removed two containers from the bag.

"And I told her I'd think about it."

"Have you?" Riley turned around and saw Kinsley standing only a few feet away. "Kinsley, you shouldn't be standing up."

"You heard her. I'm healing," Kinsley replied.

"Kinsley, sit down. I'll bring you your food," Riley said.

Kinsley moved a little closer and replied, "She's a client, Riles."

"That you may or may not be going out on a date with at some point in the future," she said.

"She's not you, Riles," Kinsley said softly, and Riley met her eyes then. "She's attractive, funny, smart, kind, and she does want to go out with me. She asked me again today." She paused and shrugged. "I said no this time."

"Because she's not me?"

"Yes," Kinsley said.

Riley's phone rang just as Kinsley had taken a half-step into her space. Unfortunately, she'd placed it on the counter next to the food. Kinsley's eyes went to the screen. Then, she moved away from Riley entirely.

"I can't help that she calls," Riley said.

"You could tell her to stop," Kinsley replied.

"I have," Riley returned and hit ignore on the screen. "Kinsley, come on. We were getting somewhere here."

"I'm tired, Riley. I think I'd just like to eat in bed and call it an early night."

"That's a lie," Riley replied as her phone rang for a second time. "You want to eat dinner with me."

"I don't want to eat dinner with you while your ex keeps calling," Kinsley said and pointed at the phone just as she sat back down in her chair a propped her ankle on another.

"God," Riley said and tapped the phone. "Elena, come on. I'm busy, and I've asked you not to call."

"Riley, Margie was in a car accident," Elena said.

"What?"

"She's in surgery now. It was a drunk driver. He T-boned her at an intersection. He's in surgery, too, that asshole."

"Is she okay?" Riley asked as she leaned back against the counter again, holding the phone to her ear.

"They don't know. I just got here."

"I'm sorry, Elena." Riley looked over at Kinsley. "What can I do?"

"Can you come here?"

"To Dallas?"

"Yes. She loves you, Riley. I think she'd like it if you were here," Elena said.

"I can't just go to Dallas now, Elena."

Kinsley lowered her gaze to the floor.

"Tomorrow, then? Riley, she's my baby sister. I don't know what I'm doing. I can manage a whole town, but when I stare at those insurance forms, I have no idea what I'm doing. It all turns blurry. She's all I have now."

"I know," Riley replied. "What hospital?"

"Mercy," she said.

"I'll see if I can find a flight for first thing tomorrow. I'm not at home right now. I'll text you the info once it's booked," Riley replied.

"Thanks, babe. I love you," Elena said and then hung up.

Riley looked over at Kinsley, who was staring back at her.

"A flight to Dallas?"

"Her sister is in the hospital. Margie is my age. We were friends."

"I get it," Kinsley said. "I guess you have to go," she added after a moment.

"I should. I have to find something for early tomorrow and contact all my clients to let them know I'll have to miss their meetings. I'm sorry, Kinsley. I promise you, this has nothing to do with Elena or my feelings for her. I'm going because Margie and I were close. Sometimes, we used to talk even when Elena and I didn't."

"She's your friend. I hope she's okay. I really do," Kinsley told her and appeared to mean it. "Thanks for bringing me dinner."

"I'll call you," Riley replied, grabbing her food and her purse.

***

"How is she?" Riley asked when she saw Elena standing just outside the family waiting area of Mercy hospital.

"She's in her room," Elena said and reached for Riley, pulling her in for an unexpected hug. Riley patted Elena's shoulders a few times and pulled back. "Thank you for coming."

"What's wrong? Is she awake?" Riley asked.

She'd texted Elena later last night, after booking her flight, to ask more questions. Elena hadn't been able to answer them, since Margie was still in surgery. Riley had texted Kinsley as well, to let her know that she was on a six o'clock flight and would be back as soon as she could. It was strange. Kinsley wasn't her girlfriend. They hadn't even gone on a date yet. But it felt like she needed to let Kinsley know about her plans. Kinsley had replied. It had been a brief text, telling her to be safe, but at least she'd replied.

"She's awake." Elena was smiling. "How are you?" She took Riley's hand and moved them into the family waiting room where they were alone.

"How am *I*? Elena, Margie was in an accident. I flew here because you said she'd want to see me."

"She does. I told her you were coming."

"Okay. What room is she in?"

"Give me like five minutes, Riley. I'll take you to her. I haven't seen you in—"

Riley dropped Elena's hand and said. "Elena, this isn't even close to the longest amount of time we've gone without seeing one another. What room is Margie in?"

Elena gave her the passive-aggressive eye-roll Riley did not miss.

"I'll take you to her," she finally said.

They walked down the hall and turned left. When Riley entered the hospital room, Margie was lying with her leg in a cast and elevated.

"Hey, Margie."

"Riley, hi," Margie greeted her with a smile.

"How are you feeling?" Riley asked when she approached the bed.

"I'm on pain meds, so I'm feeling okay. I'm going to have to be in this cast for three months, which will not be fun."

Riley looked her over, and besides looking a little bit tired and having the cast on her left leg, the woman looked fine. She turned to see Elena scrolling through something on her cell phone. Riley regretted not asking more questions last night.

"How'd the surgery go?" she asked.

"They had to put a few pins in and move the bone back in place. I guess it took a while, but I'm only in here for the next day or two. They ran a lot of tests. They just want to get those results back, and I'm out of here. Did you fly here just for me or were you already visiting Elena?"

Riley turned back to Elena, who had looked up at the sound of her name.

"I'm just here to see you." Riley turned back to Margie. "I'm glad you're okay, Margie."

"Well, at least my pain gave you an excuse to visit her. She's been miserable without you. Even the campaign hasn't made her happy."

"We're not getting back together, Margie," she said.

"*Back* together?" Margie's eye got big.

"She didn't tell you?" Riley asked her.

"Elena, what's going on?" Margie asked her sister.

Riley moved aside to give them the chance to look at one another.

"Nothing." Elena moved next to Riley and placed her hand on the small of her back. "We're just going through some stuff right now, but we'll be fine."

"We're not–" Riley stopped herself, remembering they weren't alone. "Margie, you don't need this right now. Why don't we go and let you get some rest?"

"Riley, I'm calling you when I get out of this bed and they give me my phone back."

"And we can talk as long as you want," Riley told her and kissed her forehead. "I'm flying right back home. Will you be okay?"

"It's just a broken leg with some cuts and bruises," Margie said.

"Is it?" Riley met Elena's eyes. "Elena, can I talk to you in the hall?"

"Of course," the woman said and smiled.

Riley smiled at Margie, left the hospital room, and stood in the hall, waiting for Elena to emerge. When she did, Riley thought about screaming at her in frustration, but when two doctors walked between them, she remembered her surroundings.

"Are you fucking kidding me, Elena?" she asked softly.

"Riley, I didn't lie. She was in a car accident. When I called you, I didn't know how bad it was. They told me she was in surgery. They were worried they'd be close to the femoral artery, with the break. I honestly thought my kid sister might die. I called you, and you came." Elena moved toward Riley and placed her hands on Riley's hips.

"We're in public, Elena," Riley replied instinctively.

"There's no one watching us," Elena said. "You came, Riley."

"I came here for Margie." Riley moved away from the hands trying to touch her. It felt so wrong having Elena's hands on her body. They'd spent three years together. But now, the idea of Elena touching her made her want to shower. "She's okay. I'm glad she's okay."

"She is, and now that you're here, we can really talk. I've missed you, Riley. I've been thinking a lot about how to make this work."

"There's nothing to make work. God, Elena... You don't get it, do you? We're not together anymore. We broke up."

"What if I don't run for office?"

Riley stared into Elena's eyes, trying to figure out if she was just saying that or if she actually meant it. She realized then how wrong she'd been. She'd never been able to read this woman. She'd fallen for her tricks time and again. This trip was one of the many times she'd ended up doing something she didn't want to do because she'd given into Elena.

"What are you even talking about? You *are* running."

"Not for long," Elena said. "I'm giving it up for you."

"Don't," Riley shot back. "I need to move up my

flight. You can tell Margie to call me whenever she wants."

"Riley, I love you. I'm giving up the governorship to be with you. I'll move to Tahoe. We'll buy that house."

Riley pulled her phone out of her purse to find the airline app. She ignored Elena for a moment until Elena's hand moved to her cheek. She looked up at her and stepped away from her hand.

"What really happened?" Riley asked her.

"What?"

"Elena, you wanted this for some reason. There's no way you've just given it up for me."

"I just told you; I love you," she replied.

"Maybe you do, but not enough to give me everything I need."

"I'll move to Tahoe," Elena said.

"I don't love you, Elena. I'm not in love with you anymore." She shrugged. "I thought you understood that."

"I thought you needed some time," Elena replied defensively. "That you'd get on board with the campaign. It's governor, Riley."

"I thought you weren't running," Riley fired back.

"I'm not." The woman lowered her head.

"And I repeat, what happened?" Riley asked and lifted Elena's head with a thumb and forefinger to her chin.

"The party decided to go with someone else."

"Why?"

"I told a couple of advisors about you. It didn't go well."

"Why'd you do that? We're not together. You could have married some rich white guy and completed the perfect picture."

"I don't want some rich, white guy. I want you, Riley." There were tears in her eyes. "I miss you. I didn't mean to mislead you about Margie. I called you in panic. I know I messed up, but I'm ready now. Riley, I'm ready now."

CHAPTER 18

"THANKS, MORGAN."

"You're welcome. Where's your doctor? Has she made another house call?" Morgan asked as she laid Kinsley's ankle back on the pillow before she moved to the chair in the living room. "Dr. Courtney Ash. It's such a cool name."

"She's not *my* doctor," Kinsley replied.

"She's been by a couple of times, right?"

"To talk about office buildings for her medical practice," Kinsley explained.

"And ask you out. Didn't she do that, too?"

"She did, yes. I told her no. I'm still trying to figure things out with Riley."

"What's to figure out?" Morgan took a drink of her bottled water. "Riley's in Dallas. You're here. You told her you weren't ready."

"And she ran back to her ex. Turns out, I was right to be concerned," Kinsley said.

"Her friend was in a car accident, James. Remy and I are friends outside of my past relationship with Reese. If something ever happened to her, I'd be at that hospital in a heartbeat. When you end a relationship, you don't break up with the family, too."

"I don't fault her for going to visit a friend, Morgan."

"You just fault her for having an ex; which all of us – including you – do have, by the way."

129

"It's been two days. She hasn't called. She's sent one text message telling me Margie was doing well and was getting out of the hospital."

"Well, that's good news," Morgan said.

"It is, but she's not here. She's still there. What am I supposed to think of that?"

"You don't really have the right to be jealous, James. You're not together. Because you're not together, you might have just driven her back into the arms of her weird, closeted ex-girlfriend."

"You are not cheering me up." Kinsley pointed at her.

"I came here for dinner and a movie. I didn't come here to cheer you up." Morgan pointed back at her. "And are you really not going to go out with the doctor?"

"My ankle's doing a lot better. I'm off the crutches. I just have to keep it bandaged for another day or two as a precaution. I told her I'd meet up with her to go see three of the properties she's interested in."

"When?"

"Tomorrow."

"But you're not going out with her?"

"No, but she did mention lunch," Kinsley informed. "She's a client, though."

"Riley was a client. You still had a thing for her."

"I like Courtney. She's great," Kinsley said. "I don't know what I'm doing, honestly."

"You're attracted to her?"

"A little."

"But you like Riley?"

"Yes."

"But you're not ready to date Riley?"

"I'm not convinced Riley's ready to date me."

"Bullshit, James." Morgan stood abruptly. "You're actually pissing me off now."

"What? Why?"

"You have two women into you. One of them is a hot doctor. I know she's hot; I looked her up online." She paused. "One of them is a hot lawyer. Yes, I think Riley's hot. I thought that before you did, because I've known her forever. You have two women interested in you, and you can't make a damn decision. Meanwhile, I'm over here single, waiting for *just one* woman to be interested in me enough to want all the things I want. I can't find that, but you can find two, and you're complaining about it."

"Morgan, this isn't my fault."

"Oh, yes, it is," Morgan replied with another finger-point. "Who do you want, James? If you want Courtney, go out with her. Give it a shot. If you want Riley, stop acting like you don't. Take the leap and try, James."

***

"I like the second place we saw the best," Courtney said as she ate her salad. "I think I'd like the third one as well, but I am concerned that it would only have three exam rooms. The second place has enough room for six."

"That's true," Kinsley replied. "But how soon would you need six rooms? You could easily remodel the third space and include at least five rooms within the year. The good thing about that place is that it's unattached, so you could always build out. The second place is sandwiched between two locations. You'd max out at six exam rooms."

"I'd like to bring on a partner soon. I love volunteering at the clinic." Courtney smiled. "It has its benefits."

Kinsley smiled back at the obvious remark about meeting her at the said clinic.

"Outside of meeting new, interesting people, I love the work. We get a lot of tourists, and I enjoy meeting them, finding out where they're from, what brought them to Lake Tahoe. My practice is really locals only, and I love that, too. But if I expand, I'd need a partner. I can't volunteer two days a week forever. Right now, I'm in the black financially, but if I keep doing this and not expand, I won't be."

"So, the money to expand exists, but you would run

out of it quickly after if you don't have another doctor?" Kinsley asked and sipped her iced tea. "Let's check out the third location, then. I think the first one's out. We'll compare the second and the third again after we've seen them both. The second one is $20,000 over the asking price. The third is, obviously, cheaper, but it would require work pretty immediately, it sounds," she said. "You'll have to weigh those options."

"I guess so," the woman replied and lowered her fork. "Can we talk about that other thing?"

"The roof on the second place? They said they would include a repair in the asking."

"No, Kinsley." Courtney chuckled lightly. "That thing where I keep asking you out, and you say you'll think about it. Then, you said no, but... I don't know, it just feels like there might be something here. Am I completely misreading this? I've done that before."

"You're not misreading it," Kinsley admitted. "When I first saw you, I thought you were attractive."

"Attractive?" Courtney laughed. "Really?"

"Beautiful. Is that better?" Kinsley laughed back. "You're beautiful; you know that." She paused. "And I've enjoyed spending time with you."

"But?"

"But nothing," she replied. "I have. I think you're smart and funny. I know you're a nice person, since you drove all the way to meet me in South Lake the other day, because of my ankle, which is healing well. So, I know you're a good doctor, too."

"A sprain is pretty basic," Courtney replied with a wide smile. "I can handle a lot more than that," she added.

Kinsley wasn't sure if there was something more to that comment, but she decided to breeze right past it.

"There's someone else," she said after a long moment.

"Riley?"

"How'd you know?" Kinsley asked.

"Well, her face, when she picked you up at that bar,

was a pretty big indicator. Her face again, when she saw me at your house, was another one."

"Her face?" Kinsley asked as she laughed.

"She's totally into you," Courtney said. "That's obvious. I just wasn't sure if you were into her. You told me you were single. If you would have told me about her, I wouldn't have asked you out. I definitely wouldn't have asked you out three times." She shrugged. "I'm not a masochist."

"I *am* single. The story between Riley and I is long," she said.

"We have all day," Courtney replied as she picked her fork back up.

"I don't really think that's fair to you."

"Because I like you?"

"I wouldn't have put it that way, but yes, I guess." Kinsley picked up her own fork.

"I do like you," Courtney replied. "As soon as I saw you looking all adorable in the waiting room, with your hair pulled back and slightly messy, I thought you were cute."

"You thought me sitting there with a swollen ankle and bleeding from my leg was cute?" Kinsley asked.

"Yes," Courtney replied. "I still think you're cute."

"But I'm all healed," Kinsley said with a laugh. "You're still interested?"

"I am, but it appears you're not," the woman said and pushed her salad away. "Which is fine; I can move you into the friend zone."

"Wow. That didn't take long," Kinsley teased. "I guess you didn't like me that much after all."

Courtney stared at her for a moment and replied, "I'm not great at relationships. Through college and med school, I had to be so focused on studying and preparing that I didn't really do them. I had one-night stands, mostly, with a few, let's call them, repeat sessions. Since I've been in my own practice, it's been much of the same, if I'm being honest. Rarer, though." She paused to take a drink. "I'm at a point in my life where I do want more. But I have to tell you that, right now, if you told me you didn't want anything serious, you could just have some fun with me tonight. I'd absolutely be interested and would give you my address right now."

Kinsley swallowed hard at that, "Oh."

"You are totally sexy to me, Kinsley James. I would happily have one night of fun with you. And if it repeated, that would be great. If not, that would be fine, too."

"But you said you're ready to—"

"Settle down? I am. I do want to find someone to share my life with. But if you can't give me that, I'd be fine with whatever else you could give me." Her eyes darkened. Kinsley knew that look. Courtney's eyes traveled down the part of Kinsley's body she could see with the table between them. "But if that's not for you, I can put you in the friend zone." Then, she added, "For now."

***

"Jesus, she said that?" Reese asked her.

"She did."

"What did you say?"

"I'm here, aren't I?" Kinsley said as she helped Reese carry bowls to the dining room table for dinner. "She *is* hot, Reese."

"But you didn't want to have sex with her?"

"No, I did." Kinsley sat at the table across from her. "I'm not blind."

"But you're here." Reese picked up her glass and took a drink. "Riley?"

"I'm giving up the possibly hot sex for a woman that left for Dallas three days ago," Kinsley said.

"But Riley wants you, James. It's obvious."

"I know that. I want her, too. I just also want her to want *only* me, and I don't know if she's there yet," she replied.

"You love her, don't you?"

"Did Morgan tell you that?" Kinsley shot back.

"What? No. Morgan's been super busy at work lately. I don't think I've seen her since that night at the bar. Why?"

"She thinks I'm in love with Riley," Kinsley said.

"She's right, though."

"How do you know that?"

"Because, you just gave up a night of potentially hot sex with a beautiful woman, and you can't stop checking your phone for a text from Riley. I'm guessing at that last part, but you've looked at your phone ten times since you've been here." She nodded toward Kinsley's phone, which she'd placed on the table.

"I just need to go out with her, don't I?"

"Who? Riley or Courtney?"

CHAPTER 19

RILEY WALKED into the office, hearing the bell chime overhead, and looked at Kinsley, who sat behind her desk. She smiled wide. She couldn't help it. She hadn't seen Kinsley in five days. She held up the cardboard cup holder with two coffees and the white paper bag with two bagels. Kinsley's eyes met her own, and she smiled softly.

"Can you take a break?" Riley asked and moved toward her.

"Yes," Kinsley replied. "Have a seat." She motioned to the chair in front of her desk. "How's your friend?"

Riley placed a cup of coffee on Kinsley's desk, along with the bag of bagels, before she took her own from the holder and sat in the chair opposite her.

"She's good. She's out of the hospital."

"That's good," Kinsley said.

Something was off. Things felt different now. *Awkward* would be the word Riley would use to describe this exchange.

"So, how have you been?"

"How have I been?" Kinsley's eyebrow lifted.

"I'm sorry. I don't know how to do this. You seem weird."

"You left to spend time with your ex-girlfriend and her family. How am I supposed to seem?"

"I left because Margie is a close friend. I stayed because even though her initial injury seemed fine after the surgery, she ended up with complications and an infection. They released her once they got that under control. I stayed to make sure she was going to be okay. Then, I caught the first flight back home."

"Did you see Elena?" Kinsley asked and lifted the coffee to her lips.

"Yes." Riley took a sip of her own scalding coffee and regretted it immediately. "Did you see Courtney?"

"Yes," Kinsley replied. "I helped her settle on an office."

"I helped Elena settle on something, too," Riley said.

Kinsley's smile disappeared. She lowered her coffee cup to the desk.

"Oh, yeah?"

"Kinsley, she's not running for governor," Riley replied. "She told me she still loved me and wanted to move here, like we'd planned."

"Got it." Kinsley turned her face to her computer. "Thanks for the update, Riles. I really appreciate it," she said sarcastically.

"I told her no, Kinsley."

Riley watched Kinsley's expression as she turned back to her. There was a small, almost imperceptible smile for a moment. It was a cautious smile. Riley knew it well, coming from Kinsley.

"You did?"

"I did. She tried a few times. She asked me to give her another chance, promised me she'd move here and make me a priority. Hell, she even said she'd consider kids now."

"And you still—"

"Said no, Kinsley," Riley interrupted. "I took care of

Margie. Then, I took a ridiculously early flight back home this morning and came here first thing. Well, I went to the café for this first." She lifted the coffee cup. "I haven't even been home yet."

"When you didn't really keep in contact while you were there, I just assumed…"

"That I got back with Elena?"

"Yes."

Riley swallowed hard and felt the burn on her tongue from the coffee.

"Did you…" She paused and looked down at the floor. "Did something happen between you and–"

"Courtney?"

"Yes."

Kinsley stared at her as Riley raised her eyes to hers.

"I helped her find an office, like I said before." She smiled. "Nothing else happened."

"Really?" Riley smiled.

"She tried. And if I'm being honest, I considered it. But that was mostly about you. It wouldn't have been fair to her."

"You considered sleeping with her because I didn't call?"

"No, Riley. She wanted that; and she said as much. I considered *going out* on a date with her. But I don't do one-night stands. I'm not interested in just sex with anyone. I want more than that." Kinsley leaned forward. "This is probably the least romantic way to do this ever, but I'm just going to do it, because this has gone on long enough. I've been stupid and a coward." She took a breath. "Will you go out with me, Riley Sanders?"

"Yes, I would love to go out with you," Riley replied, her heart thundering in her chest.

"Maybe if I would have just done that in college, we could have avoided all this," Kinsley remarked.

"I doubt it," Riley replied.

Kinsley looked a little confused and asked, "You do?"

"I didn't give you the time of day back then, remember? You like to point that out whenever you can." Riley winked at her.

***

"When is this date happening?" Kellan asked her.

"Saturday night," Riley replied with a wide smile.

"It's only Thursday. You look like you're about to burst. How are you going to make it until Saturday?" Kellan laughed at her.

"Kinsley is helping Courtney finalize some paperwork tomorrow and won't get back into town until late. Saturday night was the first night we could make it happen. To answer your question, I *am* about to burst. How did I not see it at first?"

"What?"

"Kinsley James," she answered. "How long have I known her?"

"Years," Kellan replied. "Since you were eighteen, apparently."

"And I'm just now realizing how much I like her," Riley said. "God, telling Elena I don't love her like that anymore was easy." She paused. "It was easy, and it's because of Kinsley."

"That's good, right?"

"It's very good. You should have seen Kinsley's face when I told her Elena wanted to get back together with me."

"I don't think I'd want to. She was probably heartbroken, Riley. Why are you smiling right now, thinking about that?" Kellan asked, pointing at her face.

"Because it means she really does like me that much. Just the thought of me getting back together with Elena was enough to do that to her. Don't get me wrong: I don't ever want to hurt her or see her hurt like that. But, coming back to town, all I wanted to do was to see her. I needed to tell her it was officially over. I'd had the chance to get back with

Elena. I could have said yes. She would have moved here. We would have bought that house."

"But you didn't."

"I didn't." Riley smiled at her friend. "And it's at least partly because Kinsley showed me what it's like to really have someone who lov—"

Riley's eyes got big. She'd almost said something there.

"Who loves you?" Kellan asked.

"I don't know about that. I think I got a little ahead of myself there," Riley said. "I know she likes me, though, and that's enough for me." She glanced at her phone on the coffee table. "Do you think I should text her? It's not too late. Maybe I should just text her good night or something. Do you do that when you haven't even gone on a first date yet?"

"I think you do that if you want to," Kellan replied. "I should probably head on home. Reese is waiting."

"That's adorable, Kell."

"Yeah, I love her. She loves me. It's very adorable. She and Remy had a sisterly dinner tonight; no significant others allowed," Kellan said as she stood. "I'm happy for you, Riley. Kinsley's crazy about you, and I can see you're crazy for her, too."

"I am," Riley said. "I didn't know it until recently, but I am."

"Tell her that," Kellan said.

Riley walked Kellan out of the apartment, moved back to her sofa, and picked up her phone. She considered texting but took what Kellan said to heart and clicked on Kinsley's contact instead.

"Hey," Kinsley greeted. "You're not calling to cancel Saturday, are you?"

"You wore a black V-neck and jeans," Riley said.

"What?" Kinsley laughed.

"That day on the futon, when you came out to me; you wore a black V-neck shirt and jeans."

"Okay. Riles, what's—"

"Kellan was just here. I asked if I should text you good night even though we haven't had a date yet."

"You asked her if you should text me good night?" Kinsley asked.

"Yes."

"That's cute, Riles. You're cute."

"What are you doing right now?" Riley asked with a smile as she settled into the sofa further.

"Talking to you."

"And?"

"And working in bed."

"On what?"

"Prepping for the meeting with Courtney tomorrow. What are you doing?"

"Talking to you."

"And?"

Riley smiled even wider, "And calling you to tell you good night, because I really wanted to do that."

"That's still cute."

"And to tell you that I like it when you call me Riles," she said.

"You do?"

"Yes."

"I like it that you call me Kinsley even though most people call me James."

"You do?" Riley asked.

"Yes."

"Hey, Kinsley?"

"Yeah?"

"You gave me your sweater that time we all went to the movies and I was cold."

"What? When was this?" Kinsley chuckled.

"Freshman year."

"College?"

"Yes, college."

"So, now you remember me?" Kinsley teased.

"I can't wait until Saturday, Kinsley. I feel like I'm that

freshman again, all excited for a first date with the girl I like."

"Thank God we're not still in college, though," Kinsley said.

"I do not want to relive undergrad or law school," Riley agreed.

"But will you tell me all about them on Saturday? I'd like to catch up on all the years I missed."

"Yeah?"

"Yes, that's how this works. You tell me all about you; I listen. Then, I tell you all about me; you listen. We see if there's something here."

"Oh, there's something here, alright," Riley said before she could stop herself.

Kinsley laughed and said, "Oh, yeah?"

"I told you, I can't wait until Saturday."

CHAPTER 20

KINSLEY STOOD just behind her front door, looking through the peephole for the tenth time in about a minute. She backed away from the door, paced the foyer, looked into the mirror on the opposite wall, tried to put an imaginary rogue strand of hair back in place, turned back around, and returned to the peephole. No Riley yet. Technically, she was staring a good five minutes early. Riley had said she'd be there at seven, and there were still four more minutes of waiting. Truthfully, though, Kinsley was kind of hoping Riley had the same problem she did: she just couldn't wait. This date, it had been years in the making.

They'd spoken on the phone Friday night as well, after Kinsley returned from her meeting with Courtney. While Courtney hadn't asked her out again, since Kinsley had filled her in about her feelings for Riley, she also hadn't backed off completely, either. She'd found ways to brush Kinsley's hand with her own or bump lightly into Kinsley's shoulder. She hadn't said anything, but she had invited Kinsley to dinner after their last meeting. They'd put in an offer on the second location they'd visited previously. Courtney wanted to celebrate. Kinsley wouldn't normally decline a client wanting to celebrate a potential purchase. In fact, she had often taken clients to a celebratory lunch, dinner or, occasionally, drinks to congratulate them on their new place. With Courtney, though, she'd decided to go with the fruit and cheese basket once they closed on the building instead. It seemed safer that way.

Saturday morning, Kinsley had woken with purpose. She wanted her house to be clean, since Riley had asked to pick her up for their date. She had dusted, vacuumed, cleaned all the windows, and washed and dried all the towels and sheets. She also made sure to clean the bedding in the guest room just in case. She didn't want to be presumptuous and assume that Riley might stay over. If they happened by the guest room, she wanted it to look like she'd cleaned that, too. Then, she showered, making sure to shave. She used her coconut-scented shower gel. And she actually blow-dried her hair, which she rarely did. She curled the ends and left it down. She put a little makeup on her face, but not too much. She straightened the princess cut button-down she'd chosen specifically because she'd always gotten compliments on the color that matched her eyes. She threw on a pair of form-fitting jeans and boots that went over them at the ankle. She unbuttoned the second button from the top, choosing to show a bit more cleavage, took a deep breath to try to calm her heart, and returned to the front door just in time to see Riley approach through the peephole and ring the bell.

"Shit," Kinsley said to herself. She took another deep breath, gripped the doorknob, and opened the door. "Hi," she said. "Damn," she added when she noticed how hot Riley looked.

"Good damn or bad damn?" Riley asked with smoky eyes.

"Good," Kinsley replied; her eyes were raking over Riley's body, and she was not even trying to hide it.

Riley was wearing a slinky cocktail dress. It was a deep gray. She had on a pair of heels that only worked to accentuate her legs in that short dress. Kinsley gulped when she noticed Riley's long, elegant neck, and that she'd even brought a clutch purse with her, as if they were going out for a fancy night on the town.

"That good?" Riley asked with a smirk.

Kinsley's eyes met Riley's as the woman took the step over the threshold. Kinsley knew what was about to happen. This kind of exchange could only go one direction. Before she could overthink it or try to talk herself out of it, she reached for Riley's clutch, tossed it on the table next to them, and pulled Riley into her by the hands. Her arms went around Riley's waist just as their lips met for the first time. Kinsley's lips touched soft and warm lips that had been ready for her. Riley's arms moved around Kinsley's neck. Her feet started moving Kinsley backward. Kinsley didn't work to push back. She let Riley move them back toward the staircase, knowing full well where Riley wanted to take them.

Kinsley's feet hit the side of the bottom stair. They stopped their movement for a minute while Riley's tongue played against her own. It was good. It was really good. Kissing Riley Sanders in her fantasies during these many years had been enough to make her wet; but kissing her in real life had her soaked through the panties she'd picked out specifically for their night in case something like this happened. She hadn't expected it to happen this quickly, though. They'd planned to go to dinner and see how things went after. But this was better. This was much better.

Riley gave her a slight push, indicating she wanted them to continue in the direction of the bedroom. Kinsley took the stairs one at a time, trying to keep their lips connected, which turned near impossible. Riley's lips moved to Kinsley's neck instead. Kinsley stopped their progress at the first connection of Riley's tongue to her throat. She leaned against the wall and let Riley do whatever she wanted to her. The picture of the lake she'd had framed and placed on that wall, fell off said wall and clanged down the stairs. Good thing she decided to leave out the glass on the front. Riley stopped to watch it fall. Her eyes returned to Kinsley's. There was a smirk on her face that matched the darkness of her eyes. Her hands went to Kinsley's buttons. Her lips and tongue went back to work on Kinsley's neck.

Kinsley felt her shirt pull apart once the buttons were mostly undone. The keyword there was *mostly*, because

Riley hadn't been able to wait until she could get the bottom two undone. She'd yanked at the shirt, causing the last two buttons to drop to the floor and bounce down the stairs. That was what it sounded like, at least; Kinsley's eyes were closed. Riley's hands were on her breasts over her bra, and her mouth had returned to Kinsley's. Kinsley's hand was on the back of Riley's neck, pulling her in closer as she tried to find the zipper to Riley's dress by searching with two hands all over her back. Realizing it wasn't there, her hands went to Riley's sides. She found the zipper on the left side. She pulled down hard until Riley stopped kissing her to step back. The dress fell to the floor. Riley was standing there in a matching bra and panty set. Her lips were wet and swollen. Her breath was coming in short bursts. Her eyes told Kinsley that she hadn't had nearly enough yet.

Kinsley's hands remembered how to move. Her feet did, too. She moved her body into Riley's, loving how their skin looked and felt together. She kissed Riley softly this time. As their lips moved together, they continued their dance up the stairs and toward Kinsley's room. Riley clearly had a thing with walls, because she had Kinsley up against the one next to her open bedroom door. Riley's hands pulled away the shirt she'd already unbuttoned. It fell to the floor. Her fingers found the button of Kinsley's jeans, popped it open, and unzipped them all within seconds. Kinsley couldn't keep up with everything. Riley's hand slid under her jeans and cupped her over her panties.

"Okay. Hold on," Kinsley said, pulling her mouth away from Riley's. "Inside."

"No problem," Riley replied and slid her hand under the fabric, moving to cup her again.

"Not what I meant," Kinsley said. "Wow," she added when Riley's index finger slid between her folds. "Bedroom. Inside the bedroom."

Riley's smirk hadn't disappeared yet, but it widened as she removed her hand and replied, "I want you."

"Let's go to bed, Riles."

Kinsley kissed Riley, coaxing a soft moan from the woman as she backed into her bedroom, bringing Riley along with her. When she made it close enough to the bed, she turned them around, gave Riley's shoulders a shove, and watched as she fell to the mattress, making the pillows behind her rise slightly and fall again. Kinsley stared longingly at Riley's body. She'd seen it like this twice before. Once, Riley was wearing a bathing suit at the lake with all their friends. The second time was when Reese was helping Riley get ready for a party back in college. She'd been in her underwear then. Both times, this woman's body was perfect to Kinsley. She couldn't believe she could actually touch her now.

She leaned down, placed one hand beside Riley's head, and used her other hand to trace the skin of Riley's abdomen with her fingertips. She dragged them slowly up and down before circling Riley's belly button. Her fingers trailed up to the cups of Riley's bra. She grazed the nipples beneath and felt them turn to rigid peaks. Riley stared up at her while she continued the exploration. Kinsley felt Riley wiggle a little beneath her. It spurred her on, but she was more than content being above Riley like this, touching parts of the woman's skin she'd long to touch.

"Babe?" Riley asked. "You've waited over a decade for this, and I've come to realize I've basically been waiting just as long. Any chance we could speed this up? I got pretty turned on just getting dressed to come over here tonight, so I'm—"

Kinsley kissed her, pressed her body fully down into Riley's spread legs, slid her hand under the cup of Riley's bra, and grasped her breast. If Riley wanted to go fast, Kinsley could go fast. She lifted up enough to lower the straps of Riley's bra and kiss the skin beneath. Riley didn't wait. She lifted enough to unclasp her bra hastily. Kinsley tossed it somewhere next to them. While she wanted to take her time with Riley's breasts, she needed something else more. She lowered herself to the floor, kneeling between

Riley's legs. She took another moment to stare at her before she reached for the final barrier to Riley's skin.

"Riles..." she uttered the moment Riley's body was completely unveiled to her.

"Kinsley, just–"

Kinsley kissed her inner thigh once before moving to the other side. A moment later, she licked her center, and Riley's hips lifted instantly. Kinsley wanted to moan at the sensation of finally touching Riley this way, but she held it in. She wanted to focus on Riley. Her own moans would come later, hopefully. When she heard Riley's sounds after her tongue slid through her again, Kinsley nearly slid her hand inside her own panties to relieve some of the pressure building from the sensations. Her hands gripped Riley's hips, pulled her closer to the end of the bed, and lifted her body up slightly for a better angle.

Her tongue slid through Riley's wetness one more time before she circled Riley's clit. She sucked it into her mouth while both of her hands moved to Riley's breasts, squeezing them softly a few times. Then, she squeezed them harder, tweaked Riley's nipples, loving how hard they felt, and squeezed the woman's breasts again. Riley's hips were lifting and falling back with every movement of Kinsley's tongue. Kinsley wanted this to last forever. Riley's hand pressed the back of her head down further before it tugged at Kinsley's hair enough to lift her head.

"Are you–" Kinsley started to ask when she opened her eyes to look up at Riley.

"Come here," the woman ordered with impossibly dark eyes.

Riley slid all the way up onto the bed. Kinsley joined her, but stopped with her head between Riley's legs, choosing to suck her back into her mouth again. Kinsley wanted to make her come this way, but she also loved touching Riley like this. Her mouth was on Riley's most intimate body part. There was something so unbelievably remarkable about that to her, that she wasn't ready to stop yet. Before she knew it, though, Riley had used her hips to flip them over. Kinsley was now on her back. Riley's center was above her face. She smiled at what Riley had just done before her mouth went back to work. Riley's hips rolled above her while Kinsley held onto them with both hands, encouraging them along. Her tongue slid lower to the woman's entrance. She slid inside, earned a gasp, and repeated the action. When she pressed her tongue to Riley's clit, Riley moved faster. Kinsley knew what was coming next. Riley reached forward and pressed both hands to the headboard. She gripped the edge of the wood and rocked her hips quickly while Kinsley kept her tongue in place. Riley's loud moans caused Kinsley to lower one of her hands to her own center, slide under her jeans and panties, and touch there. She couldn't stop herself. Her clit was throbbing too much for her to be able to withstand it any further without contact. She moaned, unable to stop herself, as Riley came above her. Her own strokes on her clit were faster, needier. Riley's rocking slowed. Her hands moved from the headboard, and she sat back enough to stare down at Kinsley. That was when she realized what Kinsley was doing.

Her eyes went wide. She turned her head and watched Kinsley's hand moving fast beneath her jeans. She turned back to look down at Kinsley's face while, at the same time, she slid her hand on top of Kinsley's. Kinsley stopped her touches. She was so close. She needed to come. Her hips lifted up when Riley's hand moved her own out of the way and stroked her instead. Kinsley was staring up at Riley's perfect sex, coated in arousal, while Riley touched her. Kinsley lifted her head enough to lick Riley once, indicating her intentions. Riley twitched as she stared down at her, but she lowered herself. Kinsley moaned as she sucked her back into her mouth. Riley moaned, too. Then, Kinsley came. It was a thunderous crash of sensation. Riley's clit was still swollen and hard, needy for another orgasm, and she tasted so damn good. Kinsley's clit was swollen and hard, too, enjoying the release of coaxing fingers as her hips rose and fell in rapid succession.

When she came down fully, Riley's hand remained. She continued to stroke Kinsley softly as Kinsley brought her to another orgasm. When she came down, Riley moved off the bed entirely. She stood at the end of it, slightly wobbly from what Kinsley could tell. Of course, that could have just been her own labored breathing and blurry vision making it appear that way. Riley yanked Kinsley's jeans and panties off her legs while Kinsley removed her bra. Within seconds, she was naked. Riley slid back on top of her and wasted no time.

"God," Kinsley gasped as Riley thrust two fingers inside her.

Riley moved her hips as she moved her fingers. Kinsley closed her eyes to fully take in the sensations of being filled by this woman. Riley's thumb flicked her clit occasionally. It was a perfect combination. It didn't take long for Kinsley to feel the building orgasm deep in her gut as Riley's fingers curled, straightened, and pushed deep inside to take her over the edge.

"We're doing that again," Riley said moments later as she pulled out, hovered over Kinsley, and kissed her. "And again, and again."

"I thought *I* was a top," Kinsley teased.

"I am not a–" Riley smiled down at her and rolled her own eyes. "Okay. I guess I am." She kissed Kinsley's lips. "Is that a problem?" she asked with a lifted eyebrow.

"Not a problem at all," Kinsley replied as her hand slid between Riley's legs.

Riley reacted by sitting up and straddling her. When Kinsley moved her fingers to her entrance and slid inside her, Riley rocked forward and lifted to allow her better access.

"I think I need to change those dinner reservations," Riley said as she rocked.

CHAPTER 21

"THIS IS MUCH BETTER than some fancy restaurant," Riley said as she and Kinsley sat facing one another, naked on her kitchen island. "Couldn't eat naked there."

"We could have. We just would have gotten arrested," Kinsley replied.

They each had a bowl of something Kinsley had thrown together at the last minute when they'd decided they were definitely not making their dinner reservation. It was after eleven when they'd finally made their way downstairs. Kinsley had cooked while Riley had watched. They still had yet to put on clothing, which was fine by Riley. Kinsley looked good in clothing, but she was sexy without anything on. Her hair was down and completely mussed. Her eyes were practically glowing in the way that told Riley she was happy. Riley was happy, too. They explored one another for hours. They'd probably do more of that later, too, and likely, wouldn't get much sleep. Riley would gladly stay up all night making love to Kinsley James. She'd also stay up all night just talking to her.

She realized in Dallas that she missed that the most. She missed talking to Kinsley, sharing coffee with her while they ate bagels at her office and talked about work. When Elena had tried to get her back, not once but repeatedly, while Riley had been there to help Margie, she'd wanted to call Kinsley and tell her what had happened. She'd wanted to tell her then that Elena wanted her back, but she had said no. She wanted to tell Kinsley then that she wanted her and only her. But she knew the woman well enough by now. She knew she needed to tell Kinsley in person. When she caught that early flight back to Tahoe, all she could think about was what Kinsley would say. Would she continue pushing her away? Would she be so angry that she'd just left that day that she wouldn't even hear her out? She bought coffee and bagels to help remind Kinsley what she'd done before in an attempt to spend time with her. She hadn't expected Kinsley to ask her out, but she was glad she had. She also hadn't expected them to just jump into bed. But, God, Kinsley had looked good when she'd opened that door.

"Sorry about that canvas print I may have knocked over. Is it ruined?" Riley asked, setting her bowl down between them.

"I don't know. Honestly, I don't care right now. You're eating dinner naked on my counter, Riley. I have priorities," she said with a smile.

"Are you almost done over there?" Riley asked, pointing at Kinsley's bowl.

"Yes. Why?" Kinsley lifted an eyebrow at her. "You don't expect me to have sex on this thing, do you?"

Riley laughed and answered, "No. But I would like it if we could go back upstairs and outside just like this. You could wrap your arms around me, and we could bundle in a blanket and just talk for a while."

Kinsley nodded with a smile and said, "That's a great idea. My body could use a break."

"Break?"

"Riley, I haven't had that many orgasms in a long time."

"Long time?" Riley teased.

"Maybe ever; I don't know. I don't normally keep track," Kinsley said as she slid off the island and stood in front of it, leaving her bowl in her place.

Riley turned and spread her legs. Kinsley's eyes went between them on instinct before they lifted to meet Riley's smirking face.

"What were you looking at, little miss needs a break?"

Kinsley wrapped her arms around Riley's back and pulled her closer to herself. Riley's went around her neck, and they just stayed there, staring at one another, sharing short kisses, and enjoying this night, because it was the most important night both of them had ever experienced. Riley knew this was the night her entire life changed. She had been in love before. She had been in long relationships before. But she had never felt this complete before.

***

"James, why is there a button on your floor?" Morgan asked as she bent to pick up the small circular object that immediately made Kinsley blush.

"Must have fallen off or something," Kinsley replied and stole the button from Morgan, tucking it into her pocket as they made their way further inside the house.

"When is the future Mrs. James joining us?" Morgan asked when they entered the kitchen.

"What? Why are you–" She dropped the grocery bag on the island. "What made you think of Riley just now?"

Kinsley was thinking of Riley, too. She was thinking of the sex they'd had on this island the previous Sunday morning.

"What made *you* think I was talking about Riley when I said future Mrs. James? I could have meant anyone joining this little party you're having," Morgan said with a wink as she pulled items out of the grocery bag she'd carried in. "I guess Saturday night went well?"

"It went very well, yes," Kinsley said.

"Your face is, like, burgundy now, James. You're blushing that much. Something you want to share with the best friend? Juicy details, perhaps?"

Morgan stopped unloading to meet Kinsley's eye. Kinsley folded the reusable grocery bag she'd just emptied and tossed it on top of the other counter.

"No juicy details," Kinsley replied. "But it was an amazing first date."

"That's great, James." Morgan smiled at her and finished emptying the bag. "But, were there no juicy details because there was nothing to have juicy details about, or no juicy details because you just don't want to tell me?"

"Objection," Riley said as she entered the room.

"Hey, Riles," Kinsley said with a chuckle. "I like that you're a lawyer," she added as Riley approached, carrying a paper bag in one hand and bottle of wine in the other.

"I like that you're not the kind of girl that kisses and tells," she said. "Hey, Morgan." She turned to Morgan to greet her. Then, Riley's eyes turned back to Kinsley. She dropped the bag and wine on the island and moved into her. "Are we at that stage where I can just walk into the room and kiss you now?"

"Still waiting on an answer to my question," Morgan interrupted their moment.

"Hi," Kinsley said and kissed her on the lips. "Morgan, do you want to, maybe, go start the grill?"

"No, I'm good." Morgan stared at both of them. "You guys look good together."

"She's cute, isn't she?" Riley asked as she turned around to face Morgan, pulled Kinsley's arms around her waist, and leaned back into her.

Kinsley hadn't known what to expect when she suggested this party to her friends and, obviously, invited Riley. They'd spent nearly every night together for the past week. Things between them were going so well. They'd talked about the fact that everyone knew that they'd gone on a few dates, but they hadn't talked about how much touching they'd do with everyone present. This was better than she expected. Riley had no problem advertising that they were dating. Her arms moved on top of Kinsley's, and she squeezed. Kinsley squeezed Riley's middle at that before she lowered her head to Riley's shoulder.

"Took you long enough to see that," Morgan teased.

"We're here," Reese called from the foyer. "And I brought Remy and Ryan, too."

"Also, her girlfriend," Kellan added.

"You're included by default." Reese entered the kitchen with a bag, placing it on the counter. "You two look comfy," she added as she pointed to Kinsley and Riley.

"When will we get to the default status?" Riley asked, turning her head to Kinsley slightly.

"I don't know," Kinsley replied, kissing her cheek.

"Now, it seems like." Kellan entered. "Happy for you guys. Where do I put the burgers I'm carrying?"

"I can take them and start the grill," Ryan offered after entering with Remy.

"I'm grilling," Morgan said, taking the bag from Kellan. "You can assist," she added to Ryan.

"Go on out. I'll bring you a beer, babe," Remy said and kissed his cheek.

"Happy to be the assistant, but don't overcook my burger, Morgan."

Ryan and Morgan went out to the backyard, where Kinsley had set everything up for them to enjoy a leisurely lunch and then head down to the pebbled beach and play in the water. They hadn't had a fun day like this in a long time. Everyone had gotten so busy recently. Remy and Ryan had been occupied with redoing their house. Reese and Kellan had been building up Kellan's vet clinic. Reese was also doing a trial for a disorder she'd only recently shared with everyone. Morgan was trying to expand the family business while also trying to meet someone. Kinsley had noticed now that the members of their group were starting to finally pair off. Morgan, more than ever, seemed interested in finding a partner of her own. Even Kinsley had thought of doing the same thing once Kellan and Reese met and started dating.

"What can I do?" Riley turned in Kinsley's arms. "I

brought the chips and stuff you asked for. Want me to pull it all out?"

"Sure. We'll get everything together and take it outside," Kinsley replied.

They all worked to get their meal put together before they moved out to the table Kinsley had ready for the dishes, bottles, and bags. Kinsley sat next to Riley. Reese sat next to Kellan, across from them. Morgan was on the end of the table in a chair while Remy and Ryan were at that end across from one another. As they talked and ate, Riley's hand occasionally ended up on Kinsley's thigh. Kinsley was happy she'd chosen to put a table cloth over the picnic table, because Riley's hand had gotten greedier with each touch. One moment it was close to her knee. The next, it was on the inside of her thigh, near her center. The final time she did it, her pinky finger reached to stroke Kinsley through her jeans. Kinsley nearly jerked but managed to keep herself together. Her body was thrumming. She'd been fine before Riley had arrived. They'd made love that previous night. She'd been sated. Now, all she could think about was how much she wanted Riley to continue to stroke her. She couldn't stop thinking about how much she wanted to touch her in return.

"Can we clean up later, James? I'm ready to go toss the ball around. I also brought a couple of kayaks from the rental shack, in case anyone wants to go out on the water," Morgan said.

"I didn't bring my suit," Riley said and stroked Kinsley softly again.

"You can borrow one of mine. We're about the same size," Kinsley replied. "I'll get it for you."

"Okay," Riley replied.

They both knew they weren't just going up to grab their suits. Kinsley didn't even care if anyone else knew; she just wanted Riley alone. They walked inside the house slowly, patiently. As soon as they were out of eyeshot, Riley smirked at her and rushed to the staircase. Kinsley followed close behind. The moment the bedroom door was closed behind them, Riley's lips were on hers.

"We don't have long," Kinsley said as Riley's lips met her throat.

Kinsley practically tossed Riley onto the bed at the same time Riley was trying to undo her jeans. They worked together to get them off. Moments later, Kinsley was on top of her, stroking between her thighs.

"Yes," Riley muttered. Kinsley felt the vibrations against her lips as they traveled along Riley's skin. "Inside."

Kinsley lowered her fingers, slid them inside, and thrust. She used her hips to push deep inside Riley. She moved fast, not wanting to give them away by taking too long. Luckily, Riley had come quickly nearly every time they'd done this. The one time she'd taken a while had been by Kinsley's design. A few more thrusts, and Riley was coming around her fingers. Her muscles clenched, inviting Kinsley even further inside. Kinsley used her thumb to stroke Riley's hard clit as she rode out her orgasm. She came again, or maybe it was one orgasm but a very long one; Kinsley didn't know. She didn't have time to ask, because Riley had flipped them over, tossed her t-shirt aside, removed her own bra, and managed to undo Kinsley's jeans all within what felt like seconds. She let Kinsley pull out of her and slid her own hand to Kinsley's needy clit.

"You were torturing me downstairs," Kinsley said as her hips lifted.

"You didn't exactly push my hand away."

Riley stroked her harder. Kinsley came almost immediately. She needed that release more than she needed air. She stared up at Riley, who'd managed to get completely naked while Kinsley was still fully dress. Kinsley kissed her softly. Her hand went to the back of Riley's neck, and she pulled the woman down closer.

"Stay tonight," Kinsley said.

"Happily," Riley replied.

CHAPTER 22

"KINSLEY, that's your phone," Riley muttered against Kinsley's chest the following morning. "Babe, your phone is ringing."

"What?" Kinsley opened her tired eyes, turned her head to the table to see that it was past eight in the morning, and reached for her phone. "We overslept."

"Shit." Riley shot up immediately. "I turned off the alarm yesterday, when we decided to go into the office later. I forgot to reset it."

"Hello?" Kinsley said into her phone as she sat up. "Hey, Courtney."

"Courtney?" Riley turned her body back to Kinsley's.

"They turned down the offer?" Courtney asked.

"Did you just get my message?" Kinsley asked back as she slid out of bed.

"I was with patients all day yesterday and then had a family dinner. I got it late last night, but I didn't want to call you until this morning."

"They got a competing offer," Kinsley said as she reached for the clothes they'd left strewn about the floor the previous night. "It's fifteen thousand over asking."

"What?"

"I guess they really want it."

"I can't afford that *and* the remodel I'd need to do."

"The other place you liked is already off the market."

Kinsley turned to see that Riley was still sitting naked on her bed. She lifted an eyebrow as she took in the woman's body, leaned over her, and kissed her.

"What do we do now? There aren't that many locations for sale up here. Should I just wait it out?"

"There's another place about ten miles away from the place you wanted. We can keep an eye on the current offer while you and I go take a look at this new place," Kinsley suggested.

Riley stood then. She wrapped her arms around Kinsley's waist, leaned in, and kissed her cheek.

"I'm hopping in the shower," Riley said.

"What was that?" Courtney asked.

"Sorry, I'm not in the office yet. Slow start to the morning," Kinsley replied.

"Oh," Courtney said. "Sorry, I didn't mean to interrupt your morning. Was that Riley?"

Kinsley didn't exactly know how to answer that. Courtney was a client, but she was somewhat of a friend. She was also a woman that had expressed interest in her in a more than friendly way.

"It was, yes."

There was a moment of awkward silence before Courtney said, "When can we see the other location?"

"I have a busy day today, but I can do tomorrow. Can you get away? Afternoon?"

"Around two?"

"I can meet you at your office, then," Kinsley said, making her way into the bathroom, where Riley had started the shower and was already brushing her teeth.

"Great. See you tomorrow," Courtney replied.

Kinsley hung up, set the phone on the counter next to Riley, kissed her naked shoulder, and then, without a word, hopped into the shower.

"Did you just steal my shower?" Riley asked after she rinsed.

"No, I just joined it," Kinsley said.

Riley climbed in and stood in front of her.

"What did Courtney want?"

"To see another property, since the one she wanted is probably going to someone for way over asking." She paused. "Any chance I can convince you to let me put my hands all over you right now?" She lifted the corner of her mouth into a smile.

"We're already running late." Riley smiled back, wrapped her arms around Kinsley's waist, and pulled her in closer. "So, we'll need to be quick."

Their touches were hurried, but no less intense. After they finished with their now, much longer than intended, shower, Kinsley dressed for work. Riley had brought a bag and dressed in her usual elegant suit.

"You and I dress very differently for work," Kinsley commented.

She'd worn a pair of nice fitting khakis and a polo for her day. Riley looked like she was going into court later, which she wouldn't be today.

"I like how you dress." Riley pulled her in for a hug. "I have to go, though. I have a meeting with a client in twenty minutes."

"Dinner tonight?"

"I can't. I have dinner with a woman who runs a shelter for victims of domestic violence. I'm trying to learn more about how to help these women and children when I represent them."

"You're a good person, Riley Sanders. That is definitely an acceptable reason to miss dinner." Kinsley kissed her.

"Tomorrow night?"

"Maybe. I have that showing for Courtney at two. Depending on how that goes, I might just have dinner over there, to avoid rush hour traffic."

"Dinner with Courtney?" Riley pulled back to meet her eyes.

"I don't know. If she wants to do dinner, I might go. But I was just thinking of looking over paperwork while I ate by myself."

"Maybe I can wrap up my last meeting early, drive over, and meet you. We could have dinner there," Riley suggested.

"Just so that we'd both have to drive our cars back?" Kinsley checked.

"So you don't have to eat alone." Riley smiled at her.

"So that I don't have to eat with Courtney?"

"She's been more than obvious about how she feels about you," Riley said.

"I've been more than obvious with her about how I feel about you. Nice job making sure she heard you when we were on the phone earlier, by the way."

Riley lowered her head for a moment before lifting it back up and looking at her seriously.

"We haven't talked about this yet, but you know I'm not seeing anyone else, right? It's just you for me."

"And it's just you for me, Riles." She smiled at her and kissed her on the lips. "We both need to get to work. Can we talk more about this later?"

"That's fine," Riley said, but Kinsley wondered if there was something more to that answer.

They didn't have time to address it now, though. They left the house, made their way to their cars, and each drove to work.

***

When Riley got to the restaurant, she saw Kinsley leaning over the table, looking at something on Courtney's phone. Courtney was leaning in, too. Then, Courtney's eyes lifted from the phone and met Kinsley's. Kinsley was still laughing, but Courtney had stopped. Her face had turned serious in an instant. Then, her lips parted. Riley watched as those lips moved in just a few inches more and pressed to Kinsley's. Riley turned away. She turned completely away, because she thought she might vomit. Never in her life had she felt like this. Her stomach rumbled. Her heart burned with pain. She rushed back outside. She needed fresh air. She needed to erase that vision from her mind. She wished then that there was bleach for eyes, because she couldn't stop seeing Courtney's lips just parted enough to take Kinsley's bottom one between them as she kissed her.

She hadn't told Kinsley she was coming. She now viewed that both as a mistake and as possibly one of the best decisions of her life. If Kinsley was a cheater, it was better that she knew now. She just hadn't seen this coming. Kinsley hadn't seemed the type. She'd been so interested in Riley, that she'd waited this long for Riley to be ready. Apparently, though, while Kinsley's friends thought Kinsley wasn't the one-night stand type or casual relationship type, Kinsley was someone who could do that while she was lying to Riley at the same time.

"Riley?" Riley turned around at the sound of Kinsley's voice. "What are you doing here?"

"I came to have dinner with you. I didn't realize you'd have company," Riley said as she fought back the vitriol she wanted to hurl at Kinsley.

"You saw Courtney?"

"Yes, I saw Courtney," she yelled and was glad the parking lot was empty at that moment; the only other sounds were coming from the cars driving past on the main road beyond them. "I saw it, Kinsley."

"Riles—"

"I can't believe this. I trusted you," she interrupted.

"And you should have trusted me. Did you miss the part where I pushed her away?" Kinsley asked.

Just then, Courtney Ash emerged from the restaurant, looking slightly off-kilter while holding her purse against her chest.

"Oh," she said when she noticed Riley.

"Oh? That's all you're going to say to me after you kissed my girlfriend?" Riley asked.

"Girlfriend?" Courtney asked back. "She said you two were dating."

"I said we were dating exclusively," Kinsley corrected her. "Courtney, can you just go, please? I need to talk to Riley."

Courtney didn't say anything else. She nodded and walked off toward her car, leaving them alone again.

"Dating?"

"Exclusively." Kinsley moved toward her. "Riles, I swear, she kissed me. I pulled away as soon as she did. I told her before that I was with you. I didn't expressly state the word *girlfriend*, but I told her I was with you. She wanted to show me a picture of her niece on her phone, and then she kissed me out of the blue. I moved away, grabbed my stuff, and left. I didn't even pay the bill, Riley. I just left."

"Why did she kiss you, Kinsley? You've told her you're with me, but she still tried to kiss you."

"I don't know. But Courtney and I are done, Riles. I'm not going to be her agent anymore. She can find someone else to help her get a new office."

"When you texted where you were going for dinner, you didn't tell me she'd be here." Riley began to calm down.

"I didn't know she would be at the time. Then, she said she had no plans and asked if we could go over the options again. There's another place that's just popped up on the market a little further outside of town. She hadn't been interested in moving that far away the other times we had talked about it. Then, suddenly, she was." Kinsley let out a deep breath. "I guess she was just pretending, to get a dinner invite."

"Maybe," Riley said.

"Riles, did you really think I would do that?" Her eyes squinted. "That I'd cheat on you?"

"We haven't talked about what cheating is to you or to me. You haven't called me your girlfriend."

"I'm happy to call you my girlfriend, Riles." Kinsley moved into her then, took Riley's hips, and held onto her. "I'm sorry if you didn't think that was the case."

"I've done this before, Kinsley. I think that's why it's bothering me."

"Done what before?" Kinsley asked as she ran her hand up into Riley's hair.

"With Elena." She shrugged both shoulders.

"I'm out, Riles. Everyone knows I'm gay. I have no

problem being out."

"Elena didn't call me her girlfriend for over six months. It took her a year to introduce me to Margie. Even then, she called me her close friend at first."

"I am not Elena," Kinsley insisted. "I would never deny you to anyone." She pressed her head to Riley's. "Riley, you're my girlfriend, okay? I don't want Courtney or anyone else. I'll pay for a billboard in South Lake, if that's what you want. My parents don't live close, but I'll take you to meet them whenever. I'm not hiding this from anyone." She paused. "I'm proud to be with you."

"I'm not used to that," Riley replied, falling into Kinsley's arms.

"Riles, literally every single friend we share has known for years that I had a thing for you." She chuckled. "I won't treat you like she did. You're too amazing to hide. I still can't understand how she did that."

Riley pulled away and stared into her now girlfriend's eyes to say, "You didn't eat yet, did you?"

"No, I was busy pushing Courtney away." Kinsley smiled sweetly at her.

"I think I'd like to try cooking for you again," Riley said. "Can you wait to eat until we get back to my place and possibly be prepared to order a pizza if I mess it up?"

"Yes," Kinsley replied as she smiled.

"And will you stay at my place tonight? I think I really need to fall asleep next to you."

"This is coming from the girl who hardly paid any attention to me for years," Kinsley teased.

"I am one to learn from my mistakes." Riley moved to meet Kinsley's lips. She kissed her softly and pulled back. "I'll meet you at my place. I need to stop by the store. I wasn't prepared to cook tonight."

"I'll go to my place and pack a bag then," Kinsley said. "And maybe bring a frozen pizza I have in my freezer."

"Shut up." Riley shoved her playfully.

CHAPTER 23

THREE WEEKS. She'd been in a relationship with Riley Sanders for three weeks. She liked saying that to herself. She'd found every opportunity she could to use the word *girlfriend*. When one of her clients asked if she had a special someone, Kinsley said she had a girlfriend. When Kellan asked if she wanted to go kayaking with her, Morgan, and Reese, she asked if she could bring her girlfriend. When her mom called to talk to her, she told her she had a girlfriend. She loved using that word to define her relationship with Riley. Truthfully, she also couldn't wait to use other words to define their relationship. She didn't want to get ahead of herself, but she knew she loved Riley. She could see a future with her. She could hear herself calling Riley her fiancée. She could hear herself introducing Riley to people as her wife. That thought made her smile as she sat behind her desk at the office.

"Coffee and bagel delivery," Riley said as the bell chimed over the door and she walked in hurriedly.

"If you keep doing this, I will gain a hundred pounds," Kinsley said with a smile.

Riley moved behind her desk, leaned down, and kissed her as she placed the cardboard tray on the desk along with the bag of bagels.

"You've said that before. Also, I doubt it. At the rate we've been having sex, you'll probably lose a bunch of weight," Riley replied with a wink. "Not that you need to, because you are perfect." She kissed Kinsley again. "Plus, doesn't Morgan have you hiking this afternoon?"

"She does. She's trying out a new tour with some;

birdwatching. Kellan, with her vast knowledge of animals, has been helping her find the best spots where they congregate. We're going out to plan the thing. I volunteered to attend, even though I am useless."

"You are definitely not useless." Riley sat on the edge of Kinsley's desk. She'd taken to doing that now that they were together. This was both a good thing and a bad thing. It was nice, being close to Riley whenever she got the chance. It was also way too tempting, because her girlfriend mostly wore skirts. "I didn't completely ruin dinner on my last attempt, but I'm still thinking it might be safer to order in tonight."

Kinsley wasn't listening, though. She and Riley had spent the past two nights apart. She'd gone without really touching her for far too long. Today was one of those days when Riley had on a skirt that made it almost to her knees. While her legs were crossed at the ankles, Kinsley knew all too well what was between those thighs. She stared without thinking before her eyes flitted to the glass front of the office. It was mid-morning. Most people were at work. The streets were relatively deserted, save a few cars driving past too quickly to catch what she was about to do.

She slid her hand up Riley's ankle, watching Riley's expression lift as she moved it up to her knee. Riley's eyes met her own. She lifted an inquisitive eyebrow as Kinsley slid her hand further, causing Riley to instinctively uncross her ankles. Kinsley's eyes remained on Riley's as she moved her thumb to Riley's clit over her panties.

"Can you come fast?"

"I think you know I can. But are you sure? What if someone sees?" Riley asked as Kinsley began flicking her thumb over her clit. "Never mind."

Kinsley smirked up at Riley as the woman spread her legs more. If the wall, leading to the street, wasn't made of glass, Kinsley would have her head buried between them right now, coaxing an orgasm from her girlfriend. Instead, she'd settle, without really settling at all, for touching Riley with her fingers covertly while appearing to be working or talking to a friend. Riley's eyes closed. Her head went back a little, though not enough to give away what they were doing. Kinsley's fingers moved the panel of her panties to the side. She stroked the gaining wetness from her entrance up to Riley's clit and pressed her thumb firmly against it.

"I've missed you," Kinsley said.

"Don't stop," Riley managed to get out. "I wish your mouth was on me right now."

"If I make you come like this, I'll lock up and take you to the bathroom, where I'll take you with my tongue," Kinsley replied, feeling the warmth and wetness begin to take over all her sensations. She clenched her thighs together to try to keep her own need at bay. "You can even tell me step by step what you want me to do to you. I know how much you like that."

"I do like that," Riley gasped out. "I like this, too, though. Harder."

Kinsley pressed her thumb harder. She watched Riley attempt to move her hips without moving them too much. Kinsley glanced toward the front. Noticing no one around, she flicked Riley's clit with her finger, squeezed it, and watched Riley writhe as much as she could.

"Like that?"

"Yes. I'm coming." Riley's hips jerked once and then again as she came silently.

"Wow," Kinsley said as she watched her girlfriend come on top of her desk.

"Bathroom now?" Riley said as she opened her eyes, slid her skirt up her thighs enough to make Kinsley's mouth water, and leaned down preparing to kiss her.

"Hey," Morgan said as she entered. The bells chimed a moment too late for Kinsley to hear them. "What's—"

"Hey, Morgan." Riley stood quickly and straightened her skirt.

"I thought you were stopping by later." Kinsley attempted to regain her composure.

"I think I need to go into that bathroom and puke, but my guess is, both of you need to wash up first. Am I right?" Morgan scrunched up her face.

"What? No." Riley grabbed her coffee cup. "I was just dropping off coffee for my girl. Heading back to the office now." She leaned down and kissed Kinsley. "Tongue," she whispered into Kinsley's ear. "Tonight."

Kinsley gulped, nodded, and whispered back, "Really not a problem." She glanced up at Morgan. "Bye, babe."

"Bye. See you later, Morgan."

Morgan nodded. Riley left. The bell chimed over her head. Kinsley met Morgan's eyes.

"Did you two just—"

"You're early," Kinsley interrupted her.

"I didn't realize the open sign on the door meant your girlfriend's legs, James."

"Hey," Kinsley stood up.

"Sorry, that was rude. I meant that to be funny; not judging." She held up her hands in defense. "I'm tired. Please excuse the tone."

"Why are you tired?"

"I had a terrible date last night." She sat in the guest chair across from Kinsley's desk as Kinsley sat back down in her own chair. "Last blind date I'd ever go on."

"What happened?" Kinsley laughed.

"She planned a scavenger hunt, James. It was a first date. We were supposed to meet at this restaurant at seven. When I got there, the hostess handed me a card. It was a clue. I got a text from her at the same time, explaining her plan to meet me at the final clue's location. Who does that for a first date?"

"You did it?"

"This regular customer, who owns a ski lodge, suggested I go out with his niece. I've known him for years. He's been coming to the store for at least a decade. He gave me her number. I've been kind of desperate lately, watching you all find your soulmates. I called her. She seemed nice. I didn't realize she'd go this crazy, though. There were ten clues. I ended up at her house in Truckee."

"The opposite side of the lake?"

"Yes," she began. "She'd made me dinner, but by the time I got there to eat it, it was after ten. She was nice, but she's a talker. It was a four-course meal, James. She had appetizers before the soup, too. Then, there was dessert and coffee. By the time we got to the movie she'd planned for us to watch, I was already over the whole thing. I can appreciate the effort, but this is not the woman I'm going to spend my life with."

"I guess not. Sorry, Morgan." Kinsley sipped her coffee, and as she did, she realized she'd yet to wash her hand. She choked slightly. "Wrong pipe," she said as Morgan gave her a curious glance.

"I didn't get home until after one in the morning. I was up at five this morning to do the inventory before the store opened. Anyway – long story incredibly long – I was thinking about canceling the hike thing later. My dad's closing tonight. I think I'd rather just head home and take a nap. Can we do it some other time?"

"No problem. I wasn't really going to be helpful anyway."

"You're good company, at least," Morgan said as she stood. "Besides, now you have more time to have sex with your girlfriend." She winked. "At home and in private, Kinsley James."

***

"Babe?" Kinsley opened the door to Riley's apartment. "Riles?"

"Kinsley, hey. I didn't expect you until later. I thought you were hiking with Morgan and Kellan." Riley emerged from her bedroom. Her eyes were wide. She was moving very quickly toward Kinsley, who still stood near the door. "I thought we were going to—"

"Riley, I don't think the outlet next to the bed works. My phone isn't charging."

Elena Rivera walked out of the guest room and stared at Kinsley before looking at Riley.

"What the—"

"Kinsley, you remember Elena?"

"Yes, I—"

"Elena, you remember my *girlfriend*, Kinsley James?"

"I do," Elena replied with a glance up and down Kinsley's body. "It's nice to see you again."

Kinsley knew it was not nice for Elena to see her again, in the same way it wasn't nice for Kinsley to see Elena again. Kinsley gulped when she noticed Riley's jeans' button was undone. Her top two shirt buttons were also buttoned wrong.

"Kinsley, let's go in the hall and—"

"No," Kinsley interrupted as she saw red behind her eyes. "I should go."

"Babe, just hold on," Riley replied. "Elena, do you want to, maybe, help me out here?" She turned around. Kinsley watched her button her jeans. "Kinsley, I realize this looks—"

"Very bad?" Kinsley asked as her heart thundered in anger. "Your jeans are—"

"No, babe." She turned back to Kinsley. "I was getting changed. I was about to put on something for our date later." Her eyes widened at Kinsley as she lowered voice. "I bought something for tonight. I was going to try it on. When she showed up, I put this on quickly. Nothing is happening here."

"Elena is in your living room," Kinsley said loudly and pointed at Riley's ex-girlfriend.

"She just showed up," Riley replied. "Elena, I swear to God, if you don't start explaining, I will kick your ass out of my apartment." She turned her head to Elena.

"Kinsley, I've had a bit of a rough week." Elena approached. "I needed to get away from Texas. I took a last-minute flight to Tahoe today. I still had the key to Riley's apartment. I let myself in and caught Riley by surprise," she explained.

"You just flew here to surprise your *ex*-girlfriend?" Kinsley moved around Riley, who was straightening her shirt buttons. "Who does that?"

"Kinsley, she came out," Riley answered for Elena. "She came out publicly on Monday."

"Why do I care about that?" Kinsley asked, feeling her skin turn a deep shade of red, but not out of embarrassment. It was out of anger. "What does that have to do with her being in your apartment, Riley?"

"She needed a place to hide out," Riley replied.

"There are hotels. There are hotels that *aren't* in Tahoe. I'm pretty sure the state of Texas has hotels."

"I needed to get out of Texas. I'm a public figure there. No one knows me here."

"*I* know you," Kinsley said to her. "And what I know about you, I don't like."

"Well, at least she's honest. I'll give her that. I'm going to try a different outlet," Elena replied and moved back into the guest room.

"Why is she going into your guest room, Riley?"

"Babe, I—"

"Please don't 'babe' me," Kinsley said softly. "I'm not really in that kind of mood right now."

"Kinsley, I am so sorry." Riley moved toward her and spoke softly. "I had no idea she'd just show up like this."

"She still had your key, Riles."

"Accident. I took my key back when she left the last time. She had a spare, which I'd forgotten about."

"Conveniently," Kinsley said.

"No, not conveniently." Riley moved a step back. "God, Kinsley, I watched another woman kiss you and listened to you tell me you didn't want it and you pushed her away. I'm trying to talk to you and explain this. You won't even hear me."

"Courtney isn't my ex-girlfriend."

"I can't help what Elena is to me, but she is my *ex*. You are my current," Riley replied.

"She's in your apartment," Kinsley reminded. "How ex can she really be when she just keeps popping up?'

"Kinsley, I told her she could stay here for a little while," Riley said. When she noticed Kinsley's eyes nearly burst out of her head, she added, "I'm staying with you. She's staying here, but I'll stay with you. It's just a place for her to crash until the media frenzy around her dies down."

"She can't stay at a hotel? There are thousands of rooms in Lake Tahoe. Hell, there are remote rental cabins out in the woods. No one would even know who she is."

"Do you really think Elena is someone that will stay in a remote cabin?" Riley asked with a small smile.

"I'm not smiling about this, Riles. This isn't entertaining to me. You knew about my issues with her. We almost didn't get together because I thought you weren't over her yet."

"And I am," Riley replied. "I am over her. I am completely over her and entirely into you, Kinsley. This doesn't change that."

"I don't think I'd be completely out of line asking you not to do this," Kinsley said. "Make her leave."

"I'm not going to kick her out on the street," Riley said. "She may be my ex-girlfriend, but she's still a person, Kinsley. She's going through something. Margie texted me a little while ago to tell me how bad it's been for Elena there. She tried staying with Margie, but the press caught up with her. She was running for governor of the state." She paused and took a deep breath. "This is kind of my fault."

"What are you talking about?" Kinsley asked. "How is her deciding to come out of the closet your fault?"

"She'd told me she'd do it when I was there visiting Margie. She'd said she would drop out of the race and come out for me."

"So, she *is* here to try to win you back?" Kinsley

grunted in frustration. "I need to get out of this apartment."

"Kinsley, come on. Just give me a minute. I'll pack a bag, and we'll leave together," Riley said, trying to take Kinsley's hand.

"Riley, I need some time alone."

"Please don't let this get in the way of us."

"I'm upset. I need to be alone right now," Kinsley replied.

"I told her she could stay here, but that I was staying with you," Riley reminded.

Kinsley thought for a moment before she pulled out her key chain. She removed her spare key from the ring and passed it to her girlfriend.

"I'm going to go. You can stay, but I don't think I'm ready to talk about this just yet. Let yourself in later. Give me a little time, okay?"

"Am I sleeping next to you, or are you putting me in the guest room because I let someone who needed a place to crash, stay in my apartment?"

"I don't know," Kinsley said.

She then turned and left the apartment.

CHAPTER 24

RILEY SAT ON THE SOFA for a while. She stayed there staring at the key Kinsley had given her so reluctantly. She'd hoped that, one day, she'd be given this key because Kinsley wanted her to use it. She stared at that key and wished she could give it back to Kinsley and ask for a do-over. Instead, she placed it on the coffee table.

"I'm sorry, Riley," Elena said.

Riley looked up and realized Elena was standing in the doorway of the guest room. She had her arms crossed over her chest. Her expression appeared genuine. Riley leaned back on the sofa and sighed.

"No, you're not."

"I know you think I did this intentionally. I'm sure Kinsley thinks that, too. I didn't." She sat on the sofa next to Riley but left enough space between them for Riley to feel comfortable.

"Why'd you come out now? There wasn't a point, Elena," Riley said, turning her head to Elena.

"Margie didn't tell you everything, did she?" Elena lowered her head to stare at her hands.

"No, apparently not."

"I didn't do it voluntarily, Riley."

"What?"

"I wish I could say I'd had the courage to do this on my own, but I didn't."

"What happened, Elena?"

"I told you the party wasn't interested in me any longer. Unfortunately, my potential opponent didn't get the memo."

"What did he do?"

"This is the part I'm really worried about. I know you

174

think I'm this selfish person. I'm not. Things were good with us once. You remember that, don't you?"

"Elena, come on."

"I'm not trying to get you back." She held up her hands. "I get it, you've moved on. That's obvious. I was watching you stare at that key for about ten minutes before I said anything."

"Then, why?"

"I tried to keep you out of it, but it didn't work."

"What do you mean?" Riley asked.

"I'm going to ask you to do something. You're going to say no, and you'll probably freak out, but I'm going to ask anyway."

"What now, Elena?" She sat up.

"I know you're with Kinsley. I'm just wondering if you'll, maybe, join me for a press conference." She paused as she appeared to check Riley's initial reaction. "And pretend we're still together."

"You want me to fake being your girlfriend?"

"Just hear me out." She turned entirely to Riley. "The press has a picture of us at the hospital. It's nothing racy, but I am holding your hand, trying to get back together with you. I didn't see anyone in the hall. I don't know how they got it, but they have it."

"Tell them I'm a family friend who was there for Margie," she replied.

"There's more. My would-be opponent found your name and did a background check. They know you're gay. He had someone on your social media accounts. There's a video of you and me there."

"I didn't put a video of you on my social media pages. I knew the rules, Elena."

"Someone put it on their page and tagged you." Elena rolled her eyes. "I hate the internet. Anyway, it's us in the background at Margie's birthday party. It's pretty grainy, but you can tell it's you and me. We were in that corridor where-"

"We thought no one could see us," Riley finished for her. "I remember."

"Someone did see us."

"I'm hardly ever on social media. I don't pay attention to people tagging me. I'm sorry, Elena. Am I responsible for this?"

"It's not your fault, but we were kissing in the video. It's out there, Riley. They know who you are, and they know about us."

"Should I worry?" Riley asked.

"I don't know. I guess that kind of depends on what I do next," she said.

"What's that mean?" Riley lifted an eyebrow.

"The media has been following me around this past week. I finally confirmed that I am a lesbian, thinking that it would all die down. I'm not running anymore. My time as mayor is almost over. I'm not running again. I could just fade into obscurity. They'd leave me alone."

"And then?" Riley asked, guessing where this was going.

"And then, I got a call from the party. Suddenly, they're very interested in me running after all. They said they'd like to help me become the first lesbian governor of the state of Texas."

"Which means what to me, Elena?"

"I have to make a choice, Riley. If I choose to run, there will be a press conference announcing my candidacy. Ideally, my girlfriend would be standing beside me."

"You don't have a girlfriend, unless there's something you haven't told me." Riley leaned forward again, looking at the key on the table.

"It would be temporary. It's just to solidify that you and I have been together for a while now. You'd make a few appearances, and then I could announce that we've gone our separate ways."

"Elena, that's—"

"Crazy? A lot to ask? I know" She paused. "I could

also choose not to run, and we could avoid at least that part. Your name is still out there. I can't guarantee the press won't come here to try to get a comment. But if I run, and you're not around, I think that will make them more interested."

"Then, you're not running, Elena. Doesn't that seem like the best solution to all of this? They stop caring about you and leave me alone. You can start a law practice in Texas. I can be here and continue my life."

"I want this, Riley," she said. "I didn't mean for it to impact you, now that we're not together, but I do want this."

"They want you to be their token, Elena. You know that."

"Token or not, I'd be the first lesbian governor of a massive state, Riley. I could help change laws that would impact people like you and me. Maybe I could make an actual difference."

"Elena, I can't pretend to be your girlfriend. It doesn't work like that. If you want to run for office, you can run. I'll deal with the press if they decide to stalk me."

"If Kinsley weren't in the picture, would–"

"She *is* in the picture," Riley stood. "Jesus, she's been so worried that you and I weren't finished. And here you are. It's like, every time I get her to a point where she believes me, something happens, and you're a part of our relationship again, which you shouldn't be, Elena."

"I'm not trying to be in your relationship," Elena returned.

"But you are. You're sitting on my sofa, asking me to pretend we're still together, when my actual girlfriend is off somewhere, wondering when I'll be able to let this go," she said and motioned to Elena. "But I'm not the one that needs to let this go. You are. She is."

"I told you, I'm not here to try to win you back." Elena stood. "You like this Kinsley woman; I'm trying to be respectful of that."

"I love her," Riley said.

"You just met her," Elena said.

"Elena, I've known Kinsley James for over ten years. I guess, it's closer to fifteen now. She's always been a friend of a friend, but she's liked me since college, and I didn't know." Riley paused as she smiled. "Spending time with her when I started looking for a house, made me realize you and I weren't working. I wanted her." She shrugged.

"I get it, Riley." She waved off. "Glad you've found someone you love while I'm struggling to get over this girl I used to date, who once planned a life with me."

"Hey, you did this to yourself." She bit her lower lip in frustration. "You weren't there, Elena. You were never there toward the end. Longer, if I'm being honest. You were too focused on staying in the closet and on work to realize that we'd grown apart and no longer wanted the same things."

"Please, pour it on me, Riley. I don't have enough to worry about." She moved to the kitchen. "Do you have anything stronger than wine or that terrible beer you like?"

"You never worried about us when we were together. Why start now?" Riley said as she followed her into the kitchen. She crossed her arms over her chest. "God, I think this is what I needed to finally put this crap behind me: I needed to yell at you."

"I flew here for solace, Riley. I didn't come here to get yelled at by my ex."

"You shouldn't have come here at all." She paused as she uncrossed her arms. "I can't be your solace anymore, Elena. That's not my job."

"What am I supposed to do, Riley?" She slammed the refrigerator door. It was then that Riley noted the tears welling in the woman's eyes. "I can't go home until I make a decision about whether or not I'm running for office. I need you beside me. I love you. I know I made mistakes. I'm sorry for that. If you tell me right now that I shouldn't run, that I should move here, and we can start again, I'd do it now. I didn't do it then, but I'd do it now."

"You can't go back and forth like that, Elena. Don't

you see that's the problem? You clearly want to run for governor. You were willing to lose me to do that. You can't take it back now. If you want this, you need to do it. It will have to be without me. Even if I wasn't with Kinsley, I still wouldn't pretend to be your girlfriend just for a campaign." She paused. "Now, I have to go. I'm packing a bag and staying at Kinsley's tonight. I hope she talks to me and forgives me for letting you walk back into my life again, because this is the last time, Elena. You can stay tonight, but you need to find a hotel or something tomorrow. I'd like you to be gone by then. Good luck in the governor's race."

"What about the press? If they come here, what will you tell them?"

"Nothing."

Riley moved quickly to her bedroom, tossed items for the night into a bag, and made her way back to the living room, where Elena was sitting on the sofa with a glass of her red wine.

"Riley, can–"

"I need my spare key, Elena." Riley held out her hand. "You can lock up when you leave without it."

"I guess this is your way of saying goodbye."

"I said goodbye to you. I've done it a few times now, but this will be the last, yes."

Elena reached into her purse, pulled out her keychain, and removed Riley's key. She handed it to her and tossed her keys back into her bag.

"Goodbye, then."

"Goodbye, Elena."

Riley marched out of her apartment, got into her car, and drove to Kinsley's. When she arrived, Kinsley's car wasn't in the driveway. She let herself in, checked the house, and realized she was alone. She gave Kinsley a few hours to be alone, made herself something to eat, and then texted her girlfriend. Kinsley hadn't replied by the time she was ready to head to bed. She called, but Kinsley didn't answer. She left two voicemails and fell asleep alone holding her phone.

CHAPTER 25

"HOW LONG DO YOU plan to crash on my couch, hiding from your girlfriend, James?" Morgan asked.

"It's been one night," Kinsley replied as she sat up and stretched her now sore back. "And I'm not hiding from her."

"That's actually exactly what you're doing," Morgan replied, passing her a cup of coffee with a glare. "I can't believe her ex has now just shown up multiple times."

"I can," Kinsley said, taking the cup. "I could just tell she'd be like that the moment I met her. Maybe even before I met her, when Riley was describing her to me."

"But you're not hiding?" Morgan sat down, moving the blanket Kinsley had used for the night. "How many times has she called? Texted?" She took a drink of her own coffee.

"I don't know. I put my phone on do not disturb after I got here." Kinsley took a sip and placed her cup on the coffee table.

"Is this about your parents? The cheating?" Morgan asked. "You know that just because that happened in their marriage, that doesn't mean it's going to happen in your relationship, right?"

"I'm aware. It's just hard to go through that and not carry that baggage with you when you find someone you want to be with, Morgan. If you remember correctly, I also had a girlfriend do this to me once before."

"Leave you for the ex? Yeah, I remember."

"It's not exactly fun, Morgan."

"You're a coward, James," Morgan uttered teasingly while giving her the Morgan Burns patented side-eye.

"I'm not a coward. I'm just not ready to talk to her yet." Kinsley laid her head back against the sofa. "I love her, Morgan."

"Obviously." Morgan took another drink. "Does she know that?"

"I haven't said it yet, but isn't it a little fast?"

"To feel it or to say it?"

"Both," Kinsley replied.

"I don't think there's a 'too fast' or 'too slow' for something like that. I guess I've seen it a bunch of different ways now. I used to think that love at first sight was a ridiculous concept. Then, I thought that falling in love with someone after knowing them forever as friends was strange."

"But you and Reese were–"

"I said *used to.*" Morgan winked at her. "I think it's just different for everyone, and whatever works for you guys is what's normal."

"But I've had feelings for her a lot longer than she has for me. What if I freak her out?"

"I bet you're already freaking her out by worrying about the ex after she's told you a million times not to worry about her. She's with you, James. If she wanted this Elena woman, she would have moved to Texas to be a governor's wife."

"Mistress, technically," Kinsley corrected.

Morgan chuckled and said, "She chose you. I bet if you check your phone, you'll have at least ten messages."

"I don't really want to check it," Kinsley said.

"Because you're afraid you'll have no messages?" Morgan guessed.

"Yes." Kinsley lowered her head. "Elena just seems like the kind of woman who could convince Riley to get back together with her."

"But didn't she try that already when Riley went to Dallas?"

"Yes, but this is, like, her version of a grand gesture."

Kinsley looked over at Morgan. "She just shows up with a crisis but tells Riley she's willing to give it all up for her. She still has a key, Morgan."

"To Riley's place?"

"Yes."

"That's probably just because she didn't get it back last time. Reese still has mine."

"You and Reese are still friends that live, like, fifteen minutes apart," Kinsley reasoned.

"True. Maybe she just forgot."

"Doesn't that say something, though?" Kinsley asked. "She forgot to get the key back because she didn't really want it back at all."

"James, you're overthinking this. When I dated Mandy, she gave me a key after like three dates, because it was just easier. I still have it, despite the fact that we only ever went on five dates."

"You still have some random woman's house key?"

"Somewhere on my keychain." Morgan shrugged. "I have like twenty keys, since the store has four keys just to run it. Then, I have my house key, the canoe rental shack keys of which there are many, the keys to the–"

"Okay, I get it." Kinsley laughed. "Any other random keys from other women on there?"

"Just yours and Reese and Kellan's place, which I've never used, for obvious reasons," Morgan replied and stood.

"How are you with all that? We talked about it back when they first got together, but we haven't talked about how you're doing in a while," Kinsley said.

"You're changing the subject." Morgan pointed at her. "But it's better." She shrugged for the second time. "It's still a little strange, seeing the person you thought you'd share your life with sharing a house with someone else. But I'm not in love with Reese anymore. If anything, her relationship with Kellan has helped me get there sooner."

"That's good," Kinsley said.

"And now, call your girlfriend." Morgan pointed again. "Better yet, go home, James."

Kinsley stayed on Morgan's couch as Morgan moved to her bathroom to shower for the day. She sipped on the cooling coffee as she tried to figure out what to do. Had she overreacted about the key? About Elena just showing up and Riley allowing her to stay? She hadn't thought so. To be honest, she still didn't think she'd overreacted to the situation. They were finally together, and happily so. They were headed in a direction Kinsley never thought she would with Riley. When she first met the eighteen-year-old girl in college, Kinsley had been more than interested. Now, she'd fallen in love with Riley the woman. It was even better than she'd imagined.

***

Riley had woken early to an empty bed and no messages from Kinsley on her phone. She did have one from Elena, telling her she'd booked a flight for the following day since nothing was available today. That angered Riley, but she had to be more concerned about her current relationship than her past one right now. She texted Elena that she should still find a hotel room for that night, since she wanted her apartment back. She assumed Kinsley had decided to sleep in the guest room. She left the master bedroom and made her way toward it to discover it was empty, and the bed was made. She checked the rest of the house. She was alone. She went outside on the second story balcony and stared out at the view from the backyard. She could make out a sliver of the lake, but not much more.

It was then that she heard sounds she didn't recognize coming from that direction. In the otherwise quiet neighborhood, they stood out. She went back into Kinsley's bedroom, searched Kinsley's drawers, and sought out a hooded sweatshirt she'd borrowed once before. It smelled of her girlfriend. She wondered how long she'd actually have that girlfriend now, given the mistakes she'd made and Kinsley's reaction.

After dressing, she made her way downstairs and outside. She had yet to travel past the tree line in the backyard. They hadn't exactly made outdoor activities a priority at the beginning of their relationship. Her face blushed at the memory of Kinsley slamming her body against the back door one day, with her fingers thrusting inside Riley. That was really as close as they'd gotten to spending any time outside unless they were on the balcony. Even out there, they'd made love once under the stars, unable to keep their hands off one another for too long.

She walked down the hill and into the trees, using the path provided. When she emerged, she was finally able to see the crystal-clear water and the pebbled beach just before it. She was also able to see Kinsley James unloading lumber from a giant pile that had been delivered at the beach's edge, likely, by a truck.

"Kinsley?"

The woman stopped when she dropped a long piece of light-colored wood closer to the water. She glanced up and wiped her brow with her forearm, which enabled Riley to see the work gloves she wore. She also wore a pair of dirty jeans and a t-shirt. She had her hair pulled back and through a baseball cap.

"Hey," Kinsley replied as if nothing had happened between them yesterday and everything right now was completely normal.

"Hey? Did you just 'hey' me? What the hell is going on?"

"I'm building a dock," Kinsley said, motioning to the wood in the smaller pile in front of her.

"You're what?" Riley moved closer to her, keeping her hands inside the front pocket of the sweatshirt she'd borrowed.

"Did I wake you?" Kinsley asked, moving to the other pile.

"No, you didn't wake me. Kinsley, stop for a minute, please. Talk to me. Tell me what's going on here."

"I was able to get this wood wholesale this morning. It was a really great deal. Basically, half off." Kinsley picked up two long boards, tossed them over her shoulder, and moved them to the other pile. Riley watched her arm muscles ripple as she dropped them down. It was difficult to keep her focus on the conversation they needed to have, because Kinsley looked pretty damn hot right now. "I found plans online, watched a few videos last night, and decided to get to work."

"You're building a dock?" Riley asked. "I keep forgetting you, basically, redid your entire house."

"Ryan and Dave are going to help." Kinsley moved back and forth between the piles again. "Dave's a contractor. He helped with the house, too. That's Stacy's husband. You know her, right?"

"You know I have met both Stacy and Dave, Kinsley James." Riley waited until Kinsley dropped two more boards before she walked around the pile and stood in her way. "Please tell me what's really going on here."

"The first time you came here, you asked me if I had a boat."

"And you said no. So, I fail to see the sudden necessity for building a dock that will have no boat attached to it." Riley motioned to the water beyond them.

"Morgan and I talked about that last night. She needs a place on this side of the lake to keep some canoes and kayaks for the store. Not all year, but during the summer, it would help them out. I told her she could use the dock as long as I could use one of their store's speed boats whenever it's not out there, giving lake tours. They have three. She'll keep one of them here, too. It's a win-win."

"So, you were at Morgan's last night?" Riley tried to pull out the most important thing from Kinsley's response and bring it to the forefront of their conversation.

"I was."

"Kinsley, I was worried. I was here last night, worried.

I called a million times. I left messages. I know you were upset, but you could have at least told me where you were so that I knew you were okay. Did you even listen to my messages? Did you hear how concerned I was? Did that not make you want to just tell me to fuck off right now but that you're okay?"

"I put my phone on do not disturb. I didn't get them until this morning," Kinsley replied, looking down at the ground. "And I figured I'd see you when I got home."

"But you're not home, Kinsley. You're outside, building a dock for some reason." She motioned again to the water.

"Dave's lumber guy told me if I picked this stuff up this morning, I'd get the deal. But he also had someone else interested. I had to get it and then have someone unload it."

"You act like that's a good excuse for not at least telling me you were here," Riley retorted.

"And you act like it's okay that when I went by your apartment this morning just to see if you'd gone back, you weren't there, but I noticed Elena Rivera getting into her rental car," Kinsley replied. "And not to leave, Riley. She was pulling out another bag. She pulled out a bag and took it back inside, like she hasn't left yet and still isn't leaving."

"She texted me this morning that she couldn't get a flight out until tomorrow. I texted her back just a few minutes ago that she needs to find a damn hotel, because she's not staying at my place tonight," Riley said rather loudly. "You'd know *that* if you came inside your house and talked to your girlfriend," she added and marched back off toward the house. "Have fun building your unnecessary dock, Kinsley."

Riley marched off back toward Kinsley's house, preparing herself to just grab her things and go. She wasn't interested in this kind of drama. She'd already had so much of that in her last relationship. She'd thought Kinsley would be different.

CHAPTER 26

"HEY," KINSLEY GREETED as she stood in the doorway of her bedroom.

"I'm just grabbing my stuff before I go home to my apartment to make sure my ex-girlfriend left my damn key on the counter and that she is no longer staying in my guest room. Then, I'll get out of your hair," Riley replied, bending over to reach for her phone charger she'd plugged in last night.

"I don't want you out of my hair, Riles," Kinsley said.

"What *do* you want? I'm not even sure if you know," Riley retorted, shoving the cord into her overnight bag.

"I never expected you to actually want me, Riley," Kinsley replied.

Riley stopped moving, turned her head to Kinsley, and said, "Well, I do. I want you. I want the woman who was there for me when I was trying to figure out what to do with Elena. I want the woman who ate naked with me on top of her kitchen island. I want the woman who told me I was worth more than what Elena would or could ever offer me. I want the woman who let me try to cook her dinner, knowing it likely wouldn't turn out well. You would have eaten it anyway, wouldn't you? Had Elena not interrupted that night, you would have eaten it and told me it was fine."

"You tried so hard," Kinsley answered with a smile.

"Kinsley, I want you." Riley threw her bag over her shoulder. "I want to be with you, but I don't want this jealousy you seem to have toward Elena. I understood it in the beginning. Elena and I were together and planning a future when you and I finally got close as friends. Elena and I aren't together anymore. You and I are. *You're* my girlfriend. God, Kinsley. You're my damn girlfriend, and you keep treating me like I'm going to run off with a woman that asked me to be her fake girlfriend yesterday, because she still wants to be the first lesbian governor of the state of Texas."

"She what?" Kinsley moved into the bedroom then. She'd removed the work gloves and her hat but was still covered in a light sheen of sweat. "She asked you–"

"You're not helping your case there, Kinsley," Riley replied.

"That's not jealousy, Riley. That's me wondering what the hell she could have been thinking, asking you that."

"Well, she did." Riley shrugged. "And I told her no and to leave. You just ran out and turned your phone off."

"I didn't turn it–"

"You stayed at Morgan's last night, instead of coming here," Riley interrupted.

"And *that's* not jealousy?" Kinsley replied.

"You told me nothing's going on there. Morgan told me she thinks of you as a sister. I trust Morgan more than you trust me, Kinsley. You don't think there's a problem here?"

"I trust you, Riley," Kinsley replied.

"Do you? It doesn't seem like you do. I watched a woman kiss you on the lips. You told me you pushed her away. You told me you wanted me. I believed you. I dropped it, even though watching someone else kiss you felt like a punch to the gut. I wanted to vomit. I've never felt that way before, Kinsley. Not in three years with Elena did I feel like I might throw up in a parking lot at the thought of someone else kissing her," Riley said.

"I know. I'm sorry," Kinsley replied. "Can we just sit down and talk? Have you had breakfast?"

"I don't want breakfast. Honestly, I want to go, Kinsley."

"Riles, are you–"

"I don't think you're ready for this. You're worried *I'm* not. You're still afraid I'm not over Elena, but it's not me that's the problem here, Kinsley. I don't think *you're* ready."

Kinsley moved toward her. Riley moved around and past her toward the door.

"Riley, let's just talk."

"You didn't want to talk yesterday, when I was trying to explain Elena's presence in my apartment," Riley said. "So, I'm not really ready to talk to you right now."

"Are we just fighting or are we over?" Kinsley asked, crossing her arms over her chest.

"I don't know," Riley replied with a sigh. "I do know that I am angry with you, and I don't want to be here right now. I'm going to go home and make sure Elena is gone."

"I guess I'll just see you when I see you, then," Kinsley replied.

"Don't get passive-aggressive on me, Kinsley." Riley turned back to her. "Even though I'm not a fan of your anger when directed toward me, it's still better than you pretending you don't care that I'm walking out right now. I know you care. Don't pretend otherwise."

Riley walked out of the bedroom. Kinsley flopped down onto the end of her bed.

"I love you," Kinsley muttered to herself.

***

"You're still here? Are you freaking kidding me, Elena?" Riley tossed her bag onto the floor.

"I'm leaving." Elena held up her hands. "I'm only still here because I wanted to apologize to you," she said.

Riley sat on her sofa and glared up at her ex-girlfriend.

"Apologize for asking me–"

"I called my sister. She told me what an idiot I am."

189

Elena sat next to her. "She said I was the dumbest smart person she knows, and then she yelled at me."

"I've always liked Margie," Riley replied.

"Better than me, I think."

"Different than you."

"I wanted too much, Riley. I'm sorry that it's impacted you. I never meant for it to become an issue between us, or for it to cause us to…"

"I know," Riley said. "And I appreciate the apology."

"Don't take this the wrong way… I get that you're unavailable now. I just want to make sure I'm not crazy." She paused while Riley stared at her in confusion. "We were good together once, weren't we?"

"We were." Riley nodded. "We just grew apart instead of together."

"And you think you'll grow together with Kinsley?"

"I don't know. I don't think anyone ever knows for sure."

"But you'd like to grow with her?" Elena asked.

"If she gives me the chance," she replied.

"She's mad at you because of me, isn't she?"

"Yes, but she's not really mad. She's jealous, I think."

"And you told her–"

"That it's over between us. And she still thinks something's going to happen."

"Sounds like she's protecting herself," Elena suggested. "We've all been there."

"Elena, she has no reason to protect herself from me. I'm her girlfriend." She turned to Elena on the sofa.

"That's usually just the person we need to protect ourselves from, though, Riley."

"You're supposed to trust the person you're with," Riley argued.

"And while you yelled at me and definitely told me we were done, you also still allowed me to stay in your apartment, failed to take back your key, and flew to Dallas to check on Margie when I called with the emergency."

"You–"

"I did all those things. I know. I did them in part because I wanted you back and, in part, because I selfishly wanted to try to destroy your budding relationship with Kinsley." She paused. "I'm ashamed of myself now, and I truly apologize to you, Riley. All I'm saying is that while you say we're over, you still let me stay here. I'm still sitting on your sofa. I can understand why she might still be worried that it's not completely over between us. Three years is a long time, Riley. We were planning to buy a house together. She was supposed to be our real estate agent, remember?"

"How are you suddenly on Kinsley's side?" Riley asked with a light smile.

"I'm not. I'm just trying to be on your side instead of my own now. I've caused a lot of problems in your life. I'm sorry. I do think you really like her, though. It's obvious she feels the same. If you and I are over, I still want you to find someone who can make you happy, Riley."

"She makes me frustrated most of the time these days," Riley replied.

"That's part of it, too, I think." Elena stood. "I used to frustrate the hell out of you."

"You still do," Riley said with a playful shove to Elena's knee.

"I'm staying at the Camden, under Margie's name. I have a flight for tomorrow. Then, I'll be out of your life. I still hope you'll call Margie from time to time, though. You broke up with me, but she still loves you."

"I will. Margie's like a sister to me," Riley replied.

"Good. She'll be glad to hear it," Elena said. "I should get going."

"I appreciate the apology, Elena." Riley stood.

"It was long overdue, I think." She nodded.

"What are you going to do about the election?" Riley asked as she followed Elena toward the front door of the apartment, her luggage in hand.

"I've made a decision." She exhaled deeply. "I'm going

to run. I'm going to run as a single, late-in-life lesbian, get completely trounced on, but try to keep as much of my dignity as possible."

Riley chuckled and said, "I think that's a good idea. It's about time you're yourself, Elena."

"I guess so. After I lose, I'll go back to practicing law in my tiny town. Who knows? Maybe you and I will run into one another on a case one day, just like when we first met."

"Don't take this the wrong way, but I hope not." Riley smiled at her.

***

Kinsley was exhausted. Her body ached. She groaned at herself as she poured cream into her cup of coffee at the little station on the other side of her office. She'd gotten the thing for clients, along with a mini-fridge filled with some soda, bottled water, and light snacks. Normally, she'd get her coffee from home, the café, or recently, from her girlfriend's mid-morning deliveries. She stretched her neck to try to ease the ache from the hard labor she'd put her body through in an attempt to distract herself from her fight with Riley.

She had called Riley a few times. She'd texted and left voicemails. She'd driven by Riley's apartment that morning and hadn't found her car. The woman was probably already at the office. Kinsley knew she needed to do something. She was the one that had caused this problem between them. Hell, she was the one that had continued to cause this problem between them. She sat back down at her desk and brought up her calendar. She needed to find time to get out of the office and go find her girlfriend. When she looked at the door the moment the bell chimed, she saw a surprising visitor.

"Elena?" Kinsley stared at the woman who stood in front of her door.

"Hello, Kinsley," Elena replied, holding her bag in

front of her. "I hope you don't mind me stopping by."

"I do, actually," Kinsley replied defensively.

"I'm here for two reasons; one is less selfish than the other. Would you care to hear them both or just the one about you and Riley?"

Kinsley was confused. Elena moved to sit in one of her guest chairs, as if Kinsley had invited her to stay. Kinsley turned her aching body toward the woman who always seemed so put-together, even though her life seemed to possibly be falling apart.

"I have a client coming in soon," Kinsley changed the subject.

"Then, I won't keep you." Elena gripped her bag in her lap with both hands. "I wanted to apologize to you. I've already apologized to Riley."

"Apologize to me?"

Elena cleared her throat and replied, "Yes. I seemed to have made a fool of myself in trying to get Riley to give me another chance. In doing that, I believe, I have caused problems in your relationship." She paused and lowered her eyes. "I love Riley Sanders. Since I met her, I've loved her. She showed me that I could be myself and be loved in return." The woman looked back up to meet Kinsley's eyes. "I squandered that love by putting my aspirations over my relationship. That's something I'll have to live with my whole life." She turned her head toward the window. "I am also sorry about that." She pointed.

"What's going on?" Kinsley asked when she turned her head to see a few cameras and people with microphones.

"They've found me."

"Who?"

"The press." Elena turned back to her and shrugged. "I noticed a few vans following me on my way here. That's my other apology. I'm sorry they're here. I'm sure they'll follow me when I leave, though."

"Does this have anything to do with–"

"Running for governor? Yes. But, I'm guessing, it

would have more to do with me running for governor as an out lesbian. You know what I asked of Riley, don't you?"

"To be your fake girlfriend while you run?" Kinsley leaned forward, suddenly tenser than she had been from hours of manual labor.

"It was foolish and cowardly of me to ask her that. I wanted someone by my side. But I realize now she'll be standing by your side." She nodded in Kinsley's direction. "I'm backing off now, Kinsley. Not that I needed to, though; Riley is already yours. I can see that plain as day." She paused when a few flashes went off outside the window. "I'll have to explain all this to those people outside, one day soon. But today, I just need to make it to the hotel, lock myself in, and catch a flight tomorrow."

"And you'll tell them you're not with Riley anymore?"

"I will. But, Kinsley, as much as it hurts me to say this, Riley is in love with you. I have this feeling that if I kept trying to win her back, it wouldn't matter. I could hire a skywriter, have flowers delivered every day to her office, build her dream house with my bare hands, and she'd still choose you." The woman stood, still clasping her bag in both hands. "Don't squander it, like I did. Whatever you're worried about, whatever issues you have, put them aside. Love her and let her love you." She turned to go but turned back quickly. "There wouldn't happen to be a back entrance to this place, would there?"

CHAPTER 27

RILEY LEFT the courthouse after spending the past few hours trying to get one client a restraining order and another client custody of her two young children. She'd been successful on both accounts and was feeling pretty good about herself, when she remembered she was still in a fight with Kinsley. Nothing deflated one's professional achievements faster than the reminder that their personal life had things that needed to be worked out. Her smile dimmed even further when she noticed the press had gathered on the stairs. She tried to think of a high-profile case going on that would have them all here. Then, she remembered Elena's warning. Once a few of the reporters noticed her, they practically rushed in her direction. They yelled her name. They asked her questions about Elena Rivera. They asked about their relationship. Riley didn't know what to do.

She hurried past all of them toward her car, unlocking it before she arrived in order to climb right in and take off. She texted Elena the moment her car was parked around the corner from her office, so as to go undetected. Elena replied that she would take care of it. Then, Riley returned to her office to find an envelope on top of her desk. It hadn't been there when she'd left. It also wasn't the standard legal envelope she'd been used to receiving. It had her first name only on the outside. It was handwritten, and it was Kinsley's curvy R and Y that extended the length of her name. She looked around the space to see if Kinsley was still there. Not finding her, Riley opened the envelope and removed the piece of paper.

Riley,

I hope you're not expecting some romantic note, because this isn't it. This is a note of apology, because I am a complete asshole. You don't normally see the word 'asshole' in a love letter, do you? I hope you'll give me the chance to apologize in person, because I so desperately want to do that. Will you come by my place later? Around seven? If you're not here by then, I'd say I'll have my answer, but that's wrong. I'll keep trying, Riley. I'll keep trying because you're worth it. We're worth it.

Kinsley

Riley folded the piece of paper and slid it back into the envelope. She glared outside and realized if she left now, she'd likely be able to get away before the press found her. They wouldn't know about Kinsley's house. She could go there directly. That would also give Elena time to fix the mess she'd caused. She grabbed her bag, left the office after locking it up for the night, and headed down the sidewalk and around the corner to get to her car. With no one around with a camera or a microphone, she climbed in and headed toward Kinsley's to hear her apology in person.

***

Kinsley was more nervous today than she'd been for their first date. It was already 7:03, and Riley wasn't here. She was worried Riley wouldn't show up. Maybe Riley wouldn't give her another chance. She should have written a better note. She should have been very clear regarding her feelings. But she wanted to say the words in person, preferably, after Riley forgave her for her stupidity. By 7:05, Kinsley reached for her cell phone on the island. She had already set dinner out on the table, and she didn't want it to get cold. She checked her phone again. Riley hadn't called or texted that she wouldn't be there at all. She also hadn't left a message, saying she'd be late. Kinsley placed the phone back down and went upstairs. She hung her arms over the railing on the balcony and stared out at the semi-darkness. The sun was still setting, and the sky was alight with oranges and purples, but the trees in and around her backyard sheltered the whole area in near darkness. She'd turned the hanging lights on, illuminating parts of her yard. She sighed and ran her hands through her hair, which she'd left down, remembering how much Riley liked running her own hands through it.

"Didn't think I'd show?" Riley asked.

Kinsley turned instantly, smiled, and replied, "I wasn't sure I'd earned you showing up."

"What do you plan to do to earn it, then?" Riley asked with a small smile as she stood in the sliding glass doorway between Kinsley's bedroom and the patio.

"I made you dinner," she said pathetically, motioning with an open hand toward the table she'd already set and lit with candles. "And I made tiramisu for dessert."

"One of my favorites," Riley replied with a seemingly hesitant smile, still leaning in the doorway.

"I also planned to be completely honest with you, which I haven't been so far," Kinsley said, clasping her hands together in front of herself.

"You haven't been honest with me? About what?" Riley moved outside then.

She'd likely come straight from work. She was still dressed in her pantsuit. Her shirt was half untucked, but other than that, she looked like she could go right into a courtroom to argue a case.

"Two things, I think." Kinsley motioned for Riley to sit. She pulled out the chair. Riley stopped to think first before she sat down. Kinsley helped her push the chair in. She moved to her own chair next and sat. "Wine?"

Riley nodded and said, "You're talking while we eat. No stalling, Kinsley James."

"There's something you don't know about me. I haven't gotten around to telling you. It's not a big deal, except it might explain a little bit of why I am the way I am when it comes to you and this Elena situation."

Kinsley poured them both a glass of wine before setting the bottle back on the table. She nodded for Riley to go ahead and start eating before she picked up her own fork and knife.

"The Elena situation? Is that what we're calling it?" Riley asked.

"My parents are divorced."

"Oh," Riley replied, obviously confused by the change in topic.

"They have a strange relationship where they're cordial where I'm concerned, but my father kind of hates my mother. Still, they live in the same city and make sure when I come to visit, they put on a good show."

"Why are—"

"The reason, or at least one of the reasons, I've had such a hard time with the Elena situation is because of the reason for their divorce."

"What happened?" Riley took a bite.

"My mother had a boyfriend before my father. They were together for nearly ten years before they broke up." She paused while she watched Riley take a drink of her wine. "He ended it. My mom moved on. She met my father, and they got married. They had me shortly after. Then, my father found out that their relationship hadn't just been in the past."

"She cheated on him?" Riley asked.

"I found out later that my father knew her ex-boyfriend. They'd been friends themselves. He'd asked my mom if they were done. He'd asked her if she was over him, and my mom told him time and again that she was. She wasn't, though." Kinsley sighed. "When I was about a year old, they started having an affair. My dad found out. They got divorced. My mom told me much later that she thought it had been over between them. She really thought she was over him, but she wasn't."

"What happened?"

"They're still together," Kinsley answered before she sipped her wine. "The boyfriend and my mom. They're married now; have been for close to thirty years."

"And you thought I was like your mom?" Riley asked, setting her fork down on the plate.

"I had a previous girlfriend do the same thing with her ex." Kinsley shrugged. "We weren't together long, but she'd just come out of a relationship when we started dating. I asked her if she was over her ex. They'd been together for two years. They lived together, for crying out loud." She took a long gulp of her wine this time. "I asked her, and she swore. She swore to me that it was over. She promised me she was ready for something else; for me."

"And she lied, too, I take it?" Riley guessed.

"I walked in on her with her ex, while the woman I thought was *my* girlfriend was going down on the woman she promised me was in her past."

Riley leaned forward and placed her elbows on the table on either side of her plate, clasping her hands together.

"I get that you've had two experiences where someone hurt you because they lied. But I've never lied to you, Kinsley."

"I know."

"I haven't made the best decisions where Elena was concerned, though, either," Riley added and exhaled.

"What do you mean?"

"I shouldn't have allowed her to walk all over me. I shouldn't have let her get what she wanted. For that, I owe you an apology."

"I do trust you, Riley." Kinsley leaned forward, too. "I just can't stand her."

"Why didn't you tell me any of this before?" Riley asked, leaning back in her chair.

"Because I thought we'd get there," Kinsley replied.

"We haven't exactly been dating long. I guess I thought I could lose you because of that. You'd been with Elena for three years. You were going to buy a house with her, and then you weren't."

"Because of you," Riley said. "I haven't been completely honest with you, either."

"Okaaay..." Kinsley lengthened the word.

Riley stood and said, "Say you're sorry for not trusting me."

"Riley, you know I am." Kinsley reached for Riley's hand, taking it in her own. "I'm sorry. I trust you."

"Good. Then, come here." Riley pulled Kinsley up by both hands.

"Riles, we haven't finished—"

"Later," Riley interrupted. "I have something to tell you, and I don't want to do it at the table."

Kinsley stared into Riley's eyes as Riley pulled her toward the lounge chair off to the side of the table Kinsley had worked so hard to make look romantic. Riley motioned for Kinsley to sit on the lounge. When Kinsley did, Riley gave her shoulders a light shove to get her to lie down. Riley reached behind the chair and pulled.

"Oh," Kinsley yelled as the chair moved into its flat position. Riley climbed on top of her, straddling her legs and placing her hands on either side of Kinsley's head. "Now?"

"I want to say something to you. This is how I pictured doing it," Riley said as she smiled down at her.

Kinsley gulped.

"I've missed kissing you," Riley added.

Kinsley wrapped her arms around Riley's neck, pulling her down, and said, "I've missed kissing you, too, but—"

Riley's lips met her own. Kinsley shut up. She wouldn't resist a kiss from her girlfriend after she'd been so worried she'd lost her. Her hands went to Riley's hair. She undid it from the tie that had it held back tightly, allowing it to fall in waves over Riley's shoulders. She moaned as Riley's tongue entered her mouth, and she ran her hands through

Riley's hair. Riley deepened the kiss in return. Kinsley moved her hands to Riley's shoulders, sliding the jacket off her shoulders. Riley shook it off and leaned up. Kinsley watched as Riley unbuttoned her blouse slowly. Her hands went to Riley's hips, and she moved them slowly up and down against her girlfriend's body, wanting her naked already, but also wanting Riley to take her time.

Riley's shirt was tossed aside. Then, her bra joined it. Kinsley licked her lips at the sight of Riley's breasts right in front of her. Riley undid the button on Kinsley's jeans and unzipped them. Kinsley lifted herself up to allow Riley to pull off her shirt. She unclasped her own bra next and tossed it on the hardwood. Riley stood, and without words, she pulled at Kinsley's shoes and jeans, until Kinsley was left just in her panties. After she was done with that, Riley divested herself of the rest of her own clothing. Then, she was climbing back on top of Kinsley. She kissed her deeply before reaching between Kinsley's legs, feeling her already wet and ready.

"That thing I want to tell you, I want to be inside you when I do." Riley slid two fingers down to her entrance and moved inside, causing Kinsley's hips to lift up in response. "I want to feel you around me."

"I hope it's good then, because if this is how you give me bad news, it wouldn't make—"

Riley thrust deeper inside her, stroking her girlfriend hard and fast as Kinsley stopped talking. Kinsley's hips were lifting up just as Riley took her nipple into her mouth. Riley sucked hard as she continued to move inside Kinsley's body. Her thumb joined in and began pressing into Kinsley's clit, creating the perfect storm. Kinsley moaned loudly, gripped Riley's back tightly, and held on as she climbed higher and higher.

Just as she was about to come, Riley said softly and into her ear, "I love you."

Kinsley came at those words. She couldn't hold it in any longer. Her orgasm tore through her as Riley continued to stroke her through it.

Riley repeated the three words over and over, "I love you. I love only you. I choose you."

When Kinsley finally came down, Riley looked down at her. Her fingers were still buried inside. Her thumb was still on Kinsley's clit, moving lazily over it, causing slight tremors with each movement. Kinsley just stared up at her with watery eyes.

"You just—"

"Said I love you. Yes, I did." Riley said confidently. "Because I do, Kinsley. I'm in love with you. I belong to you." She removed her hand from between Kinsley's legs and placed it against her own chest as she leaned up. "This is yours, okay?"

Kinsley placed her hand over Riley's. Riley moved her own hand on top of it and placed it back over her heart. She held it there tightly, allowing Kinsley to feel the thunder in her chest.

"Okay." Kinsley stared into those eyes she'd always been able to fall into. "I love you, too."

Riley smiled. Then, in rapid succession, she dropped Kinsley's hand and leaned down to whisper, "Then, stop being such a pain in the ass and just be with me." She smiled again.

"I'm sorry," Kinsley replied with a chuckle. "And I will."

CHAPTER 28

WHEN RILEY woke the next morning, it was to an odd sensation. No, it wasn't odd. It was good. It was definitely good.

"Oh," she uttered when it dawned on her.

Her eyes snapped open at the thought. She lifted the blanket that had been covering her up to her waist and looked down at Kinsley, who had just licked from her entrance up to the very tip of her clit. Then, Kinsley's eyes opened, and she smiled.

"Good morning," she said with a smirk.

"Good morning," Riley replied, lifting the blanket entirely away from Kinsley in order to see more.

"Can I continue?" she asked as she kissed Riley's clit.

"Absolutely," Riley replied with a wide smile before she closed her eyes and laid her head back against the pillow.

Kinsley's tongue went back to work. She stroked her softly, as if to welcome her slowly into the morning. Riley's hand went to the back of Kinsley's head. She didn't grip it or try to hold it in place, though. She merely played with the soft hair, enjoying the subtle caresses that had her moving toward a slow-building orgasm. Riley's eyes opened to watch Kinsley's head move up and down, and then side to side. Riley loved this woman. She couldn't help but think about how her life had changed so much in recent months.

She tried not to, as Kinsley's fingers slid inside her. She tried to only focus on Kinsley's movements and the feelings they caused, but she couldn't *only* focus on them. She thought about how Elena had initially been a decent girlfriend, but she'd never been a great one. It would have been impossible for her to be great. She was too focused on herself and her own priorities to ever be a great girlfriend; to ever view Riley as a true partner.

Kinsley, though – her jealousy aside – was a great girlfriend. Her tongue slid down and then all the way back up; again, slowly. Kinsley's fingers curled inside her, causing Riley's hips to lift. She gasped. She loved this. She loved coming slowly like this. She'd never told Kinsley that. Somehow, her girlfriend just knew. As Riley's hips lifted again, and her hand tightened in Kinsley's hair, her phone rang on the table next to the bed.

"Don't even think about it," Kinsley said, lifting her head and giving Riley a glare that told her in no uncertain terms not to pick up that phone.

The phone continued to ring until it went to voicemail. Riley didn't dare pick it up. She couldn't even if she wanted to, though. As Kinsley's tongue had sped up and increased its pressure, Riley's phone rang again.

"Jesus," she exclaimed, but not because of the phone.

Kinsley's fingers moved faster and deeper. Riley met Kinsley's eyes as they stared up at her. The phone went to voicemail again. Riley lifted herself up to increase the pressure on her clit. She was ready now. She wanted to come. The slow build was too much.

"Are you ready?" Kinsley stopped to ask.

"Yes." Riley held onto Kinsley's head tightly. "Yes. Yes," she gasped out. "Right there." She held onto Kinsley's head harder. "Deeper."

Kinsley's fingers straightened inside her. She pushed them deeper until Riley was certain she'd never felt this good, this full, this complete in her entire life. Riley came on a deep thrust as Kinsley sucked on her clit. Riley's hips lifted up higher than before. Kinsley's free arm pressed down on her abdomen, continuing her touches until Riley finally came all the way down. She kissed up Riley's abdomen, stopping at her breasts to suck on one nipple followed by the other. She kissed Riley's neck, her chin, and then Riley's lips. Riley tasted herself. She kissed Kinsley back hard and deep as the phone rang for the third time.

"I'm going to throw your phone away. That's okay, right?" Kinsley asked somewhat seriously as she stared down at Riley.

"Let me just see who it is." Riley reached awkwardly to the table as Kinsley tried to kiss her skin everywhere she could reach with her mouth. Riley grabbed for the phone. "It's an unknown number."

"Perfect. It's not important. We can keep doing what we're doing," Kinsley replied.

"We can, but we need to do this in the shower. I have a meeting this morning," Riley revealed.

"Shower sex?" Kinsley lifted up. "I can do shower sex."

Riley laughed at her adorable girlfriend and replied, "I'm glad."

Riley had her pressed against that shower wall moments later, driving her fingers deep into Kinsley. Her lips were on Kinsley's pulse point. She knew she'd likely leave a mark. She didn't care. In fact, she wanted to leave a mark. For the first time in her life, she wanted to mark a woman as her own. She sucked, lifted her lips away, and noticed the redness. She kissed the spot gently before moving to Kinsley's mouth. The water had cooled slightly since they'd climbed into the shower. They'd cleaned one another first before Riley couldn't wait any longer; her thigh pressed between Kinsley's. She applied more pressure while she rubbed her own center over Kinsley's thigh, needing to come again just from touching this woman in this way.

"Riley," Kinsley whispered. "I'm coming."

Riley thrust harder, pressing her thigh as closely as she

could to give Kinsley what she needed. Riley pressed her own center harder. Kinsley gripped her ass, helping her get that friction she craved. Kinsley moaned and said her name again, causing Riley to go over the edge right behind her. When they'd toweled off and moved back into the bedroom, Riley's phone rang yet again.

"What's going on, Riles?" Kinsley asked.

"I don't know. It's from an unknown number again. Should I just answer it?"

"Maybe it's a wrong number? Just let them know, and they'll leave you alone."

"Hello?" Riley said into her phone.

"Riley Sanders?"

"Who's this?" Riley asked.

"Cynthia Garrett from Dallas 6 News," the woman replied. "I was hoping to catch you–"

"You're a reporter?"

"Regarding Elena Ri–"

"No comment," Riley said. "And please don't call here again."

Riley hung up the phone and glanced toward Kinsley, who was pulling underwear out of her drawer.

"Reporter?"

"Yeah," Riley replied, staring at her phone.

She stood there naked, going to her voicemail app and checking the five messages she had on her phone. Two of them were from that same reporter. The third was from a reporter in San Antonio. The fourth and fifth were from two different stations in Austin.

"How'd they get your number?" Kinsley asked, moving to stand behind her, wrapping her arms around Riley's waist.

"I don't know," Riley replied. "I asked Elena to take care of this."

"Maybe she's tried," Kinsley said and kissed Riley's shoulder.

"I'm sorry, what?" Riley turned in Kinsley's arms,

tossing her phone on the bed. "Did you just assume something good about my ex-girlfriend?"

"I'm trying to be a better current girlfriend," Kinsley answered with a slight smile. "And she stopped by my office. We talked."

"What? Elena stopped by your office? When?"

"When I was being a dumbass," Kinsley said. "She apologized to me. It's clear she still has feelings for you, but she realizes it's over. I think she'll leave you alone now."

"She apologized to you?" Riley asked.

"For trying to come between us, yes."

Riley's arms went around Kinsley's waist, and she said, "I don't know how this is going to go, with the news of her running and the fact that she and I used to date, but it might require me to see her again. I told her I didn't want to. I asked her to handle this. But I want you to know."

"I understand." Kinsley kissed her lips gently. "Do what you need to. I'll be here. And I promise, I won't freak out again," she added.

Riley kissed Kinsley's lips sweetly, then pulled back and stared at her girlfriend.

"I'm sorry. I'll do what I can to keep you out of this," Riley said.

"I don't care about the reporters, Riles. I care about you. If you need me by your side, I'll be there. If this is something you need to deal with yourself, I'll give you the space to do that."

"I promise, this has nothing to do–"

"Riles, I get it. I was being stupid before. I almost lost you because I hadn't dealt with my own issues. Of course, it is a little bit your fault." She smiled playfully.

"I know. I should have–"

"Riles, I was kidding. I mean, I wasn't; but I was." Kinsley kissed her lips again. "I just meant that I don't think you really understand how much I liked you back then."

"In college?"

"Yes, in college. After college, too, though. You'd

come into town to visit your parents or something. I'd see you hanging out with Reese or Remy. It was like I'd start right up again. I'd see you laugh about something and I'd be gone all over again. You'd leave, and it would take me a while to get you out of my mind." Kinsley paused, running her hand up and down Riley's bare back. "I think part of the reason I worried so much about Elena, other than you deserve better than how she treated you, was because I wasn't sure I deserved you, either. I've always wanted you, Riley. I never thought I'd get to have you like this, though."

Riley leaned in and pressed their foreheads together before saying, "I love you. You do deserve me. We deserve each other in the best way, Kinsley."

Kinsley leaned in and kissed her once more.

***

Riley couldn't make it inside her office without being confronted by reporters. There were three news vans outside her building. She could see as many reporters standing off to the side, likely, waiting for her to arrive. Riley picked up her phone and dialed Elena's number.

"Where are you?" she asked.

"At the hotel. My flight doesn't leave for a few hours. What's wrong?" Elena asked.

"The press is hounding me, Elena. I've had, like, eight phone calls this morning alone. The reporters are outside my office right now. I can't even get inside without being asked a million questions. I have a meeting with a client in ten minutes," Riley explained.

"I'm sorry, Riley. I issued a comment last night that you and I aren't together, but they don't seem to care."

"Where'd you comment?" Riley asked, moving the phone away from her ear to open her browser.

"I had my press secretary release it," she replied.

Riley went to the site she knew and found the brief comment. She then searched Elena Rivera, and that local government website was the only result that had anything related to that comment.

"Elena, it's only on your site. It's not wide yet," Riley said. "You need to do more."

"I will, as soon as I get back." She paused. "Riley, I promise. I will take care of this for you, okay?"

"I don't want it to impact Kinsley, Elena. I'm worried they'll find out about her, and I don't want that. We're just starting out. I don't want–"

"To scare her away? I take it, you two talked."

"Yes. And she told me you apologized to her. Thank you," Riley said.

"It was the least I could do."

"Can you do the most you can do now, please?" Riley asked.

"As soon as I get back to Dallas, I'll issue another statement. I'll make sure everyone in Texas sees it and hears it. The press knows I'm here now. That's why they're in Tahoe. I'll have my press secretary issue a statement that I was taking a weekend away before the race begins. We'll leave your name out of it. I'll make sure they know I'm heading back to Dallas. That should be enough to drag them away," Elena replied.

"Thank you," Riley said. "Shit, my client is here with her ten-year-old boy. I need to go before she gets scared off. Her husband is a monster of a human being. I don't want her to get nervous about divorcing him."

"I am sorry, Riley," Elena said.

"I know you are. I've got to go."

Riley had parked down the street. She gathered her belongings and headed toward her office, inhaling and exhaling deeply as she walked. One reporter caught sight of her. She headed toward Riley, microphone outstretched. Riley walked past her and her questions. The other reporters tried as well, but Riley reached for her client's hand and pulled her and her son on through the office door.

CHAPTER 29

K<small>INSLEY AND</small> M<small>ORGAN HAD BEEN</small> working hard for the past couple of hours. The sun had set, and their lights could only do so much; they needed to stop for the night. They were also both exhausted from their long work days and hard labor.

"And where's the girlfriend tonight, James?" Morgan asked after downing an entire bottle of water.

"She's coming by later. She had to drop a client off at a women's shelter. I don't know how she does what she does," Kinsley replied.

"Does she know why you're doing what you're doing right now?" Morgan asked.

"I told her it was because it made sense," Kinsley replied, sitting next to Morgan.

"Made sense? Really?" Morgan laughed.

"It does. You get to use it. It makes sense," Kinsley said.

"And the urgency of it?"

"The deal I got on lumber," Kinsley replied.

"That was a good deal," Morgan agreed. "Isn't this a lot for something so new, James?"

"I'm not asking her to move in with me, Morgan."

"True. But I kind of think that by doing this, you're

basically saying you won't be leaving your house anytime soon. Which means, if you two do take that step one day, she's moving here. Is that part of the reason?"

"No, it's not," Kinsley began. "She loves this house, though. She's said that on numerous occasions. This isn't about trying to convince her to move in one day. It's just about showing her that I'm not going anywhere."

"Well, I'm here to help." Morgan passed Kinsley a bottle of water. "I think it's great that you've let the whole jealousy thing go. I gave her a hard time in the beginning, but I love Riley. She's great. You're great together, I think."

"You think?" Kinsley asked with a chuckle.

"I don't spend that much time with the two of you together. You guys have been holed up. I get it. Trust me, I do."

"It's not just about that," Kinsley said. "Though that is a big part, and it is great."

"I get it, James," Morgan replied laughing.

Morgan stared out at the water then. Her smiling face turned serious, and she exhaled deeply.

Kinsley took a long drink from her water and asked, "How are you?"

"I'm okay," Morgan said, obviously not saying everything. "Can I ask you something, though?"

"Of course," Kinsley replied.

"Is she the one? Does it feel like that to you?" She turned her face toward Kinsley.

Kinsley took a breath and answered, "Yes, it does. I think, in a way, it always has with Riley. I knew her at eighteen, and I was just so enamored by her. She has this way about her that made me want to know everything."

"And you wanted to touch everything," Morgan added.

"It wasn't just about that, though. Don't get me wrong, I wanted that with her. But I also wanted to just be near her. I wanted her to see me how I saw her, but I was too scared to say anything back then."

"And now?"

"Now, I want to be the last person she's with. I think she wants the same thing." Kinsley paused. "Why do you ask?"

"Because I'm tired of waiting for my own Riley," Morgan answered with a sigh. "I thought I found her in Reese, but I was wrong about that. I'm starting to worry I'm never going to find her. And that makes me both pissed off and kind of sad. Where is she, James?"

"I don't know, Morgan." Kinsley reached for and took her hand. "But I do know that you will find her. I mean, look at Kellan and Reese. Kellan had to come all the way from San Francisco to find Reese. Look at Riley and me. We've known one another for years, but we only just now got together. Stacy and Dave met in high school. Two of my clients met online. Another one said she met her husband when they were in pre-school, but she moved away after. They reconnected over twenty years later and fell in love."

"Are you trying to make me feel better or worse?" Morgan asked.

"I'm trying to tell you that it happens differently for everyone." She nudged Morgan's shoulder. "And I can't wait to see how it happens for you."

***

"Are you sure you want to watch this?" Kinsley asked her.

"I'm sure. I want to know what she says," Riley replied.

Riley clicked the mute button to unmute the TV in Kinsley's living room. They sat next to one another on the sofa. Kinsley had her arm around Riley's shoulders. Riley's head was on Kinsley's shoulder. It was exactly where Riley wanted to be and exactly who she wanted to be with.

"I'm going to make a brief statement, and then I'll open it up to a few questions," Elena Rivera said at her press conference.

"God, let's hope the questions aren't about me," Riley said to Kinsley.

"I am running for governor of the great state of Texas. I am running because I believe it's time for some changes. Before I give my full statement regarding what I plan to do in office, I wish to comment on something that's been going around regarding myself and another individual. Yes, the rumors are true. I am a lesbian. I won't comment about my sexuality beyond that. I won't, at least at this time, tell my life story about how I came to realize this about myself. I will, however, address the rumors that have me linked with a woman. I am not in a relationship with her or with anyone else for that matter. While I have been in relationships with women in the past, I am not currently. And I would be running for governor as a single woman, intent on improving her state for the citizens that make it their home." She paused. "Now, let's get to how I plan to do that."

Elena continued by talking about her platform. Riley clicked the mute button again, turning the sound off.

"Are you okay?" Kinsley asked.

"I'm with the woman I love." Riley looked up at her. "I'm perfect." She kissed Kinsley's cheek.

"Is it over now? The press packed up and moved on, but is it over?" Kinsley asked.

"That," Riley said as she pointed to the TV. "Is over." She climbed onto Kinsley's lap, straddling her. "This," she said, pointing at Kinsley's heart. "Is just beginning."

Riley leaned in and kissed her girlfriend, slow and deep. Kinsley's hands made their way into Riley's hair. Riley reveled in the feeling of having this woman in her life. She reveled in their new beginning; in the fact that they'd both dealt with their pasts and their jealousy; in how Kinsley made her feel like she was the most important person in the world to her. Kinsley was the most important person in the world to Riley. She'd be introducing Kinsley as her girlfriend when her parents came home in a few weeks. They knew

Kinsley already, of course, but not like this. They had no idea how much she meant to their daughter. Riley couldn't wait to share this with them. Riley would be meeting Kinsley's family soon, too. They'd go visit them together, holding hands as they drove. Riley would be nervous, but ready to take that step with her. Riley wanted to take every step with this woman.

"I love you," Kinsley said.

"I know. I kind of love you a little bit, too," Riley replied with a wink.

"Then, I'm not giving you your gift after all," Kinsley said with a lifted eyebrow.

"Gift?" Riley asked. "What gift?"

"No gift for you now. You said you *kind of* love me, Riles," Kinsley said with a soft laugh.

"Fine. I love you. I really, really love you." Riley leaned forward and kissed Kinsley's laughing mouth. "Come on. I don't ever make you dinner. Doesn't that show you how much I love you?"

"That's how you show—"

Riley kissed her again and said, "You love to cook."

"I do, but still," Kinsley returned.

"I could *show* you how much I love you," Riley suggested, kissing Kinsley's neck. "Upstairs, in the bedroom."

"Before or after your gift?" Kinsley asked.

"Who says it has to be before *or* after? It could be before *and* after," Riley whispered seductively as she began to roll her hips slowly.

Kinsley glanced down and watched them move. Riley was wearing a pair of boxers and a white t-shirt. Her breasts were visible ever so slightly through it. Her nipples were already erect and nearly piercing through. Kinsley's eyes met Riley's again. Her smile was infectious.

"Come with me," Kinsley said.

"I plan to," Riley replied cheekily.

"No, outside. Come with me outside."

"On the patio? Okay," Riley said. "I like having sex out–"

"Riles, put on a hoodie and some sweats, and follow me outside," Kinsley interrupted with a laugh.

"So, I'm putting clothes *on*?" Riley lifted a confused eyebrow at her as Kinsley patted her butt for her to get up. "Fine. But just remember: you're the one that told me to get dressed."

Riley slid off Kinsley's body and made her way upstairs to Kinsley's bedroom to borrow one of her sweatshirts and a pair of yoga pants. Kinsley hadn't followed her up to the room, but she was already wearing a warm sweater and pants. When Riley made it back down the stairs, Kinsley was waiting by the front door.

"Shoes, too," she said, pointing at Riley's shoes.

"Yes, ma'am." Riley moved to slide her shoes onto her feet. "Where to?"

"Backyard," Kinsley replied, taking Riley's hand.

They walked through the house toward the back door. Kinsley pulled it open and let Riley walk through first. She followed close behind, flicking a switch to turn on all the lights outside before she moved in front of Riley to lead her through the yard and down the path through the tree line. Riley knew Kinsley had been working on the dock for about the past week. It was clearly her new project for the house. Riley hadn't minded. If Kinsley wanted to add a dock to her property, it was her choice to do so.

When they arrived at the change from soil and sporadic grass to the pebbles that occupied this part of the beach, Riley watched as Kinsley moved around to turn on work lights aimed at the water. She stood still as each light illuminated a different part of a nearly completed wooden dock.

"You're almost done already?" she asked, taking a few steps onto the crunchy pebbles. "Kinsley, this–"

She stopped talking when Kinsley lit the last two lights. There, attached to the dock that had been nearly done without her even realizing it, was a twenty-foot bowrider powerboat, with an open bow space designed for extra seats. This one had four seats with a flat back for someone to lie in the sun. It was white, with faded blue trim. There was an empty space where the engine would be. There was also a bench seat in the front for those who wanted to ride with the full force of the wind blowing at them. The rest of those seats were behind the glass visor that helped protect the driver and passengers from that same wind. The boat didn't look new. In fact, it looked pretty old. She moved a little closer toward the water. She could make out in the light – now that it had some light – rusting and a lot of paint chipping. The glass visor also had a few dents and a crack along the left side.

"Remember how I told you I got a great deal on the wood for this thing?" Kinsley asked.

"Yes," Riley breathed out.

"I got a great deal on something else, too," Kinsley began. "It doesn't look like much, but Morgan knew this family that wanted to sell it. They needed the dock space for their new boat. I guess the guy always planned on fixing her up, but he never got around to it. Now, he's in his sixties, retired, and has decided to spend his time enjoying his new boat instead of fixing up his old one. He gave it to me for next to nothing."

"This is yours? You own a boat now?" Riley asked, pointing at the boat.

"It is," Kinsley replied. "It floats right now, but that's about it. I'll have to pull it out of the water to do the real work."

"You own a boat?" Riley turned to her.

"They dropped it off today," Kinsley said while chuckling at Riley's reaction. "I don't know… I thought I'd fix it up, and by the time I do, it would be *our* boat," she added.

"*Our* boat?" Riley asked.

"It'll take some time, but I think I can do most of the

work myself. Ryan actually knows a lot about boats. He's offered to help when I need it. He had a summer job, as a teenager, working on them. Anyway, I was thinking you could help, too, if you want. You could do whatever you want. You could just supervise me if you don't want to get your hands dirty." Kinsley took Riley's hand and walked her out closer to the water's edge. The dock still had some gaps where boards needed to be placed, so it appeared she didn't want them to go all the way out there in the dark. "I have a feeling you'll like bossing me around," Kinsley added.

"Kinsley, you bought a boat," Riley said as she turned to look at her. "Babe, you bought a freaking boat."

"You said you always wanted one," Kinsley replied.

"You remember that?"

"I think you know by now that I remember everything about you, Riles," she said. "I was going to wait until your birthday, but he wanted to get rid of it as soon as possible. I figured you'd notice it just sitting here."

"Kinsley, this is amazing," Riley wrapped her arms around Kinsley's waist. "I don't deserve this."

"This is how I am as a girlfriend, Riles. I like doing things for you. It makes me happy to see you happy. I love cooking you dinner, or bringing you breakfast in bed."

"You've never brought me breakfast in bed," Riley replied with a playful glare.

"There's always tomorrow," Kinsley replied, giving her a gentle kiss.

"That sounds nice," Riley said. "How about after that, I repay you with things I like to do to you?"

"Oh, yeah? What things?"

"Well, I like to tell you over and over how much I love you, since you like to forget about that," she began. "And I also love touching you. There's something about your skin that just makes me want to reach for it," Riley added as she slid her hands up under Kinsley's sweater to touch the bare skin of her abdomen. "And I also love just being with you. We could do nothing all day, and I'd love it."

"What about working on a boat?"

"Any chance I get to spend time with you, I want it, Kinsley. I didn't notice when I was a dumb college freshman who thought she knew it all. I missed out on you back then because of that. I don't want to miss out on you anymore. So, breakfast in bed." She kissed Kinsley. "Sex." She kissed her again while Kinsley's laugh nearly got in the way. "We'll lie around for a bit." She kissed her throat. "And then, we'll get dressed." She kissed her collarbone. "We'll come out here." She slid her hand up a little higher, discovering the bare breast that fit so perfectly in her hand. "And you and I will start working on *our* boat."

"Then, we'll go back inside," Kinsley started as she cupped Riley's ass through her pants and boxers. "And I'll make us lunch." She squeezed both cheeks roughly. "We'll clean up the kitchen." She kissed Riley's lips. "And have sex on the island." She kissed Riley through her smile. "We'll take a long, hot shower. And we'll invite our friends over for an afternoon because we miss spending time with them." She kissed Riley's neck just under her earlobe. "We'll spend the evening out here on the beach. Everyone will pitch in and help finish building this dock. Then, they'll all go home." She kissed Riley in the same spot. "But you'll stay."

"I'll stay?"

"Yes. And we'll fall asleep next to one another," Kinsley finished.

"And I get to hold you and tell you I love you?" Riley asked.

"Every night if you want," Kinsley answered.

"I want."

EPILOGUE

"**Y**OU JUST PAINTED this thing. Now, you have to break a bottle over it? How does that even work?" Morgan asked. "That whole tradition has never made any sense to me."

"If it can't withstand a bottle breaking on it, I think they have bigger problems," Kellan replied.

"Literal blood, sweat, and tears went into this thing. It better work," Kinsley said.

Morgan, Reese, Kellan, Remy, Ryan, Kinsley, and Riley were all staring at the finished boat they'd all had a hand in building. It was attached to the dock that Stacy and Dave also helped with, but they were out of town and would miss the ceremony and launch of the boat. They'd all gathered for its inaugural trip on the water after months and months of repair work.

"It'll work," Riley assured and wrapped her arm around Kinsley's waist. "And would you guys mind if we go out for a bit on our own first? I promise, we'll come back and pick you all up and go for a real spin."

"I can start the grill and get the food cooking," Remy offered. "Ryan can assist." She smiled at her longtime boyfriend.

"I'm a great assistant," he replied.

"You're not planning on christening that boat another way, are you?" Reese asked. "If you are, I'm not going out on it after."

"We're not," Riley replied as she laughed at her friend. "I just want to take the first trip with my girl. We'll be back in less than an hour, ready to eat lunch."

"And we're okay to make a mess in your kitchen, James?" Morgan asked.

Kinsley looked at Riley, who had a very happy expression on her face. It made Kinsley not care about anything other than getting on that boat with her. She could deal with a dirty kitchen.

"Go for it," she said to Morgan. "You ready?" she asked Riley.

"Let's go."

Riley and Kinsley headed down the dock that also had two canoes tied to the other side for Morgan's family store. They climbed into their boat. Kinsley passed Riley the keys. Riley lifted both eyebrows and gave her a smile. She sat in the chair and started the engine. When it roared to life, there was a soft round of applause that came from the shore.

"Oh, shit!" Kellan yelled over the sound. "You forgot the champagne."

She picked up the bottle off the pebbled beach and jogged toward the boat. Kinsley and Riley climbed back out. Kellan handed Kinsley the bottle and moved back down the dock.

"Do you–"

"We can do it together," Riley suggested.

Riley and Kinsley both gripped the neck of the bottle with Riley's hand over Kinsley's. They smiled at one another before they crashed the bottle over the side of the boat, spraying it with champagne and broken dark green glass. Everyone applauded again. Riley's arm went to the small of Kinsley's back.

"We'll clean up," Kellan said of the glass and mess.

"Thanks," Kinsley replied. "Now, we go?"

"I still can't believe what you named this thing," Morgan said.

"It worked for us," Kinsley replied, turning her head back to Morgan. "Get your own boat and name it whatever you want."

"*Looking for love?*" Remy teased Morgan.

"No way," Morgan replied with a chuckle. "Come on. I'll help you guys get the lunch together."

Riley and Kinsley climbed back into their boat. Riley moved behind the wheel, and Kinsley sat next to her. She pulled them not so expertly away from the dock and then onto the lake in no particular direction. They watched their friends get smaller and smaller as they made their way into the massive, clear lake. Several minutes later, Kinsley was standing behind her, with her arms wrapped around Riley's neck. They were enjoying both the ambiance and the reward for their hard work, putting the boat back together.

"Here?" Kinsley asked.

"Here's good," Riley replied.

Riley slowed and then stopped the engine altogether. They were still in open water, but near enough to the shore to not get in the way of any other boats. They'd drift for a while before returning home. Riley stood. They moved to the back of the boat. They still called it the back and the front, along with right and left, instead of using boat terminology. They probably always would. That was fine with Riley. She and her amazing girlfriend had a boat together.

"So, I know you wanted to talk before everyone else got their chance on this thing. What's going on?" Kinsley asked, taking Riley's hand in her own after they sat.

"I'm ready for our next project," Riley said. "Now that the boat's finished."

"Oh," Kinsley said, seemingly a little disappointed. "I don't have anything planned."

"I know. I was thinking we could plan something together," Riley suggested.

"Like what?"

"Like redoing my apartment," Riley answered.

"What's wrong with your apartment?"

"Nothing's wrong with it. It's just an apartment, and I think it's going to take a lot of work to turn it into offices," she explained.

"What are you talking about?" Kinsley asked. "What offices? Where would you–" Kinsley stopped as it dawned on her. "You'd live with me, wouldn't you?"

"Yes," Riley said.

"And the offices would be…"

"For us," Riley answered. "It's a two-bedroom apartment. Kellan's agreed to let us build a separate entrance and remodel the whole upstairs into a law office and a real estate office. We'd use the living room as the reception for both, or the living room for you and the dining room for me; either way is fine. We could even separate the whole space with a wall. I'm completely open to ideas."

"You want to share an office space with me?" Kinsley asked.

"Well, I think the moving in together thing is the more important piece of this conversation. Is that okay?"

"Of course, it's okay," Kinsley said loudly, causing Riley to laugh lightly. "I'd love for you to move in. This is your house already; you know that. And your office?"

"If you're interested," Riley began. "I want to do more, Kinsley. For my clients, I want to do more. I want to get more involved in the programs that benefit these women and children. I was thinking you and I could even partner on some things."

"Like what?"

Riley dropped her hand from Kinsley's cheek and placed it on Kinsley's thigh instead.

"You know about foreclosures before anyone. These women often need places to live that aren't expensive. They need places where they could start over. I thought we could let them know about the places you find. We could also buy another place of our own with my savings and trust. We could flip it and sell it."

"After your apartment, that could be our next project," Kinsley suggested.

"I do love supervising you when you do manual labor," Riley replied with a lifted eyebrow.

"And I love you," Kinsley said.

"I love you, too." Riley climbed into her girlfriend's lap, straddling her thighs. "I love our home, and I love our new boat. I love our life together, Kinsley. I want everything with you," she said.

"And to think I used to wonder if you even knew who I was," Kinsley reminded.

"Because I never gave you the time of day, right?" Riley laughed as she leaned down to kiss her.

"We cannot have sex on this thing before our—"

"Oh, we're definitely having sex on this thing. How else did you think we were going to christen it?"

They touched one another hurriedly and without losing all their clothing, for obvious reasons. When they finished by whispering their feelings to one another, Kinsley took the wheel and drove them back to the dock so that they could join their friends. They tied up their new boat and took a moment to look at it from the beach while listening to their friends, up at the house, laughing about something funny. Riley kissed her on the cheek. Kinsley took her hand, and they walked away from their finished project that they'd named *"Time of Day."*